Writing Still

New Stories from Zimbabwe

Writing Still

New Stories from Zimbabwe

Edited by

Irene Staunton

WEAVER
W
—PRESS—

Published by Weaver Press, Box A1922, Avondale, Harare. 2003.

'The Ugly Reflection in the Mirror' by Alexander
Kanengoni was first published in *The Daily News*, Harare,
25 March, 2003.
'Sorting it Out' by Yvonne Vera was first published in
World View, Fall, 1999.

Typeset by Fontline Electronic Publishing, Harare
Cover Design: Danes Design, Harare.
Cover picture: 'Planes at Headlands' by Mishek Masamvu
Printed by Bardwell Printers, Harare.

The editor and the publisher would like to express their gratitude
to Hivos for the support they have given to Weaver Press in the
development of their fiction programme.

ISBN: 1 77922 018 9

✿ Contents ✿

⚜ Notes on Contributors ⚜

Pat Brickhill is the mother of three wonderful children. She grew up in a large extended family in Durban, South Africa, where both her parents were prominent trade unionists. She has had a life-long love affair with books - her first job was working in the Musgrave Library in Durban. She lived in Zimbabwe for 21 years and co-founded Grassroots Books, now known as the Book Café. For five years she was Events co-ordinator at the Zimbabwe International Book Fair. She lives in West Sussex although her heart is still in Zimbabwe. She has recently completed her first novel – and hopes one day to write for a living.

Clement Chihota (born 1964) teaches Applied Linguistics at the Zimbabwe Open University. Currently, he is based at the University of Cape Town where he is reading for a Ph.D. in English (on interfaces between Marxist criticism and critical stylistics and the possibility of integrating them into 'Marxist stylistics'.) Clement has published a collection of poems, *Before the next Song* (1999) and seven short stories in *No More Plastic Balls* (2000), one of which (entitled 'Shipwreck') has been re-published in the San Franciscan literary journal, *Tripwire*.

Brian Chikwava was born in Victoria Falls in 1972 and grew up in Bulawayo. He completed his schooling in Zimbabwe before leaving for university in Bristol, UK, where he graduated with a B.Sc (Hon). Apart from writing Chikwava is also a blues/Afro-jazz guitarist/singer/songwriter and a keen follower of the visual arts scene. He was once a member of the now defunct Zimbabwe Association of Art Critics and has spent a lot of time collaborating with some of Harare's upcoming jazz musicians on experimental shows trying to fuse action painting and live music. Brian is currently working on some short stories and a music album.

Julius Chingono who was born on a commercial farm in 1946, worked for most of his life on the mines. A poet, he has had his work published in several anthologies of Shona poetry including *Nhetembo*, *Mabvumira eNhetembo* and *Gwenyambira* between 1968 and 1980. His only novel, *Chipo Changu* was published in 1978 and an award-winning play, *Ruvimbo*, was published in 1980. His poetry in English has also been published in several South African and Zimbabwean anthologies: *Flags of Love* (*Mireza yerudo*)(1983) and *Flag of Rags* (1996).

Shimmer Chinodya was born in Gweru in 1957 and educated in Zimbabwe. On completion of his first degree he went to the Iowa Writers Workshop where he did an MA in Creative Writing. His publications include the novels *Dew in the Morning* (1982) and *Harvest of Thorns* (1989): and anthology, *Can We Talk and other stories* (1998). *Harvest of Thorns* won the Commonwealth Writers Prize (Africa region) in 1990; *Can we Talk* was short-listed for the Caine Prize in 2000. Chinodya has also written children's books under the pen name, Ben Chirashe, and he has developed a highly acclaimed O-level textbook series *Step Ahead: new secondary English course*. Shimmer Chinodya works as a free-lance writer and consultant.

Memory Chirere comes from Mount Darwin. He belongs to the younger generation of Zimbabwean writers. Chirere published short stories in *No More Plastic Balls* (1999) and *A Roof to Repair* (2000). He teaches African Literature courses in the English Department of the University of Zimbabwe

Alexandra Fuller is the author of a memoir, *Don't Let's Go To The Dogs Tonight*. She was born in England in 1969. In 1972 she moved with her family to a farm in Rhodesia. After that country's civil war in 1981, the Fullers moved first to Malawi, then to Zambia. Fuller received a B.A. from Acadia University in Nova Scotia, Canada. In 1994, she moved to Wyoming in the United States, where she still lives. She has two children.

Wonder Guchu a freelance journalist, was born 1969 in Mvurwi area. Trained as a teacher of English at Gweru Teachers' College between 1988 and 1990. Taught in Masvingo for five years and in Harare for six years. Started writing short stories for *The Sunday Mail* Magazine in 1992. Contributed poems to *Tsotso* and *Moto* magazines. Reviewed books for *The Masvingo Star*, *The Independent*, *Parade* magazine, *The Herald*, *The Sunday Standard* and *The Daily News*. Was music critic for the now defunct *Masvingo Tribune*. Married with two children.

Annie Holmes works as an editor, writer, and filmmaker. Born in Zambia in 1958 and raised in Zimbabwe, she studied English, African and Comparative Literatures at the Universities of Cape Town and the Witwatersrand in South Africa. She returned to Zimbabwe just after Independence, taught at Highfield High School for two years, and then worked in educational publishing. Later, combining book editing with film work, she went on to make documentary films all over southern Africa and produced a number of TV series for SABC Education. In 2001, she took a temporary leave from home and a sabbatical from film to study, write and work in California, USA. She likes to write about journey, having been on quite a few.

Derek Huggins is an Englishman who emigrated to Southern Rhodesia in 1959 at the age of eighteen to join the British South Africa Police. He rode horse patrols in Matabeleland and later became a detective with the Criminal Investigation Department. He married Helen Lieros, artist painter, in 1966. Resigning from the police in 1974, he opened Gallery Delta for the promotion of contemporary painting. Concurrently, he was the Chief Executive of the National Arts Foundation from 1975 to 1988. Presently, he continues to manage Gallery Delta, and to publish *Gallery magazine* in which he is a frequent contributor. He has, intermittently, over a period of thirty years, endeavoured to write stories but which have remained unpublished until now.

Alexander Kanengoni was born in 1951. Trained as a teacher, he taught briefly before going to join the liberation struggle in 1974. After Zimbabwe's independence in 1980, he went to the University of Zimbabwe and majored in English literature. In 1983 he joined the Ministry of Education and Culture as project officer responsible for the education of ex-combatants and refugees. In 1988 he joined the Zimbabwe Broadcasting Service and worked there until 2002, when he became a farmer.

Alexander's previously published work includes the novels: *Vicious Circle* (1983), *When the Rainbird Cries* (1988) *Echoing Silences* (1997) and a collection of short stories, *Effortless Tears* (1993).

Rory Kilalea (pen name - Murungu) was born and educated in Zimbabwe. He works as a filmmaker, having picked up the skills on the anti-apartheid movies shot and Zimbabwe television. He has worked in the Middle East and throughout Africa, directing and writing documentaries and an Aid-related television series. His short stories have been nominated twice for the Caine prize and his poetry and short stories have been published in South Africa, USA, Malaysia, UK and Ireland . He is currently writing a novel based in Zimbabwe.

Nevanji Madanhire, born in 1961, has lived a varied life reflecting the restlessness of growing up in an amorphous fledgling Zimbabwe. As a teenager, Nevanji saw the political fission resulting from the dying years of the war of liberation when most of his classmates were forced to either join the liberation forces or be conscripted into the Rhodesian army. Because of cowardice he only chose to throw a few stones at the establishment from the safety of the mobs of demonstrating students. The two decades of independence saw the pain of a nation dismally failing to define itself, and became for Nevanji, a period of soul-searching during which he worked as a teacher, a curriculum theorist, an educational book publisher, a public relations executive and a journalist. He has published two books, *Goatsmell*, (1993) and *If the Wind Blew*, (1995). He hopes, when his children are through with school, to become a full-time writer.

Charles Mungoshi was born in 1947. He has written novels and short stories in both Shona and English, as well as two collections of children's stories, *Stories from a Shona Childhood* (1989) and *One Day Long Ago* (1991); the former won him the Noma Award. He has also continued to write poetry and has one published collection: *The Milkman doesn't only deliver Milk* (1998).

He has won the Commonwealth Writers Prize (Africa region) twice, in 1988 and 1998, for two collections of short stories *The Setting Sun and the Rolling World* (1987) and *Walking Still* (1997). Two of his novels: *Waiting for the Rain* (1975) and *Ndiko kupindana kwa mazuva* (1975) received International PEN awards.

Stanley Mupfudza was born in 1971 in Guruve and educated in Zimbabwe, graduating from the University of Zimbabwe. After teaching for several years he joined an advertising agency as a copywriter. His short stories have appeared in *Moto* magazine and in *A Roof to Repair (2000)*

Chiedza Musengezi is a founding member and director of Zimbabwe Women Writers, an organisation that nurtures women's voices through writing. She co-edited compilations of women's voices: *Women of Resilence, Women Writing Africa*, The Southern Region and *A Tragedy of Lives: women in prison in Zimbabwe*. Her short stories and poetry have been anthologised locally and internationally.

Gugu Ndlovu was born in Zambia in 1973, to a Zimbabwean father and a Canadian mother. She currently lives in Johannesburg, South Africa with her husband and four-year-old son. Until recently, she lived in New York City where she completed a BA in creative writing at Hunter College. She is currently pursuing an MA in creative writing from the University of Cape Town. Her writing experience thus far has included journalistic projects for magazines and newspapers to a short story published in *Opening Spaces* edited by Yvonne Vera.

Mary Ndlovu was born in Canada in 1942, and educated in Toronto and New York. She went to Zambia in 1966 as a teacher. She married Edward Ndlovu in 1972, she moved with him to Zimbabwe in 1980, where they had three children. She taught history, civics and geography at secondary schools and has lectured in teacher education at tertiary levels in both Zambia and Zimbabwe. In the latter part of her career, she worked for Legal Resources Foundation developing training programmes and materials in legal and human rights. Recently retired, Mary Ndlovu continues to live in Bulawayo and is active in promoting library services in Matabeleland South.

Vivienne Ndlovu was born in Northern Ireland and grew up during 'The Troubles'. She moved to London to complete her studies and then in 1983, travelled to southern Africa, where she met and married her late husband. She was a founder member of the Zimbabwe Women Writers (ZWW) and a participant of probably the only surviving locally based writer's group set up as an initiative of ZWW in 1991. She has published two short novels and her short stories have appeared in magazines and newspapers in Zimbabwe, in an early ZWW Anthology and in a South African anthology of womens' writing, 'The Torn Veil'. She now works for a regional NGO as an editor, having at last combined her love of writing and books, with her work.

Stanley Nyamfukudza has published two collections of short stories, *Aftermaths* and *If God Was a Woman* and a short novel, *The Non-Believers Journey*. He has also written educational books for primary and secondary schools. He lives and works in Harare as a writer, editor, translator, small publisher of children's and general books, and as a public relations and book publishing consultant.

Freedom Nyamubaya is a rural development activist, farmer, dancer and writer who was born in Uzumba. Cutting short her secondary school education in 1975, she left to join the Zimbabwe National Liberation Army in Mozambique where she achieved the rank of Female Field Operation Commander, later being elected Secretary for Education in the first ZANU Women's League conference in 1979.

After Independence, she founded MOTSRUD, an NGO that provides agro-services to rural farmers, and she has worked on attachment with the United Nations in Mozambique.

Her first volume of poetry, *On the Road Again* (Zimbabwe Publishing House, 1985) was followed by *Dusk of Dawn* (College Press, 1995), both being attempts to grapple with a brutal world using powerful images and disconcerting rhythms.

Bill Saidi was born in rural Marondera in 1937, but raised in Mbare, then called Harare. He was educated in Harare and at Plumtree. He became a journalist in 1957 and has worked for various papers in Zambia and Zimbabwe. He is currently the editor of *The Daily News on Sunday*. His first short story was published in The African Parade in 1956. Subsequently he has had short stories published in South Africa, Zambia, Sweden, Egypt, the United States, on the BBC, and in the former Soviet Union. His novels include:

The Hanging (1975), *Day of the Baboons* (1980), *The Old Bricks Lives* (1988), *Gwebede's Wars* (1989), *The Brothers of Chatima Road* (1990).

Yvonne Vera, one of Zimbabwe's best-known authors, was born in Bulawayo. She received her doctorate from York University, Canada, and returned to Bulawayo where until recently she was Director of the National Gallery. Her five novels have been translated into many languages and have won many awards, including the Africa region of the Commonwealth Writers Prize (1997, for *Under the Tongue*), the Macmillan Writer's Prize for Africa (2002, for *The Stone Virgins*) and Italy's Premio Feronia (2003, for *Butterfly Burning*).

Chris Wilson was born in Gweru, grew up on a farm near Nyazura and went to school in Mutare. He studied English Literature at the University of Cape Town. He then lived and taught English in Egypt for three years, Turkey for eleven years, Zimbabwe for two years and has now been in the Yemen for nearly six years. He has a house in Chimanimani and intends to live there permanently one day, and write lots of books.

🐾 Introduction 🐾

In *the past century* Zimbabwe has been scarred by racism, discrimination and war, uplifted by hope and self-determination, and discouraged by economic decline and political intolerance. The memories of this history have always been reflected in its oral and written literature.

Much of the serious fiction written in the 1980s and early 1990s focused on the effects of Zimbabwe's war of liberation. Little has yet been written about post-independence Zimbabwe and the complex and challenging issues that have arisen in the last twenty years. But while writers may be social commentators, their role differs from that of journalists or historians in that good writing, by definition, offers multiple meanings and invites multiple interpretations; it allows us to perceive situations from many different points of view. Indeed, fiction, to paraphrase Iris Murdoch, is a way of telling the truth, and is sometimes the only way of telling a complex truth.

The initial idea for this anthology was to provide a representative sample of the range and quality of writing in Zimbabwe at the turn of the century, and an impressionistic reflection of the years since independence in 1980. However the focus and the scope reflects a somewhat broader perspective than was first envisaged, with stories by Alexandra Fuller, Derek Huggins and Freedom Nyamubaya that remind us of the conflicts out of which Zimbabwe arose, and the memories with which we are still engaged today.

Nevanji Madanhire, Gugu Ndlovu, Alexandra Fuller and Bill Saidi have used the vivid intensity of a child's perspective on an adult world, which can seem incomprehensible, absurd, and cruel, to probe social realities. Yvonne Vera draws upon the child that lives within every grown-up through the sharp clarity of recollection triggered by a sound or a movement. Julius Chingono, Wonder Guchu, Chiedza Musengezi, Mary Ndlovu, Vivienne Ndlovu and Stanley Nyamfukudza look with sympathetic realism at situations that raise deeper issues of class, poverty, alienation, and personal responsibility. Memory Chirere and Alexander Kanengoni look to the emotive issue of land, but as a backdrop to stories of hope and renewal, bitterness and loss. Rory Kilalea and Annie Holmes raise questions of gender and sexuality, but within a perspective that does not allow them to forget their history or ethnicity. Pat Brickhill and Chris Wilson engage with the lessons to be drawn from living within a culture other than one's own; and its constant demand for self-criticism and self-awareness.

Zimbabwe's now omnipresent queue becomes for Shimmer Chinodya a symbol that winds through reflections on the interdependence of the personal and political, private and public. If our visible social selves provides the disguise for the hidden self rooted in memory, this reflection is made tangible in Charles Mungoshi's story of ruthless, if thwarted, ambition and timid self-deception that pits father against son in a tale where the past holds the present in sway.

Regret is a refrain in the anthology, but it would not be Zimbabwean without humour: Brian Chikwava's dry wit ranges over urban scapes, producing sharp caustic notes as he hones in on particular characters and situations, juxtaposing them in a manner that reveals their larger absurdity. Similarly Clement Chihota, not unaware of the larger economic issues in Zimbabwe, chooses to make us laugh by making his aspirant characters part of a grand plan that goes farcically wrong. Stanley Mapfudza blends realism with humour in his sharp perception of an urban situation in which the need to survive erodes principles of morality.

Writers of integrity become the pulse of a nation, its eyes, its ears, and the barometer of its values. Compiling this anthology has been a source of great pleasure. It reaffirms the value that Zimbabweans attach to the art of imaginative writing and demonstrates that the future of the country's literature is in good hands.

Irene Staunton
Harare, 2003

🕮 Universal Remedy 🕮

Pat Brickhill

I first met Esilina Sibanda one dusty hot Zimbabwean summer's day as I walked to my local TM at Avondale shopping centre. She greeted me politely and stopped me to tell me that she was looking for a job. I was wheeling my infant son in his push-chair, while his older brother walked by my side. I listened then told her that I was sorry but I did not need anyone to work for me as I was at home with my children and managed all my own housework. She told me that I must be a strong woman, and I chided her, telling her that she also must be a strong woman if she could take on all my domestic chores. We stood together talking before my children grew restless and irritable in the heat. Before we went our separate ways she told me she rented a tiny room behind a house a few doors from me. This meeting was the first of many. We grew to recognise each other, become gradually more familiar. We started greeting one another when we met on the grassy pavement each carrying our own shopping or when I was walking my oldest child to and from school.

Africa was my home and my birthplace. It filled my soul as only a spiritual home can. I had lived on my own since my husband left to be with a young woman, and now my three children were reaching the age when the unknown world beckons ever more persistently. I loved the sunny blue skies and the delicate green lacework of the acacia trees that filled my garden. I loved the heat so hot that it shimmered on the tarmac. I loved the fiery erithrina and the way its lucky beans were scattered like red pearls over my lawn every year. At night I loved to lie on the cool grass, my dogs lying puzzled at my side and look up at the stars until my heart stopped pounding and grew peaceful.

Esi came to my house late one very dark evening. The street lights were no longer working as the city council had put all the services out to tender and established their own private companies to serve the city's needs. I could almost hear my heart beating in my chest as I walked cautiously out, with my two dogs running, barking, just ahead of me. In the dark I did not at first recognise the short, slightly built woman at the gate. Her head was covered in the old-fashioned way, as black women in colonial Africa did before braiding and extensions became popular. She carried no luggage save a small supermarket carrier bag, and on her head she balanced a woven basket, which I would later discover contained all that she owned.

I quietened the dogs and my youngest son and daughter came out of the house and called to me to see if I was all right. I told them I was fine, and asked them to call the dogs in. I asked the woman how I could help her. People say that you can see the aura of a really good person. I knew even before she came to the end of her story that she was one of those people that some call an angel, one who comes into your life for a season or a reason. We had a small, two-roomed cottage at the end of our garden. Esi had a haunted hunted look in her eyes that I recognised from my own reflection in the mirror. Something made me offer her the cottage, which she accepted with a huge sigh of relief. She turned down my offer of bedding and said she had all that she needed but that we would talk in the morning.

I returned to my bed and slept badly. I got up early and went to the kitchen to make myself a pot of tea. The sky was dark, but the dawn was fast approaching and the birds sang in the new day. From the window I made out a small shape huddled over, digging in the back garden. I opened the door and went out to investigate. Esi held a worn hoe in her hands and she groaned with effort as she struck the ground, loosening the black clay soil.

'What are you doing?' I exclaimed. 'I have slept,' she said in a breathless voice. 'Now I must dig.'

I stood for a while then walked back to the house and poured her a large mug of sweet milky tea. She accepted it and leaned against her hoe. She thanked me and we drank our tea together standing in the early morning light of an African sunrise. She asked me to come and look at the back garden and asked me to make a mark to indicate how big the vegetable garden could grow. There are times in our lives when we do not question. Someone or something fits so neatly into our lives that we have no need to know any more. Esi came into my life like that. I did not need someone to do more than a few hours of cleaning in the house, but although I did not acknowledge it at the time, my soul was almost mortally wounded and I needed someone to nurture me and show me the way to heal myself.

Days blended into weeks and weeks into years. Esi grew older but her strength never flagged. Although she liked to talk, there were times when she preferred to be silent. One day as I walked back from work I found her walking in the road with her hoe over her shoulder. I asked her where she was going and she told me she had found a piece of unused land nearby where she was growing sweet potatoes and maize. I marvelled at her stamina and her consuming need to plant and grow things.

Often she would come and stand near me in my office, as I worked from my computer at home. I realised later that she could sense my moods and my sadness and always knew when I needed someone to talk to, just as I grew to know when she did.

I offered to hire someone to help her dig as she slowly transformed the back yard into a huge vegetable garden. She declined my offer and said most of the gardeners in town knew only about flowers.

3

She knew only about vegetables. We never discussed what she should grow or where she should grow it, but sometimes I bought seeds from the supermarket and left them on the window ledge in a small cardboard box. She took what she wanted to plant and discarded the seeds she did not want. She also taught me to save the seeds from fruit and vegetables that I bought, although some were hybrids and produced no fruit, even with the most tender care. She shook her head as I explained to her about hybrids. Sometimes I would find small red tomatoes on the window ledge, onions, carrots, a bundle of pumpkin leaves, a ripe paw paw for my breakfast.

In the spring I would also dig in the garden over the weekend, but I grew only flowers and lavender and herbs. Sometimes she would come and talk to me as I knelt, pulling out weeds. We would speak of the garden, and of life, about my children of whom she grew very fond, and whom I shared with her. Her brother had given her a baby girl many years ago whom she had raised as her own child – a common occurrence in days gone by.

At first she steered our conversations away from personal things, but gradually she shared with me her history, and I shared mine with her. Sometimes the pain of my own heartbreak grew too much, and I longed to curl into a small ball and retreat from everything. I would hear her in my kitchen moving quietly around, chopping, preparing food that had grown in her garden. Sometimes it was ground maize made into a thick porridge, pumpkin leaves with cream and onions and tiny slivers of chicken. When it was ready she would put it in the oven and silently slip away. It was as if by magic that the aroma of the food would creep down the passage, till it seduced me, and I would be compelled to get up and go to the kitchen. I would take the lovingly prepared food and eat it in the traditional way, with my fingers, all the time thinking of Esi and the way that she seemed to cope with her immense pain and loneliness so much better than I did

She had grown up in the rural areas. From an early age she fetched water and collected firewood. As the only girl in her family, many of the household chores fell onto her. She told me once that her mother had often beaten her to try and make her behave like a 'real' girl. But even then she loved to garden, to feel the earth open before her, to plant her seeds and look after them as they grew. She married a man not of her own tribe nor of her parents' choosing, and he let her down badly. When she was forty-two, he accused her of being barren, and he threw her out of the house and replaced her with a young woman. He never had any children by the new wife, or any of the subsequent women he lived with. Esi never had another relationship with a man.

Esi told me that she cried a lot over that period. She could not understand why God had not given her a child to keep her company, to help her keep her husband. Then she told me that when she went to the maintenance court to try and retrieve some of her meagre possessions she was astonished to see so many women with children who had been abandoned by their husbands.

To try and take her mind off her sadness, she told me, she grew cotton for the first time, and sold it to the cotton marketing board. She built her ageing mother a house from concrete bricks. She loved her rural home so much that my curiosity got the better of me one day and I asked her why she did not leave the city and return there. She shrugged, and then she stared hard at me, as if to say that part of the mission she was fulfilling involved looking after me. Over the weekends, when she was not digging, she walked around the suburb selling some of our excess produce. We never discussed what she would do with the money but I would see a new fork, a pair of clippers, or a brand new bucket, neatly arranged where she kept her tools in the shed. She spent hours cultivating seedlings in an army of wooden trays that I bought tomatoes in, from the supermarket.

Esi taught me much about life. She taught me how life is mirrored in nature – that everything has a time to laugh and a time to cry, a time to grow and then a time to stop growing, and to die. The cruelty of men was something that she knew only too well. But she taught me to avoid bitterness, that cruelty cannot be paid back by the women who had suffered – they must busy themselves with tending their gardens. They must plant, grow, heal. She taught me how to nurture and treasure my own little seedlings and in turn my children too kept a special place for her in their hearts. She told me once as I cried that my tears were the rain that would wash away my pain.

She loved the fact that in her garden she moved at her own pace, she grew what she chose to grow, and she decided to pull up anything she considered a weed. She loved the beauty of growth. She told me once that, given the choice, she would rather work with the soil than do any other kind of work. It was strange to think that, had she been able to have children, she might have spent a lifetime in the rural areas. Instead she had come to town to start a new life away from both her disappointed family and her former in-laws.

She knew that life was unfair, and she always finished a particularly sad conversation with 'God knows'. Her faith was the kind that could move mountains, but she accepted her life with a stoicism I found breathtaking. On Thursdays she dressed in her Methodist Church Women's uniform and spent the afternoon in church. She invited me and my children to a service when she was ordained as a preacher and I witnessed a sisterhood that sustained women in a visible way that I had only dreamed of. In the evenings she would sit in her cottage and read, or copy out passages of the Bible in her spidery handwriting. Although she had not been to school for very long she could read and write and speak three languages.

The politics of the country had taken a turn for the worse when the ruling party had decided, for a reason that I never understood, that they would never relinquish power, and were prepared to destroy the whole country to accomplish this. They relentlessly pursued their goal, crushing all opposition – whether real or perceived. White farmers left their farms. For a time Esi though that perhaps she might be able to get some land, but the land was not given to the likes of her.

My eldest son left Africa to study to become a film-maker. When my second son left school he soon grew restless and I could see his desire to join his brother. When the situation in the country deteriorated to a point beyond the comprehension of all except those who lived in Zimbabwe, my anxiety and my longing grew too much. I packed a few meagre possessions and a friend paid for me and my two remaining children to fly to England. I found a job at my local Sainsburys and rented a tiny cottage in West Sussex. I bought a spade and a fork and some seedlings. I tied up my hair and I turned to my garden to dig.

ॐ The Kiss ॐ

Clement Chihota

Hofisi, *more usually known as* Hofi, almost stopped the show before it started. The other actor who had stepped into view at the last minute did not fit the archetype he had projected. A nervous nondescript man glancing from side to side and wishing to see the whole thing done quickly – yes. But a tall, broad-shouldered, handsome man with voluptuous lips and a wicked little smile playing about the corners of his mouth? No. Not such a one. He was the kind of character who might make things a bit personal: one who might threaten the objectivity and detachment with which he had planned the whole operation. As he had explained to his wife, he was assuming the role of a Hollywood film director. A Hollywood film director could watch his own wife being 'made love to' by a male actor. 'Cut!' he would shout professionally if he thought the lovemaking was not being done correctly. Later, he would make real love to his actress wife on an expensive massage bed in a mansion paid for by the money that rolled in big-time after the show. Hofisi loved such analogies. They helped to contextualise plans. They also helped to orient visions and universalise the various roles that he had to play in life. His wife, Majaira, often had to fight both Hofisi, the man, and Hofisi the dream he dreamt up. For him, reality and dreams were separated by a thin, almost abstract line. She never won such fights.

'Mike! Mike!' Majaira shouted, just as Hofi had instructed her, then ran towards the stranger with open arms. The man called out the agreed response, left his place in the queue, and ran forward to embrace her. The two kissed passionately, perhaps *too* passionately, Hofi thought. Was it necessary, for the man to encircle Majaira's narrow waist with his right arm *and* squeeze her buttocks with his left hand? Was she warming up to the scene when she allowed her hands to slide up his neck and play with the tiny 'love-handles' at the back of his head? Hofi almost ran into the immigration hall shouting, 'Cut! Cut!' But the scene was unstoppable. Even as he hesitated, two security guards, who had been dozing on their stools when Majaira burst through the doors, jumped to their feet and ran to deal with the 'shameless couple'. Hofisi almost felt thankful to the guard who forcibly prized the big man's hand off his wife's bottom. The 'couple' had to be pulled apart, so tight had been their embrace. Majaira was scolded roundly as the security guards pushed her towards the exit.

'This is a national port of entry, not a Mills and Boon wedding!' bellowed a bespectacled official, jolted into comparing a place with an event. The guards pushed Majaira out of the immigration hall, then scowled at her for a few seconds before returning to their seats. By then Hofisi, mission accomplished, was already walking down the corridor towards the lounge. He could hear Majaira's feet pitter-pattering quickly behind him, but he did not look back. He walked straight into the lounge, found an easy chair, and sat down, waiting for his wife to come and occupy the other chair next to him. This was the moment of truth: the fruition of his plan, the moment for which he had long been waiting. He sighed as Majaira took the seat. He dared not ask the question, THE QUESTION, *THE QUESTION!* But he had to.

'Have you got it?' he asked softly, not daring to breathe.

* * * * *

The dealer unpacks the instructions, his dry voice assaulting the ear like a relentless Kalahari wind.

'It has to be done,' he repeats for the fourth time. The wife shivers. Butterflies in the belly? Cold feet? His sharp eyes miss nothing.

'Don't worry. At least four immigration people are in on the deal. The act is just a precaution in case some other officer happens to pitch at the wrong moment.'

'But … but …' mumbles the wife, pressing herself tightly against the wall like a malarial child quailing from the offer of quinine.

'Look,' the husband interrupts impatiently, pulling her by the arm. 'That diamond, safe in my hands, will fetch several millions. We need to pay something towards the mortgage. And, for heaven's sake, we are not planning to murder anyone. We are simply trying to survive these tough times.'

These-tough-times has become the devil frightening many impressionable Zimbabweans into a new creed of quick self-enrichment. The woman has heard this expression quite often. But she continues to squirm, inside. His glassy eyes miss nothing. He laughs briefly, then explains, 'You are the bait and the decoy in this operation.'

'But, but …' protests the wife, 'Couldn't you have found some other woman, I mean anyone else, to do this? And, how can you ask me to kiss a strange man on the lips like that?' Her tongue is thawing. Her soul is putting up one last fight before it succumbs to the inevitable. Patiently, like a linguistics lecturer explaining x-bar syntax to an average student, he re-explains, in his thin dry voice.

'Look darling,' he says, intensifying his concentration on her eyes, as if he would abandon the 'periscope' and leap bodily into her very soul. 'Darling, this is what I call acting. This is what I also call survival, Hollywood style. Okay, I have given you the script three times already. But I will give it to you again. You wait outside those glass doors so that you can see what's happening inside the immigration hall. You wait until the courier is about three people away from the customs desk. You will know him because he is wearing a gray suit, a white shirt, a dark red tie and black shoes. Your cue to go into action is that the courier will produce a white handkerchief from his pocket and pretend to wipe his face. Once you see that sign, you cry out loudly, then burst through the immigration doors. You rush towards him calling, 'Mike, Mike!' He will leave his place in the queue and rush towards you. The two of you then embrace and kiss on the mouth. During that all-important kiss, the diamond will quickly slip from his mouth into your mouth. By the time the immigration guys separate you and drag you out of the hall, the diamond should be under your tongue and you must make sure that you don't try to speak. I will be waiting for you in the foyer.'

'But you haven't explained why it should be me. Why *me* of all people?'

'Precisely because you *are* you, and not *all people*. You are family. You see, my dear, the source of these diamonds is a war zone. The diamond you are receiving has passed through the pockets of army generals and the briefcases of ministers of state. Such high up guys hate risks, because they have a long way to fall, in the event that something makes them slip. I don't want to be that *something*.' He pauses for emphasis, then continues, his voice becoming almost singsong, 'Now my dear, just imagine what any other woman playing this part might do. First, they will realise just how much money they are carrying inside their mouths. So, what next? Ask for a modest payment? Keep their mouths shut afterwards? No! A mouth that has carried millions of dollars under its tongue wants to eat well, and also talk about its adventure. I can't risk that. Denford is cooling his toes in Chuks because he made that kind of miscalculation. Ben was extradited back to Nigeria because of one partner he picked up from the streets.'

He is now wearing his most winning smile. Because he has finished grappling with her soul, his eyes now glisten like those of a cockerel with a cornered hen. She sighs deeply. Her husband is the kind of man who never gives up. He is the type to wallop a mountain blocking his path until it shifts its position. He is also clever. He has the kind of brain that can sift through sand and isolate camouflaged grains of gold. And he has never been to jail. A cynical idiom that once did the rounds in Harare crosses her mind like a lost cloud, racing across the sky: '*Chabhenda chabhenda, mbambaira haitwasanudzwe*. What is bent is bent, a crooked sweet potato would rather break than be straightened.' He is studying her face and smiling almost tenderly. Without a word, he leads her to the immigration doors. The arrival of the flight from the DRC has already been announced. 'Just think of Hollywood,' he whispers, before turning on his heel to walk back to the lounge. He has not gone five steps when the action starts, suddenly. Instead of walking on, he turns back to watch. He is not sure if the actors know that he is watching.

* * * * *

Majaira claimed that she fell in love with Mike the moment she saw him. 'I don't write Mills and Boon romances,' I told her, when she revealed this.

'So what do you write?' she asked, with a slight laugh.

'I am an African writer, you see, and African writers write serious stuff, okay?'

'But you said earlier you were a budding writer. I thought you wrote love stories, melodramas.'

'Budding writer is what we call junior, aspiring writers in Zimbabwe – and – budding writers are the most serious. Ask anyone in the Budding Writers' Association.'

'Okay, just write this love story for me. Just this one before you turn to your serious writing. I need to read about myself, about what happened. You see, it was different and it was wonderful and it served my husband right.'

'Okay, let's start with your background, your life with Hofi,' I say, opening my notebook to take down some notes. Mike laughs. His own story is much simpler. He was already a little in love with Majaira before he met her. But more about that later.

Majaira's life with Hofi had been a life riddled with fear. Fear is exhausting. This is why even a short journey in a car hurtling at two hundred kilometers per hour can leave one exhausted. She became a bit frightened of Hofi when he talked to her about his ideas in his almost robotic manner, staring deep into her eyes with a glassy expression: dead as a pair of camera lenses. This was not to say Hofi was like that all the time. Come most evenings, at home, he would be a completely different creature. His eyes would be softer, his voice more muted, the attention he gave her would be almost flattering. But she knew what he would be like the next morning. Sometimes, her own reticence frightened her. But the fear did not end there. A lot of the time, she was afraid *for* Hofi. This fear dated back to Hofi's *chipembere* days. Those were the days when he had started dealing in rhino horns. She remembered the time he had dramatically pulled out a rhino horn from the centre of a bale of *kapenta*, which had just arrived from Kariba. He had announced that this single horn would make more money than all the *kapenta* he had traded in the whole month. The horn had moved in his hands like a dangerous weapon, capable of exploding at any moment. Her fear had become physical, a sharp pain impaling the bottom of her chest, when they had had to co-habit with the horn for a full week before it was finally taken away. Hofi's *chipembere* days had given way to what he now called his *duula watuula* phase. This was the phase when he bought and sold everything and anything. 'The only item I don't buy and sell is a human being,' he had boasted, showing off an AK 47 rifle and a live pangolin that were both on their way to the market. She had almost screamed at the sight of the pangolin. The gun had made her cringe. He had changed the subject and asked her how business was going at the hair-salon. In fact she was quite pleased with the way her clientele was developing and she had rather proudly given him some figures. He had just laughed in his metallic way, gulped in some air then said, 'The dung produced by this little pangolin here will fetch more money than your salon can ever do in a year.' She had laughed with him but her laughter was shrill, underpinned by fear and a sense of rejection.

She is talking quickly. I am listening like one yet to hear the climax of a story. I am somehow reminded of the Chomskian non-sentence: *Colourless green ideas sleep furiously.* 'Okay, let's come to the moment when you met Mike for the first time,' I say, turning to a fresh page in my notebook. The first page is full, not of notes, but of drawings, most of which look like hearts or like diamonds.

'*Making* me receive the diamond at the airport made me feel more frightened than I had ever felt in my entire life. I felt intimidated, immoral,' she continues, frowning as she re-captures the movement, the expressions, the scents – all the nuances which that incident at the airport had evoked. The fear, which she had suppressed throughout her marriage to Hofi, had erupted, laid itself bare in all its nakedness, and in such a public place.

Majaira's heart had beaten like the site of a wrestling match, as she stood alone by the immigration doors after Hofi had turned to go. So Mike materialised almost out of a mist – the gray suit, the dark red tie, the white shirt. Her eyes slowly climbed up to his eyes, then locked, as if he was the key to her safety. This is when it happened. This is when the whole thing happened.

'What exactly happened,' I ask. Majaira and Mike look at each other then laugh.

'I think I made love to her with my eyes,' Mike confesses, blinking his eyes rapidly like someone trying to blink a sudden vision into focus. 'Mm, as I told you, I was already half in love with her.'

'How come?'

'Just like that. You see, her photograph had been faxed to the DRC. My brother, who used to be Hofi's business partner before we all became enemies, showed the picture to me. I was due to return to Zimbabwe the next day so he insisted that I do him a favour. 'How about being met with a kiss as soon as you land at Harare airport – you are still a virile young bachelor, are you not?' I had dismissed his request as a bad joke. I am not in that line of business, by the way. I actually teach at Belvedere Teachers' College. Anyway, my brother showed me the photo of the woman I was to kiss, and that's when it happened!'

'What happened?' I ask automatically.

'Well, I think I fell in love.'

I snorted. Mills and Boon had surely reached Belvedere Teachers College. Hardly surprising, I suppose, when there are no other books!

My editor (whose editing is quite brutal – especially on Monday mornings) warned me that this story would never make it, unless I attended to three fault lines than threaten its understructure. First, the woman portrayed in the first two parts is more timid than the Majaira we see in the conclusion. Well, to that I say the Majaira of the final part is a transformed woman. She is a woman who is really in love for the first time in her life. So, let's leave her alone. Secondly, I have not explained what happened to Hofi, or to the diamond that he got after his wife was kissed with his own permission. Well, to that, I say he lost his wife of course. After all, didn't I state the obvious by celebrating the serendipity of the immigration official who correctly construed the kiss in the immigration hall as more of a Mills and Boon issue than anything else? Finally, my editor says there seems to be a confusion about who is really narrating the story. Is it me? Is it Majaira or Mike or Hofisi? And why do I sidle myself into the story towards the end, even elevating myself to the journalistic writer, privileged to talk heart to heart with a beautiful woman like Majaira and the new man in her life? Well, to that I say, everyone has been free to narrate the story, except the real me. As for including myself, well, I say, who wants to be left out of the action, especially if it takes place close to *such* action: diamonds and beautiful women? I might be living in Borrowdale.

Seventh Street Alchemy

Brian Chikwava

By 5 a.m. most of Harare's struggling inhabitants are out of their
hovels. They are on their varied ways to innumerable places to waylay
the dollars they so desperately need to stave hunger off their
doorsteps. Trains and commuter omnibuses burst with exploitable
human material. Its excess finds its way onto bicycles, or simply
self-propels, tilling earth with bare frost-bitten feet all the way to the
city centre or industrial areas.

The modes of transport are diverse, poverty the trendsetter. Like
a colony of hungry ants, it crawls over the multitudes of faces scattered
along the city roads, ravaging all etches of dignity that only a few
years back stood resilient. Threadbare resignation is concealed
underneath threadbare shirts, together with socks and underpants
that resemble a ruthless termite job. In spite of poverty's glorious
march into every household, the will to be dignified by underpants
and socks remains intact.

Activities in the city centre tend towards the paranormal. A
voodoo economy flourishes as daylight dwindles: fruit and vegetable
vendors slash their prices by half and still fail to sell. The following
morning the same material is carted back onto the streets, selling at
higher than the previous day's peak rates. In some undertakings

the enthusiasm to participate is expressed in wads of notes; in some, simple primitive violence – or the threat of its use – is common currency. As the idea of ensuring that your demands are backed up by violence is fast gaining hold among the city's prowlers, business carried out in pin-striped suits is fleeing the city centre, ill-equipped to deal with the proliferation of scavenger tactics. Pigeons too have joined the new street entrepreneurs: they relieve themselves on pedestrians when least expected and never alight on the same street corner for more than two days in a row.

Even the supposedly civilised well-to-do section of the population, a pitiful lot typified by their indefatigable amiability, now finds itself anchored down by a State whose methods of governance involve incessant roguery. Instead of facing up to their circumstances with a modicum of honour, they weekly hurl themselves into churches to petition a disinterested God to subvert the laws of the universe in their favour.

At the corner of Samora Machel Avenue and Seventh Street, in a flat whose bedroom is adorned with two newspaper cuttings of the President, lives a fifty-two-year-old quasi-prostitute with thirty-seven teeth and a pair of six-inch heeled perspex platform shoes. It has been decades since she realised that, armed with a vagina and a will to survive, destitution could never lay claim to her. With these weapons of destruction she has continued to fortify her liberty against poverty and society. Fiso is her name and like a lot of the city's inhabitants she has conjured that death is mere spin, nobody ever really dies.

On the night a street kid got knocked down by a car it was a tranquil hour. A discerning ear would have been able to hear two flies fornicating several metres away. But to Anna Shava, a civil servant, soaked to the bone with matrimonial distress, the flies would have had to be inside her nose to get her attention. Her tearful departure from home after another scuffle with her husband set in motion a violent symphony of events. Security guards who scurried off the streets for safety could not have imagined that an exasperated spouse in a car vibrating to the frenzied rhythms of her anguished footwork could beget such upheaval.

Right in the middle of the lane, at the corner of Samora Machel Avenue and Seventh Street, a street kid staggers from left to right, struggling to tear himself out of a stupor acquired by sniffing glue all day. The car devours the tarmac, and in a screech of tyres the corner is gobbled up together with the small figure endeavouring to grasp reality. Sheet metal grudgingly gives in to a dent, bones snap, glass shatters. The kid never had a chance. His soul's departure is punctuated by one final baritone fart relinquishing life. Protruding out of the kid's back pocket, is a tube of Z68 glue.

A couple of blocks from the scene, blue lights flashed from a police car while two officers shared the delicate task of trying to convince a grouchy young musician to part with some of his dollars for having gone though red traffic lights.

'You've been having a good time. That's no problem. But you must understand we also need something to keep us happy while doing our rounds,' one of the officers said with a well-drilled, venal smile before continuing. 'Since you are a musician we know you can't afford much Stix, but if you could just make us happy with a couple of Nando's takeaways ...'

Anna, realising that they were not going to pay her any attention without some effort on her part, marched over to the officers. 'Will you please come to my help, haven't you seen what happened?' she said, donning that look of nefarious servitude that she often inspired on the faces of applicants at the immigration office. She knew better than anybody that being nice to people in authority could render purchasable otherwise priceless rights, and simplify one's life.

'We are off duty now, Madam, call Central Police Station,' one of the officers yodelled over. Returning to her car and periodically glancing over her shoulder in disbelief, she saw the offending driver stick out of his window a clenched handful of notes to pacify the vultures that had taken positions around his throttled freedom. His liberties resuscitated, he sped off in his scarlet ramshackle car.

Two days before, Anna, no less fed up with her errant husband, had followed him to the city's most popular rhumba club. She had found him leaning against the bar, with men she did not recognise. They talked at the top of their voices in the dim smudged lighting. Her husband, who had been tapping his foot to the sound of loud Congolese music, recoiled at the sight of her. Befuddled, he grappled with the embarrassment of having been tracked down to a night-club crawling with prostitutes. And then there was the thought of his mates saying that his balls had long been liberated from him and safely deposited in his wife's bra. His impulse was to thump her thoroughly, but lacking essential practice, he could not lift a finger.

'What do you want?' he asked, icily.

'Buy me a drink too,' she brushed the question aside.

He stared at Anna as she grinned. Outrage lay not far beneath such grins – experience had schooled him. Reluctantly he turned to the bar to order her a Coke, struggling to affect an air of ascendancy in the eyes of his peers. He tossed a five hundred dollar note at the bartender, as if oblivious to his wife's presence.

Half an hour later when Anna visited the ladies toilet, transgression would catch up with her husband. There a lady with greying hair, standing with what looked like a couple of prostitutes, cut short her conversation to remark innocently, 'Be careful with that man. He's a problem when it comes to paying up. Ask these girls. Make sure he pays you before you do anything or he will make excuses like, "I didn't think you were that kind of girl."'

Anna was transfixed, hoping – pretending – that the words were directed at someone else.

'You could always grab his cellphone, you know,' the woman added kindly.

That woman was Fiso who at the time Anna ran into a street kid, was engrossed in the common ritual of massaging her dementia. Having spent a whole day struggling to sell vegetables – a relatively new engagement imposed on her by the autumn of her street life, she was exhausted and was not bothered by the screeching tyres down the road. It did not occur to her that what had registered in her ears was an incident precipitated by her well-meaning advice. Beside her, sharing her bed, lay her daughter Sue, a twenty-six-year-old flea-market vendor. In the midst of her mother's furious campaign against a pair of rogue mosquitoes, which relentlessly circled their heads before attacking, Sue came to the tired realisation that in spite of all the years on the streets, her mother still had undepleted stocks of a compulsive disorder from her youthful days. In the sooty darkness her mother blindly clapped, hoping to deal one or both of them a fatal blow. Precision however remained in inverse proportion to determination. The mosquitoes circled, mother waited, her desire to snuff out a life inflated. They would dive, she would clap. Sound and futility reigned supreme. At last, jumping off the bed, Fiso switched on the light. A minute later one of the mosquitoes, squashed by a sandal, was a smudge of blood on the president's face, but Fiso could not be bothered to make good the insignia of her patriotism. A few months before, she would have wiped the blood away. But the novelty of affecting patriotic sentiment in the hope of dreaming herself out of prostitution to the level of First Lady had long worn off.

The following morning Sue switched on her miniature radio, to be confronted by the continuously recycled maxims of State propaganda, which ranged from the importance of being a sovereign nation to defending the gains of independence in the face of a 'neo-colonialist onslaught'. Leaning against the sink, she failed to grasp the value of the messages to her life. She gulped her tea and went to the Union Avenue flea-market. There, among other vendors slugging it out for survival, she could at least learn where to get the next bag of sugar or cooking oil.

On the same Saturday afternoon that marked the climax to Anna's marital woes, Stix, a struggling, young jazz pianist, had a call from his friend, Shamiso, inviting him to an impromptu dinner at Mvura Restaurant. Her friends and elements of her 'tribe', as she liked to refer to her cousins, were to be part of the company. With only the prospect of being part of a nondescript crowd at a glum, low-key music festival in the Harare Gardens, Stix committed himself to Shamiso's plans. At 7.30 p.m. he made his way to the restaurant. By midnight he had made a pathetic retreat to his flat, having shared part of his meagre income with two police officers fortunate enough to witness him driving through red lights. From his flat he had called Shamiso, and threatened to cremate her for inviting him to a restaurant where they would be saddled with a bill of over $15,000 each. That it was a restaurant with 'melted mars bar' on its dessert menu wickedly swelled his appetite for arson.

'So don't say you have not been warned about Mvura Restaurant,' Stix said to Fiso the day after the incident. 'If, however, out of curiosity you decide to go there, your experience will approximate to something like this: you get there, the car park is full of cars with diplomatic registration plates and there is not even space to open the car doors. At this point a security guard …' Stix pauses to light his cigarette. '… will run like a demon to find you parking space – but since you don't own a car, Fiso, you won't experience that bit.'

'So you're not going to take me there?' Fiso asks, but Stix ignores her and continues.

'You may be at a table where you sit back to back with the Japanese ambassador, and you will be confronted by a waiter wielding a menu without prices. By the end of the evening you will be sorry. Never assume that such restaurants price their food reasonably!'

Fiso listened, thinking what a curious person Stix was, and well aware that save for living in the same dilapidated block of flats, they did not have much in common. The nice restaurants, élitist concerts and well-dressed friends, existed only in the stories that Stix told her on their doorsteps on sluggish afternoons. They were just another spectral reality that Stix was fond of invoking. And after an hour or two of reciprocal balderdash, one of them would just stand up and walk into his or her flat, leaving the other to wean themself from that hallucinogenic indulgence.

Defining one's relationship with the world demands daily renegotiating one's existence. So far-reaching are the consequences of neglecting exigencies imposed by this, that those unwilling or unable to participate eventually find themselves trapped in a parallel universe, the existence of which is not officially recognised. These are the people who never die, Sue and her mother being a quintessential sample. Sue has no birth certificate because her mother does not have one. Officially they were never born and so will never die. For how do authorities issue a death certificate when there is no birth certificate? Several other official declarations only perfect the parallel existence of most of Harare's residents. Officially basic food commodities are affordable because prices are State-controlled. Officially no one starves because there is plenty of food on supermarket shelves. And if it is not there, it is officially somewhere, being hoarded by Enemies of the State. With all its innumerable benefits who would not want to exist in this other world spawned by the authorities – where your situation does not daily remind you what a liability your mouth and stomach are. It was therefore towards this official existence that Sue and her mother strove. Fed up with galloping food prices in their parallel universe, they took a chance and tried to take the leap into official existence.

It was an ordinary Monday morning when mother and daughter walked to the Central Registry offices hoping to get birth certificates, metal IDs and, eventually, passports. Sue had been told she could make a good income buying things from South Africa and selling them at the flea markets. But because the benefit of her deathless existence did not also confer upon her freedom of movement across national boundaries, she needed a passport. Fiso had decided to assist her daughter and get herself a passport too. Little did they know that they would find the door out of their parallel existence shut, and bolted.

By mid-afternoon Fiso was on her doorstep relating the events of the morning to Stix. Back in her humble flat, she felt better having spent half a day surrounded by the smell of dust, apathy and defeat.

Such were the Central Registry offices: an assemblage of Portakabins that had outlived its lifespan a dozen times over. With people enduring never-ending queues, just to have their dignity thrown out of rickety windows by sadistic officials, inevitably a refugee camp ambience prevailed.

'If your mother and father are dead and you do not have their birth certificates, then there is nothing that I can do,' the man in office number 28 had said, his fat fist thumping the desk. He wore a blue and yellow striped tie that dug painfully into his fat neck, accentuating the degradation of his torn collar.

'But what am I supposed to do?' Fiso asked, exasperated.

'Woman, just do as I say. I need one of your parents' birth or death certificates to process your application. You are wasting my time. You never listen. What's wrong with you people?'

'Aaaah you are useless! Every morning you tell your wife that you are going to work when all you do is frustrate people!' Fiso stormed out of the office. Having learnt the false nature of authority and law from the streets, she was certain that he was her only obstacle. Men, she knew, could have the most perverse idiosyncrasies and at least one vice. In her experience, doctors, lawyers and the most genteel of politicians could gleefully discard their masks to become the most brutal perverts. It was a male trait, an official trait, and it accounted for her failure to acquire the papers she and her daughter needed.

Fiso's parents had died long back in deep rural Zhombe where peasant life had confined them to a radius of less than a hundred kilometres, and where an innate suspicion of anything involving paperwork was nurtured. Back in the forties, stories of people having their names changed by authorities horrified semi-literate peasants such as Fiso's parents, who swore they would never have anything to do with the wicked authorities of that era.

'We were told to go to office number 28, but there was no one there. After about forty minutes, we went back to the office that had referred us, but there was no one there either. Returning to office number 28, and seeking help from an official who was strolling past we were told, 'Look? Can't you see that jacket? It means he is not far away. Wait for him.' So we waited – for three hours – only to be told to bring one of my parents' death or birth certificates.'

'Civil servants are like that, Fiso. They all have two jobs you know,' Stix said, mildly. Fiso was being too naïve for a seasoned sex purveyor, he thought.

'Look: a Japanese firm is making big money generating electricity out of sewage waste. All you have to do to bring your electricity bill down is shit a lot!' Stix, his eyes on the newspaper, was trying to steer the conversation in another direction.

That afternoon, it was Fiso who disappeared into her flat first, inexplicably regretting that she had let Stix have sex with her a couple of months before. They had been drunk, and she had found herself naked and collapsing onto Stix's bed, his fiendish shaft plumbing her hard-wearing orifice. 'Ey, you! That's not a good starting point!' was her only protest, and she cursed the alcohol that still swirled inside her head.

'If you'd been a virgin, Fiso, I would have washed my penis with milk, just for you,' Stix said after contenting himself. Fiso ignored the remark. More incensed with herself than with Stix, she simply decided to sleep over the anger in the hope that it would go.

In Harare, vegetable vendors can yield useful connections. After Fiso and Sue had failed to get their papers, a woman at the Central Registry was brought to the attention of Fiso by a fellow vendor. This woman, a relative, could assist her to get any form of ID for a fee. Because the vendor and her relative went to the same church, she suggested that this would be the ideal place to introduce Fiso.

Less than a hundred metres from the church building, a man of Fiso's age stood by a corner selling single cigarettes and bananas. Fiso, sensing her increasingly disagreeable nerves, sought to calm them down with a cigarette.

'Sekuru,' she addressed the man 'How much are your cigarettes?'

'I'm not your Sekuru. Harare does not have any Sekurus. They are all in the rural areas. If you desire a Sekuru then make one for yourself out of cardboard.'

'How much are your cigarettes?' she asked again avoiding the contentious term.

'Fifteen dollars.'

She quietly retrieved three brand new five-dollar coins from her purse, handed them over and picked a Madison Red from among the many on display. Contentedly lighting the cigarette and avoiding eye contact, she heard the man ask, 'What time is it?'

'If you need a watch why don't you make yourself one out of cardboard?' she retorted, and walked away, victorious.

With what panache does fate deliver the person of a harlot into a church building? Cockroaches appear through the cracks in the walls and wave their antennae in response to an almost primeval call. The priest, beneath his holy regalia, shudders, aware of the relative paleness of his cloistered virtues in the face of a salvation cobbled together on street corners. Against the tide of attrition of the human condition, what man of cloth can offer a soul a better salvation than the sheer dogged will to live? In the priest's mind, however, such sentiments only manifested themselves in vague notions of jealousy and contempt. As Fiso strolled in carefree, the holy man recoiled, the congregation's heads turned, and the devil chuckled. A Dynamos Football Club T-shirt, fluorescent green mini-skirt and six-inch high perspex platform shoes upstaged the holy word.

Destructive distillation is a process by which a substance is subjected to a high temperature with the absence of oxygen so that it simply degenerates into its several constituent substances without burning. After her silent confessions and having received the body and blood of Christ, Mrs Shava found herself subjected to destructive distillation by an ogling congregation. Like anyone being introduced to a person of dubious appearance on sanctified premises, she degenerated into her constituent attributes of self-righteousness and caution.

'The church services are short here – or was I late,' Fiso remarked after being introduced to Mrs Shava by her vending friend.

'No, we're not like those Pentecostal churches, we're less fanatical.' Mrs Shava said, unable to look Fiso straight in the eyes and bewildered, her mind whirling with an elliptical sense of *déjà vu* as she wondered where they had met before. She could also feel the stares of the congregation pecking at her back from several metres away. She resented them but neither did she like talking to Fiso. However, having listened to her plight, she agreed to help her out. Everyone had to live, after all.

'Eeeek, ahh, it's complicated.' Mrs Shava moaned, a technique that she had perfected after helping several people. 'It's no easy task,' she continued, wanting to justify her fee.

'I understand, but I must have a birth certificate. And my daughter cannot get one if I don't have one – and she needs a passport.'

'I can try, but it is a risk, I could lose my job.' Mrs Shava assumed a pious expression. Fiso knew that it was time to tie up her end of the deal. She understood what Mrs Shava meant when she said that success depended on a number of factors; Fiso knew it meant one thing only.

'I understand it's a big risk, but I intend to reward you for your efforts.' Fiso glanced at her friend for clues but the vendor's face was as blank as a hospital wall. 'I don't know what you would like, but I'll leave you to decide, my sister.' Mrs Shava's lips parted dispassionately to reveal her white teeth. 'Okay, call me on Wednesday and I will see if it's all right for you to come to my office. People at my workplace will be on strike but I can't risk my job. If it's okay, I'll give you the forms, you fill them in and I'll take them back. And don't forget my fee: $15,000!' She smiled for the first time and turned to walk away.

'Uhh, huh, your phone number at work?' Fiso stammered

'Nyasha will give it to you, I have to see someone else,' came the reply.

Fiso turned to Nyasha, and they smiled at each other.

Contentedly walking off, Mrs Shava could not have guessed that in less than a minute she would be caressed by more poltergeistic echoes of a recent past. She was walking out of the church premises when Stix stopped by to pick up Fiso in his scarlet car. A shiver descended Mrs Anna Shava's spine as she recalled the night she killed the street kid. Fiso's face, though, defiantly refused to fit into the jigsaw puzzle, and Mrs Shava could only watch in bewilderment, as old harlot jumped into the car, which rattled away, accelerating sideways like a crab.

In a mortuary at the central hospital, clad in a blue suit, white shirt, and seemingly asphyxiated by the tie around its neck, lies a slightly overweight corpse. A cellphone is still stuck in one of the pockets and when it rings for the third time, it is answered by a being who, after years as a mortuary cleaner, picking his wages from its floor, has become indifferent to death.

'Hullo, Central Hospital,' he answers.

'Hullo, I'm looking for my husband, is that his phone you are using? Who are you? Is he there?'

'Aah, I don't know, but unless this is the body of a thief who stole the phone from your husband, your husband is dead. The police shot him in the head. They said he was rioting in the city centre.'

The previous night Anna's husband had not returned from work. That he would have come to such a rough end, no one could have guessed. But being in the insurance industry he would have appreciated it, if he'd been told that the value of his life was equivalent to twenty condoms, and in all likelihood would not have contested such a settlement being awarded to Anna. His death, though, had consequences that reverberated through to Fiso, because on the day she was supposed to call Mrs Shava, grief and its attendant ceremonies had already claimed her. Then on Monday, having spent all night at Piri-Piri, the city's sleaziest night-club, Fiso decided to take the central registry juggernaut head-on. Suffering from a hangover, and caring not about consequences, she went straight to the Registrar General's office.

'I've been trying to get a birth certificate and can't, because your staff members only care about getting bribes!' The Registrar General's secretary remained calm, picked up the phone and dialled, but before she had uttered a word, the RG had emerged from his office. Being a constant target of ridicule by the press as the man heading one of the most inefficient and corrupt government departments, he was very sensitive to criticism.

'How can I help you, lady?' he demanded impatiently.

'I only need a birth certificate, but your staff is only interested in frustrating people into paying bribes!'

'Those are serious allegations.' The RG's interest lay only in smothering public objections.

'All I want is a birth certificate, Sir. My womanhood is an old rag. I've paid the price of living. Please do not waste my time, I'm too old for that.'

The Registrar nearly had convulsions. 'Sandra, call security!' he ordered.

The secretary fumbled, dropped her pen and spilt her coffee.

'Your staff members all want bribes. I come to you and all you do is get rid of me! I suppose you want a bribe too? What else can you do apart from sitting on your empty scrotum all day?'

In a little less than half an hour Fiso was behind police bars facing a charge of public disorder. The police, however, soon found their case stalling. There was no way of establishing her identity because she did not have an ID. After she told the investigating officer that she was trying to get just such an ID when she was arrested, the officer called the Registrar General who offered to quickly process an ID, if it was in the interest of facilitating the course of justice. That afternoon Fiso was bundled into the back of a Landrover Defender in handcuffs and taken to the Central Registry to make an application for an ID. Predictably she refused to co-operate, so she was later thrown back into the vehicle and taken to the police cells.

Two days went by, each bringing a new face into the cell she shared with six other women. On the third day two cellmates went for trial and never returned – either freed or sent to Chikurubi Maximum. Then a new inmate arrived. From her appearance one would have surmised that she was a teenager picked up from the vicinity of a village while herding goats. It was her carefree disposition that won her the attention of her cellmates.

'What are those for?' she asked, looking up at the left corner of the cell. The officer who had brought her had hardly locked up. No immediate answer came until the officer had disappeared.

'Those are CCTV cameras,' someone finally answered her.

'What is CCTV,' the girl asked again.

'Closed Circuit Television. It enables them to watch us from their offices all the time on one of their televisions.'

Later in the evening when another new face was brought in, the goat-herd girl asked the officer: 'Is it true that you have a TV and that you are watching us?'

The officer just continued with his duty of locking up the gate as if nothing had been said. Goat-girl was, however, unfazed.

'I think you people are going to be in trouble when the president finds out that you are wasting TVs on criminals. I'm sure he would like to be watched on TVs too. Or watch himself so that he's safe from assassins and perverts?'

After five days in the cell Fiso was cautioned and released without charge – not even that of failing to produce an ID. The investigating officer, seeing that the case was going nowhere, had managed to convince his superior to release her with just one statement: 'It's only an ageing whore.'

✂ Maria's Interview ✂

Julius Chingono

Maria arrived at No. 28 Shava Road, a house at the top of a hill in the plush suburb of Highlands to the north of Harare, to find an unwelcoming entrance. She looked closely at the wooden plate posted on one of the brick pillars that held the rusting steel gate. The plate read O and S Ga.adzi.wa, the paint was peeling and letters were missing. She put down her two green canvas bags and noticed that they were already blotched by red soil. The gate was not locked but a big key hung on a chain from the gatepost that tilted a little inside the yard. There was no one in sight. A driveway of concrete blocks stretched away from the gate and was flanked by huge jacaranda trees. Maria, stretching, stood on her toes and peered through the overgrowth of trees and shrubs, squinting in the haze of the hot afternoon. A white house peeped through the fading green of trees and wilting flowers. But Maria did not dare walk through the gate. She feared dogs although she saw no sign of life beyond the gate. The yard was hot and lifeless, except for the faint twitter of birds, and the drone of vehicles behind her on the access road.

With difficulty, Maria shook the chain strung around the gatepost. It was the only way she could draw the attention of the people in the house, if there were any there. Then she hit the frame of the gate with the hanging key, and the metal clanged through the air, disturbing the birds in the cool shadows of the trees.

She took a handkerchief from the hip pocket of her faded blue jean skirt and blotted the sweat that ran down behind her ears and above her eyes. She rubbed her bare arms. She straightened the cheap pendant that fell from her neck, arranged her skirt and brushed away the loose strands of her permed hair with her palm.

A girl in a green tracksuit appeared in the driveway. She stopped when she saw Maria and stared at her silently. She wore rubber slippers of different colours and her hair was uncombed. She was about eighteen years old, Maria's age. Maria raised her hand. She did not find the strength to shout. The gesture shook off the girl's hesitation and she walked towards the gate.

'Can I help you?' she said abruptly, standing well back. Maria wondered how the girl was managing in the glaring heat – a zipped-up track-suit, goodness she must be hot.

'Good afternoon, I would like to see Mrs Gahadzikwa.'

'Is she expecting you?' The girl looked at Maria, shading her eyes from the sun with the palm of her hand. She shrugged lightly when her eyes shifted to the big bags lying beside Maria. She did not seem to like visitors whom she could not recognise.

'I hope so.' Maria's voice was shaky. She moved nearer the gate, moistening her lips with her tongue.

'She is not in.'

'I have got a letter for her.' The girl stretched out her hand to receive it but Maria did not give her the letter that was tucked in the hip pocket of her skirt. Instead, she tried briefly to explain how she happened to be enquiring about Mrs Gahadzikwa.

'I understand Mrs Gahadzikwa is looking for a housemaid. My previous employer referred me to her.'

'Okay, you can wait. She'll be coming any time from now,' the girl said, 'She is somewhere in the neighbourhood.'

'Thank you.'

Maria watched the girl walk away fast, wiping her face with the front of her track suit jacket, and disappear at the bend in the driveway. She hoped her manners were not those of her prospective employer's.

She turned and found herself some shade below a big gum tree across the road. The late September heat was dazzling to the eye above the tarmac. She sat down on her handkerchief, spread over the resinous leaves of the tree and inhaled the aroma of mint. Her bags kept vigil at the gate. She whiled away the time by combing her hair behind her ears and touching up her dark face with a brown powder and red lipstick. She waited. The traffic droned up and down the access road. She thought of the reference letter from her previous employer. She felt it was written in the right language and tone to impress her prospective employer. Hardworking. Honest. Reliable. Mrs Mukoko, her previous employer, had given her the letter to read before she sealed the envelope. She smiled at herself in the small mirror of her handbag. The job was hers, she thought.

A tall fat woman without an evident waist-line approached the gate. She wore a baggy blue flowery dress. A big straw hat tilted to one side of her head blocked Maria's view of the woman's features. Her body seemed to sway with the effort of walking. Reaching the gate she observed the two large bags and raising the front brim of her straw hat, looked around. Maria rose and swiftly carried her 4 foot 2 inches of height across the road towards the woman, trying quickly to close her handbag as she moved, but leaving her handkerchief behind her.

'Good afternoon.' Maria's voice was more than polite.

'Afternoon. Can I help?' The woman quickly proceeded through the gate, then half-turned and spoke to Maria through the rusty bars, eyeing the bags as she did so. Maria suspected that this was her prospective boss, though she seemed strangely unreceptive. Her voice was barely audible. Sweat dripped heavily from her chin, in the afternoon heat.

'Mrs Mukoko sent me with this letter.' The woman arranged her hat to shade her face, then she rested her hands on the gate and immediately jumped back with a cry. The metal was burning hot. She seemed entirely pre-occupied as if Maria was no more incidental than a fly. The girl fumbled in the pocket of her skirt and pulled out a crumpled envelope. She curtsied as she poked the envelope through the bars. She needed the job. She had left her previous place of employment without being paid her last salary and she badly needed money, let alone food and accommodation. She knew how interviews for domestic employment were conducted. Politeness and servility were often key.

'Let's see.' The woman did not take long with the letter; Maria watched her fat fingers grasping it and observed the woman's bare plump shoulders rippling under her skin. She concluded that she did not resemble any of her previous employers and she would have to tread carefully.

'Uhm, come through!' The woman sounded pleased but she did not open the gate; instead, as if she was expecting Maria to follow her, she began to make her own way up the drive, the open letter and torn envelope pinched between her fingers.

Maria threw the bags inside the gate and forgot to close it when she hurried after the woman. The woman did not look back as she swayed heavily up the drive, her brown leather slippers pattering steadily ahead of Maria.

'What's your name?' she called out.

'My name is Maria.' Maria trotted up behind to fall within hearing distance. The weight of her bags grew heavier on her small arms. She fell in behind the woman listening hard for any further questions as she struggled to stop the bags from dragging on the ground.

Beyond the bend in the driveway, the white house exposed itself. It was evidently bigger than the one she worked in before. The white paint on the walls and the blue of the gutters appeared new. She hoped white was not the woman's favourite colour. Maria's eyes did not dwell much on the garden. A quick look showed that it needed work: the shrubs were overgrown, the wilting flowers needed water, the lawn wanted cutting, and ant-hills sprouted in the red earth A big munhondo and another musasa tree stood tall in the front yard.

But Maria did not pay the garden much attention. She hoped there was a gardener. There was certainly work to be done. She stumbled up the steps of the porch, staggered forward and fell on her bags but the woman did not turn to investigate the cause of the slight commotion behind her. She opened the door and walked into the house. Maria picked herself up and quickly squeezed herself and bags through the door before it closed.

'Take a seat.' Maria sat down on a sofa nearest to the door. The woman disappeared into a passage that led into a room where Maria could hear children playing. Their noise was interrupted by the voice of a woman, but Maria did not hear what she was saying, though she recognised the voice of the girl who came to the gate.

The women did not take long. She came back holding a baby boy aged about two, Maria thought. A wet towel hung around the woman's neck. The woman fell into a sofa directly opposite the one that Maria was sitting on. She switched on a big blue fan that ran noiselessly behind her. Maria observed her quietly. She seemed more yellow than brown with thin lips that slanted downwards. Her nose was small below a pair of sleepy eyes. When she breathed she let out a slight whistle. She had no visible eyebrows and her hair was tied into a ball at the back of her head.

'By the way what's your name, Sisi?'

'Maria Mhofu.' Maria sat at the edge of the sofa pulling her mini skirt that was exposing her young thighs. 'I will not mind if you call me Sisi.' Her voice felt unnecessarily loud and she looked at the woman with concentration. She knew the interview was still in progress. She did not want to miss a word uttered by the woman's discontented mouth.

'Okay, that makes it easy for the kids. Have you been to school?' While she waited for Maria's reply, she introduced her light brown child, whom she called Di. The child was only wearing diapers. He played with his mother's big straw hat. The mother stretched the child's hand towards Maria. 'Say Sisi ... Sisi!' Her tone was English and the baby laughed looking at its mother with interest and waiting for her to repeat the unusual sound. 'I passed two, two O-level subjects, English and Fashion and Fabrics,' Maria said without regret.

'You are the girl I am looking for. You may as well call me Amai.' Maria thought with relief, 'the job's mine'. Amai stared at Maria.

'I will,' Maria replied looking down at her bags.

'What I would like you to do is talk and teach my children English – I mean, your medium of communication should be English.' A smile slid down her slanting lips.

'I will.' Maria nodded her head slowly thinking that if Amai was now giving instructions the job must be hers. She liked her new boss's manner of recruitment, it was at least fast. 'I can show you my certificate when I have unpacked.' Maria did not keep her school certificates handy because she never expected anyone to ask to see her educational qualifications. Most prospective employers bothered about experience and nothing else.

Amai handed Di to Maria. Then she struggled to rise. She held on to the armrest of the sofa with both hands and pushed her body upwards; standing, she panted and complained about the heat, wiped her face with the wet towel and moved towards the kitchen. Maria thought she must be about thirty years old, though her feet were swollen – maybe she was suffering from some overweight disease. She embarked on an English lesson with Di.

'Say Dhe e..e..dhi?' She lifted the child by his armpits and plonked him securely on her knees facing her. Di was too heavy for his age. 'Say siii si.' Di found Maria's tone interesting.

The child laughed and waited, looking at Maria for more funny sounds.

Amai returned cuddling a smaller baby, one about nine months old. Maria's heart sank. Amai sank down on her sofa and started to breast-feed the child who was called Kuku. The baby sucked noisily as if she was not finding enough milk.

'Your other duties will be cleaning every room in this house. We have four bedrooms, a kitchen, a dining room and a lounge.' It sounded like an achievement. Maria took a brief look around the room they were in. There were four big black Dralon sofas, a colour TV and video set. A big brass flower-pot with an exuberant green climber popularly known as 'money-maker' sat at the back of the door to the porch. Its branches trailed around the top of the window-sills. The leaves were covered with dust. A mahogany display cabinet with glasses and ornaments occupied half the width of the room behind Amai. The furry carpet was brown, brilliantly decorated with flowers that blew out from the centre. The radio, stereo, a table with a vase of plastic flowers, a coffee table, three stools, a small table for the telephone, were scattered around the rest of the spacious lounge. Two big photographs hung on opposite walls: one of Amai, in colour, and one of a bearded man of about thirty-five years of age in black and white.

The room was too big for Maria's liking. She sighed and arranged her skirt, which had slipped to her pelvis. Amai noticed and glared at Maria. She did not utter a word but her glare said it all. That such dressing was not acceptable.

'After cleaning the house …' Amai stopped: the manner in which she emphasised 'cleaning' showed that she had a keen taste for cleanliness. Maria imagined that the girl in a tracksuit must have been doing the cleaning because one could not expect Amai to do much, given her weight. The room appeared tidy but she knew that she was expected to do better, judging from the voice of her new employer. 'The household linen and clothes.' Obviously Amai did not own a washing machine or a hoover. 'We will appoint set days for the laundry – washing clothes and household linen.' Amai closed her sleepy eyes as if she were trying to remember some more instructions, while giving her breast a good squeeze for the still-sucking Kuku.

'I hear Amai.'

'Sisi, you must be very careful – how you handle the different fabrics.' She opened her eyes and stared at Maria.

'I will – er – I know.' Maria stammered, nodded and looked away shielding her face with Di.

'Sisi, if you are not sure of something, please ask.' Amai had forgotten that Maria passed Fashion and Fabrics at O-Level.

'I will.' Her tone was that of a bride exchanging marriage vows.

'My husband has a mammoth appetite for well-prepared food. He does not just complain but he refuses to eat badly prepared food. And I do not want him to go to work or to bed on an empty stomach.' From the kitchen Maria heard the clanking of a spoon and the spatter of frying meat. Maria imagined the girl in the tracksuit sweating before a hot stove.

'Is that meat cooked, Munya?' Amai swallowed, and then shouted in a voice that managed to be heard. She seemed fond of abbreviating names: Kuku, Di, Munya. Maria bit her lip when she imagined how Amai would shorten her own name. Her mind trailed away to her previous employer who never believed in taking short cuts to anything.

'I boiled it for an hour.' The girl with the husky voice appeared at the lounge door. Her tracksuit jacket was unzipped, exposing a pair of small, upright unbrassiered breasts. Her face was moist from the heat but her dark skin seemed to have been in some cold shower. Maria watched the girl she then knew as Munya hold the spatula like a cricket bat. She had a very forgettable face. The smell of frying beef seeped through the door where she stood.

'You know your brother-in-law – how he is with food?' Amai glared at the girl but her voice was low.

'I know he is a toothless hyena.'

'Let him hear you call him names,' Amai shouted to her retreating back. Munya gave a loud chuckle as she disappeared back into the kitchen.

'Sisi, what's in your bags? Are they both yours?' Amai's glare fell hard on Maria, who talked from behind Di.

'Yes, my blankets and clothes.'

'Sisi, you will have to open your bags – and show me what you have brought.'

Amai's eyes grew larger and her slanting lips were pursed. 'Sisi, put Di down on the floor and unpack.' Maria stared at Amai from behind Di in disbelief. How could the woman make such an order?

'It is not my fault. A girl I engaged last year stole from her previous employer and hid the clothes in this very house when the police were after her.' Amai's voice grated. Maria moved backwards in her seat. She did not put Di down.

'Here? Now?' Maria's voice was faint.

'Yes. I do not want to get up over such a petty matter. Place the child on the floor. And unpack so that I can see.'

The order was accusing.

The nipple of Amai's breast slipped out of Kuku's mouth but Amai did not realise it. She latched her eyes onto the bags. 'Open your bags.' She pointed. Her voice had gained volume.

Maria bit her lip, set the child on the floor like a doll and tore open the first bag, near to her. Her hands trembled. 'Tse.' The angry sound escaped her. She threw out her clothes, one by one, shaking each one with trembling vigour. Blouses, skirts, dresses, petticoats, knickers, bras, shoes, sandals. Some of the items fell into Di's hands and Di pulled them with his sticky fingers. Ha. This was fun. Birth control pills. Sanitary pads. Cotton wool, soap, two towels.

'How old are you?'

'Eighteen.' So what? Maria's stare did not distract Amai. She seemed to be looking for something in particular, as if Maria was already a thief. Then a small bottle appeared.

'Perfume. Let's see.' Amai reached out for the tiny bottle with both hands. 'Did you …?' she asked when she held the three-cornered miniature bottle above her head, glaring suspiciously at the name. 'Narcisse', she read the faint label on the bottle. A triumphant smile replaced her suspicious glare. Maria did not look up. She produced another bottle. It was even smaller. It appeared more expensive than the first, the label was new. Amai temporarily forgot about Kuku who slept buried between her thighs. She was turning the first bottle round and round and viewing it from all sides, and then seeing that Maria had produced another one, she lunged forward and seized the small glass bottle by its golden top. Amai placed both bottles in the palm of one hand and observed them as if they were rare jewels. 'Mrs Mukoko gave them to me because she could not pay me off.' Maria's voice choked.

The first bag was empty and Maria pulled the bigger one, unzipped it, but Amai's attention was consumed by the perfume that she was inhaling from the second bottle. She breathed in the scent as if she was drawing in a life-saving vapour.

'How could she pay you with such expensive perfume?' She did not look at Maria, who threw her blankets out, oblivious to the fact that they fell on Di.

'She did not have the money and I did not like the dresses she offered.' Maria talked fast; she did not care whether Amai heard or not. Di cried forlornly under the weight of blankets but Amai took no notice. Maria pulled the small boy out from under the blankets.

'How much did she owe you?' She inhaled the scent again from the bottle, closing her small eyes. A heady aroma filled the room as it was dispersed by the fan.

'One thousand three hundred dollars'. Maria said quietly. She had finished removing her blankets from the second bag. Amai did not look down at the floor that was now covered with Maria's belongings.

'How many months?' Amai took another deep breath from the three-cornered bottle. It seemed she thought of perfume as the physic of perpetual life.

'Two.' Maria sat back and watched Amai go through another ritual of drawing in the scent with her eyes closed; and releasing her breath with her eyes transfixed by the two tiny bottles in her hand. There was silence. Di was attracted by the blue plastic pack of birth control pills; he reached across and seized the packet and then tried to open it with his teeth. Very little attention was accorded to him behind the heap of clothes and blankets.

'I will have to check on you.' Amai put the miniatures carefully on the floor. She laid the sleeping Kuku on the sofa and heaved herself up from her seat. Seeing what Di was up to she grabbed at the packet of pills. Di screamed. She thrust her breast back inside her dress. 'I will have to phone Mrs Mukoko.' She walked heavily past Maria towards the phone. Maria watched and waited. She felt blank. Di continued wailing. Maria seemed not to hear. But Amai expected Maria to care for the child. The child rose, grabbing at a chair leg, still crying.

Maria did nothing. She did not even look at it. 'Get a hold of that child, Sisi,' Amai ordered but Maria looked away. She was not concerned any more. Job or no job. She only wanted Amai to discover her innocence. And then she would leave. 'Maria, mind the toddler.' But the child made its tearful way over to its mother and clung to her leg. 'Yes,' Mrs Mukoko was available. The niceties of housewives' chat were briefly exchanged.

'That girl is here. But I find she has valuables. She has some very expensive perfume.'

'Perfume? Ah you know how it is with girls, and this one has a fancy for expensive things.' Mrs Mukoko's voice echoed faintly down the line.

'Yes, but did you give her the two perfumes?'

'Yes. I gave her.'

'I just wanted to check, you know what happened to me last year.'

'No, she is okay, I – I – gave her – no problem.'

Mrs Gahadzikwa thanked Mrs Mukoko for sending the girl Maria, and put the phone down. She picked up Di who was now anchored to the lower part of her dress. She moved very slowly.

'All clear, Sisi. Before I sit let me show you your room.' Maria did not look up. She remained huddled in her seat, her hands crossed at her knees. 'Here you are, Sisi.' Ama tried to hand the two perfume bottles to Maria. The girl rose and took them. Tears escaped from her eyes.

'I did not want to be paid in perfume.'

'I have to be careful…' Amai's voice faded as she left the room, but Maria did not follow. She began slowly repacking her clothes.

☙ Queues[1] ☙

Shimmer Chinodya

Some time in the early prime of my life I lost faith in myself.

In the mid-seventies Sisi Elizabeth earned twenty-two dollars a month working for white people. I hauled my trunk, black like a coffin and heavy with books, into her little wooden cabin at the back of that hideously large yard. I arrived bruised and sore, expelled from school, utterly desperate, banished for raising my tender adolescent fists against Rhodesia. Sisi Elizabeth returned every now and then from the white mansion and wiped her creased brow with her apron and adjusted her nanny's cap and said, 'But cousin, you must be starving. What will you have to eat? Don't be afraid, they are not here. They are away on holiday in Cape Town. Monkey Valley or something.' I shoved my modesty into my shorts and she took me to the house and showed me a 'dick freeze' loaded to the neck with steaks. I reclined in a resplendent lounge, timidly sampling Dolly Parton records and *Illustrated Life* and *Personality* magazines in that strange superior house. Later I gorged myself on the spaghetti and mince and cheese she had prepared. For a week while I waited for the news of this latest disaster to get through

---

[1]   This story was written at the Caine Prize Workshop, Monkey Valley, Cape Town, 4 – 13 March 2003.

to my parents, I lived in that white house, eating rich strangers' food, listening to rich strangers' records and writing angry stories on a strange typewriter.

Rudo said I had to believe in myself. Expulsion sometimes felt like a bad start.

I was on the plane fleeing from I know not what going to I know not where and I know not why. I saw her profile and black-stockinged legs and short hair and the rings on her fingers and I recognised her at once. University. A quarter of a century ago. Sociology or Law. Probably now some NGO chef. She was dozing, her face turned up to the ceiling of the plane, perhaps meditating in the peaceful way people do when they are flying among the clouds, miles above the world. I mastered the courage to accost her. She spoke to me with the quick shallow warmth and precocious airs of women who become widows too early in life, of women who clutch at the tattered shreds of perceived bliss, of single mothers who cling to files and reports and Bibles to bolster their waning sanity in a vicious world. She baffled me with her newly acquired strength. I tried to be level with her, to hide the horns of my chauvinism. I tried to be honest and serious with her, with myself; not to flirt; not to patronise or to be frivolous; to avoid shocking her with the depth of my depression. She said earnestly, 'Call me any time and we can talk. But don't you have a wife to love?'

Once upon a time in the days of Sisi Elizabeth a loaf of bread cost twelve cents and you could buy a kilogram of meat for a dollar. Twice upon a moon your father sent you, by registered mail, two dollars pocket money to last half a term. Thrice upon a star you ate chicken and chips for twenty-five cents, and with Sidney at the end of the term you patrolled the train at night, munching five-penny mints and Choice Assorted biscuits. Four times upon a sun your father sent three siblings to boarding school on a milkman's pay. Five times upon a galaxy you had rice and chicken for Christmas. Six times upon the universe you were poor, but you survived.

The rains came. Rivers gurgled and dams burst, but not all the time. Hippos waded out of the rich mud. The spirits of the land smiled, and sometimes frowned. Without fertilisers you could reap thirty bags of maize and thirty-five bags of groundnuts from ten acres and the GMB sent you back with your unwanted produce, or with peanuts in your pockets. If you reaped nothing you pawned a beast for a bag of grain. You were dirt poor, but you seldom starved.

I told Rudo that I wanted to believe in myself.

I told her I wanted a good woman to help me do that, that the best thing for a man was a good woman. A good, funny, honest woman. A woman to enjoy, to like, to love, to talk to, to laugh with, to devour, to feast on. A soul- and brain-mate. A woman who does not take herself too seriously and does not do too much of the church stuff. An intelligent woman who knows what she's about and has many layers to her that I can slowly peel off. A woman who is dependable, yet will allow me the foolishest of my fantasies. A woman who will help me organise myself. A woman who will let me talk to Hazvina or Memory or Nontokozo, and will not imprison my imagination.

'You must be an aspiring polygamist, then,' laughed Rudo.

'I suspect so,' I replied. 'My grandfather had two.'

'And what became of him and his wives? Did he become another statistic in a classic case of poisoning?'

'OK, things did not work out well. They never do, but polygamy could be beautiful. If I had two wives we would live and love and laugh together, dress to kill and go out as a threesome.'

'Where would you find women like that?'

'They must be there somewhere in this universe.'

'You, an educated man, saying such things. The feminists will immolate you.'

'I hope not.'

'Do you see a woman merely as an object?'

'God, please no.'

'OK – but why do you want to be mothered so much? Why do you want to define yourself in terms of another person?' Why why why?

In '67 and '73 there was drought, but that was before independence. Our mothers served us yellow sadza on the tables – the infamous 'Kenya' – so called because some of that brand of maize was imported from East Africa. In 1980, the year of our independence, Chaminuka and Nehanda smiled and released a deluge of rain to wash away all the blood and pain of the war. Crops flourished. Livestock lowed and baa-ed and bleated joyously in the plains, munching luscious grass. Even the backyards of township houses and the scrapland between factories and townships boasted greenly of abundant harvests. Silos filled fatly, trains thundered thankfully away to foreign lands, laden with exports. We were given sweet reprieve. We were declared the bread-basket of the region.

I met Rudo for lunch a few weeks after we got back home. She had on a black see-through blouse and an ankle-length denim skirt with a long slit on the side. She wore lipstick and a dark eye-shadow; her short hair had a special glow. I could tell she had done something to make herself look OK. She possessed a quiet simplicity that made me ache longingly within, that made me gasp at the degree of my despair, at the extent of my famine. She drank mineral water and ordered a cheese and tomato sandwich, which she carefully nibbled. She staunchly refused to take wine or spirits or beer, saying that she drank only on very special occasions and when she didn't have to go to work, saying that her late husband had only persuaded her to take the occasional glass. I somberly sipped my beer and fingered the bank notes in my pocket and tried to be engaging. Her answers were short. She seemed to be hovering on the borders of her own dilemma, waiting for some decided declaration from me. She laughed briefly and politely at my jokes, judging me, trying to fathom the reasons and nature of my interest in her. I wondered if she was worth the effort, if she was not chained too much to propriety; why I needed to be with her, why she readily let me pay the bill, what it would take to make her unshackle herself from herself.

We declared independence, after that long bitter war, in 1980. In the late 80s we tried to unshackle ourselves from the past. Out went the chains of the old constitution and in came the new. Out went the premiership and in came the presidency. We ploughed forward with a show of fisted arms, with calls for reconciliation, a brave new unity and work. Of course, there weren't enough funds. It wasn't easy. We massacred each other. We manufactured enemies. We squandered resources. There was mistrust, gangrene setting in. There were die-hards who chose to shit in the face of forgiveness. We fumbled with propriety, with new challenges. The world was watching, avariciously. We invited the world out for dinner and she coyly agreed. The world came with a wig and sweet-smelling musk, large round earrings, a black T-shirt, a short denim skirt and black *gogo* shoes. She was bra-less and pant-less and we leapt to her, our mouths drooling. The world ordered a rock shandy and a tuna-fish sandwich and watched us while we knocked back lager after lager and gorged ourselves on sadza and cows' hooves. The world watched as we paid the bill, then she gave the waiter a little tip.

Rudo wanted me. She wanted to win me over bit by bit. She called me day in day out. She left innumerable messages with my maid and my children asking me to call her. I think my estranged wife saw the messages. I feared for myself. I suspected that like me, Rudo wanted to believe in somebody else so that she could believe in herself, and redefine herself. I suspected she did the church stuff, however mildly, in order to belong to something. She declared she was Catholic, that she had a rabid mistrust of the new born-again churches. I didn't believe in myself and I didn't belong to anything. But I knew I could not leave her; that I had started something that I could not stop. Rudo wanted me but she really did not want me. Her sudden change of heart bothered me. She wanted me to respect myself, to help me salvage myself from what she thought was self-

imposed gloom, but she wanted to own me like a toy. She even called me Teddy Bear. Teddy Bear! I felt a kind of pity for her. She lived with her eight-year-old daughter, her only child, in a two-bedroomed flat in a well-to-do block in the Avenues. The flat was cosy and tastefully furnished. I played CDs of the Beatles, Fleetwood Mac, Elton John, Joan Armatrading, Thomas Mapfumo, Miriam Makeba and Chiwoniso Maraire. She also had several gospel CDs by Mechanic Manyaruke and Shuvai Wutaunashe, and when I ignored the latter I told her that God had eluded me, had been too hard on me and my family.

People are defined by the music they keep and play but she confused me because of the ambiguity of her choices. I suspected some of the older music had been merely left by her husband and now she was using it to bait men. She drove an old-model Mazda which, perhaps, like her, was rust-eaten but efficient. I asked if some of her property had been left to her by her late husband, but she would not be drawn to tell me. Her daughter was beautiful and intelligent and liked me at once. Her name was Tariro. Tariro saw me like a father figure, a friend. I could tell she needed a father to cling to, somebody to love her, somebody who did not, like her mother, just order her to wash her feet or eat all her vegetables or switch off the TV and go to bed. Tariro loved books and I brought her some of the ones I had written. She curled up on the floor, between my legs, with her head in my lap and asked me to read to her. She told me the stories that she liked. She and her friends in the block decided to act out one of my children's plays. She wanted them to stage the play for me but two members of the group were away and they could not do it. When she went to bed she hugged me and kissed me on the lips and her little tongue touched mine.

Rudo smiled at me and said, 'But did you ever do this to your own children?'

I stood up guiltily and went to change the CD.

We bit off more than we could chew. We started starving bit by bit. Our teeth ached from raw meat and bone and there were not enough carcasses, not even enough dentists, so we went for the soft stuff. The national cake was getting smaller, but suddenly everyone wanted a piece. The bakeries hiccupped and coughed and sent out frantically for more wheat. The teachers wanted the cake, before it was even baked. The nurses wanted it. The doctors wanted it. The soldiers wanted it so badly that they sent in battalions in brand new Bedfords to bring it back in truckloads. The ex-combatants wanted it. The farmers wanted it. The peasants wanted it. The workers wanted it. Little children in the schools cried for milk and soup, for buns, for books. Pastors and priests in the pulpits of poverty pined for Lazarus' pitiful morsel. We squandered the national cake then turned to ordinary bread, but even that was not enough. We put up impressive schools, clinics, roads and dams. We gazetted new minimum wages, instituted quotas in workplaces, demarcated growth-points. But the new classrooms pleaded for desks; clinics squabbled for food and medicines, sun-baked roads yawned for bridges and asphalt. We printed more money. We imported doctors and teachers from other lands. We sent out planeloads of our own school-leavers to train in foreign languages, on foreign islands, so that they could come back to teach their own. We thirsted for education.

I had begun to thirst for her. She was slyly putting me through some kind of probation, as if to test me. She wanted to see whether I would behave myself and prove to be worthy of her. She deliberately called it a probation and it lasted weeks. She was clicking me off in the computer-brained folders of her psyche. I was sure she wanted me too. Perhaps it was true she had lain fallow for years, that she had survived the droughts and famines of her life, that she was now waiting dangerously to be ploughed up and seeded and fertilised. But she was holding on. Hanging in there. I felt we were both too old to pretend, that we did not need to follow any cardinal rules, that we could pass the litmus test of morality as long as we did not rob or envy or steal or maim, or do or wish anybody ill; that we could commit the lesser offences with reasonable impunity.

Our probation with the world was interminable. Night after night we took the world out for dinner and she ordered a shandy and a tuna sandwich while we knocked back lager after lager and wolfed down platefuls of cows' hooves. We would pay the bill and she would give the waiter a tip. At weekends we would order whiskies then after several glasses we became incomprehensible and had to order a taxi home. We paid the fare and the world gave the driver a tip. Later on the world would agree to go upstairs for a cup of coffee. She took off her earrings and slipped out of her *gogo* shoes and wiped off her lipstick and eye-shadow and let down her hair and perched on the edge of the bed and chirped, 'Not quite yet, not quite yet.' She counted off on her fingers our crimes and shortcomings and reproached us but we did not listen. She said, 'Stop giving ex-combatants grants,' but we did not listen. She said, 'Stop subsidising commodities,' but we did not listen. She said, 'Stop controlling prices,' but we did not listen.' She said, 'Devalue your currency,' but we did not listen. She said, 'Stop tampering with the land,' but we did not listen. She said, 'Stop grabbing farms,' but we did not listen. She said, 'OK, reimburse the white farmers you kicked out,' and we said, 'No, *you* do that. They are *your* offspring; your kind. Great-grandchildren of red-necked boys who called themselves policemen and armed themselves with rifles and rode shamelessly into our villages at dawn and planted the Union Jack and each earned themselves miles of savanna from some dainty little woman called Queen Victoria. *You* give us money to buy them out.' She said, 'But we've already given you the money for that,' and we said, 'Peanuts!' She said, 'You squandered that money. And there already is lots of government land lying unused,' and we said, 'Nonsense.' She said, 'But you've got to look at things differently. This is not the twentieth century any more. You can't go on flogging the colonial horse. The colonial horse is dead. You've got to find yourselves new horses, new *mules*. You've got to survive. You've got to change your ideas. You can't go on excusing your corruption and inexperience forever, and persecuting each other. You've got to have the rule of law.'

We were confused. We did not speak with one voice. Some of us said, 'Leave the white farmers alone,' and others said 'No way!' Some of us said, 'Don't destroy the soul of this land, the farming industry, the economy – don't turn this gem of a country into a land of peasants,' and others replied, 'Better be poor on your own land than be slaves forever.' In the towns sleek residents clicked their tongues in disapproval. In the country tottering grandmothers and grandfathers and newly reformed rustics rejoiced at the pieces of their ancestral land that were restored to them, at the little seed packs, thrifty bags of fertilisers and itinerant tractors that were availed to them. In disbelief they partitioned pastureland, dairy fields and miles of tobacco. They put up little pole and dagga huts and tilled the land with cattle and donkeys and iron ploughs. Other new farmers came purely out of greed – veritable new settlers, with not an iota of the farming instinct in their veins. Some ex-combatants and chefs were among that lot. They bullied peasants out of furnished farmhouses and barns and eyed rich valleys and well developed properties the way pot-bellied, cigar-smoking, inebriated businessmen eye virgins selling snacks outside beerhalls. Aggrieved white farmers packed up and abandoned their houses and lands to seek refuge in city flats or hotels or neighbouring countries. Highways and country roads were littered with tractors, harvesters and irrigation equipment, abandoned, pillaged or lined up for sale. The borders of chiefdoms were expanded and redefined – unwary chiefs suddenly found themselves in a quandary as their chiefdoms suddenly shrank or expanded, some of their subjects dispersed and some became victims of new ever-changing laws. The world did not speak with one voice either. It quarrelled with itself. Some voices pleaded, 'Leave this little country alone,' and the most strident among the other lot shrilled, 'No, this precedent is bad for the world, a prescription for chaos and disrespect for the rule of law. This country must be stopped at all costs – punished, humiliated, isolated, starved and squeezed until it goes down on its knees and accepts defeat.'

Rudo lies on her back on top of the sheets, spent, nursing her new dilemma. Her hair is damp, her forehead laced with sweat, her eyes blank and her mouth half open. She is half facing me, with one arm thrown in wild abandonment over my chest. My heart is slowing and stilling; I am almost numb, pervaded by a deep sense of emptiness and loss. Our clothes are strewn all over the red-carpeted floor; her elegant clock clucks three on the wall. In the adjacent bedroom little Tariro coughs and moans in her sleep.

There is something ambivalent about conquests and defeats. Something innately sad.

'You never talk about your wife,' Rudo smiles, weakly.

I don't answer. Some pain is beyond words. I am stripped of all my defences. Rudo continues, 'Why don't you just divorce her if she doesn't make you happy? It's bad for you both and it's bad for your children. Many people like you suffer because they don't opt out, because they live their lives for other people, for their parents or children or neighbours and the like. Why don't you go and get yourself a hot-blooded young lass from the high density areas – the kind with O-levels who work as typists and will serve you fried lizard tails to soften up your brain?'

'Suppose I've already had one?'

'Have you? What was her name?'

'Nontokozo.'

'What was she like? What does she do?'

'Never mind. Just don't talk badly about other women. Don't look down on other women because of their class or education or whatever. Never ever ever.'

'Does it bother you so much?'

'What about you?' I croak back. 'Who are you living for?'

'Myself.'

'Are you using me?'

'No.'

'Do you want me to marry you?'

'Of course not.'

'Is it friendship you want, then?'

'Maybe.'

'Are you a feminist?'

'Maybe. Maybe not. I was never a textbook person. I never blindly believed in any "isms". And besides, who says a feminist doesn't need a good lay?'

We never truly believed in any *'isms*. We were born capitalists, raised capitalists; we lived with racism; we flirted with Marxism; we heard about humanism and *hunhuism*,[2] we briefly espoused socialism, in lecture theatres we even dabbled with feminism and classism and ageism and now we are squashed again with the capitalists. Full circle. Perhaps the only *'isms* we truly knew were chauvinism and sexism. Maybe one day the good old world will agree to knock back several lagers and scuds and wolf down a few cows' hooves for an aphrodisiac and agree to go home with us and she will take off her earrings and rip off her wig and slip out of her *gogo* shoes and wipe off her lipstick and eye-shadow and, lo and behold, slip out of her bra-less, pant-less dress and tuck herself into bed with us and she will dream us up a brand new *'ism*. For *bitter* or worse, till death do us part, as Clopas Wandai J. Tichafa wrote.

Rudo and I did not part easily. Oh no, she didn't die. Not yet anyway. On the contrary, she started showing me off to her friends. She started saying, 'Let's go and see so and so.' Or, 'Let's go out with so and so.' Or she would say, 'Tariro is lonely. Why don't we take her out to meet her cousins?' She introduced me to people as her friend, which was fair enough, but there was always a question hovering over our relationship. People knew I was attached, that what I had going on with her could at best be described as an affair. But sooner

---

[2] Zimbabwean belief in the humanness of people propounded by the late Stanlake Samkange.

or later we would have to come to terms with ourselves, with each other. She had a special friend that she liked, a beautiful nurse called Jean. Jean was pregnant, expecting a baby – her second – anytime. Jean was our age, perhaps a bit younger, and I thought she was taking a big gamble having a baby. Perhaps the baby was an accident, or she had done it willingly. She said the man had run off somewhere or other. I didn't ask. I couldn't ask. There are things you don't ask. We went out together, Rudo and Jean and I, and had drinks and she made us a delicious pot of oxtail, tripe and intestines. We listened to rumba and jazz and talked. I asked Jean if it was OK for the baby if she drank wine and she said, 'No problem. You can't live by the book all the time. After all, rules are meant to be broken.' I wanted to believe her. After all, she was a nurse. The wanted, hunted kind who were fleeing our ramshackle clinics and flocking out to the world to work in lavish, well-lit hospitals. I liked Jean. She was a survivor. She laughed a lot, a tinkling little laugh. She and I created a wicked camaraderie and we fenced Rudo in with it, into our circle. She wanted Rudo to be happy. She nursed Rudo out of her loneliness. She had small features, a kind of quick precariousness. I knew what she would be like once she delivered the baby. She was going to have a Caesar. I did not ask why she was going to have one when she looked so healthy. I couldn't ask. There are things you don't ask. Rudo glowed with pride. She was happy to have me, to have Jean. To have friends.

After the thorny land business, we quickly lost our friends. One by one they packed their bags and left, most without saying goodbye. We woke up in the morning and found their houses and offices empty and their doors and windows wide open. There was rubbish on the unswept floors, cracked windows in the bathrooms and some of the toilets did not flush. We wrenched out their drawers and found condoms. We flung open their cupboards and found only paper-clips and pins. We raided their kitchenettes and found remnants of mouldering meals. We rummaged through their trashcans for valuables and found useless coins. The world phoned back long-distance with a crackling voice and said, 'Look, you little truant, just say you are sorry and we will come back,' and we sulked. The world said, 'Look, we want to come back and play with you. We'll give you back your marbles and bring you many more. We'll give you liquorice and candy and cake and teddy bears,' and we sulked some more. The world said, 'Now you are going to be really sorry.'

Now we were really sorry. The banks ran dry. We queued helplessly for cash that wasn't there. The industrialists went off to visit our neighbours. We ran out of foreign exchange. Our friends said, 'Enough is enough. You are a bad friend. You don't pay your debts. Now we can't give you any more fuel. Now we can't give you any more food,' and we cried,' We'll give you half our estates – we'll mortgage them to you,' and they said, 'OK, but that's not enough.' We ran around borrowing. Borrowing and borrowing. Borrowing from other friends. Borrowing from ourselves. We borrowed and borrowed until we borrowed the word borrow. Now we were really, really, sorry. We had no power. We had no electricity; aeons of coal lay unmined beneath our trees and rocks and mountains. Our own spirits, Chaminuka and Nehanda, sulked and turned against us. They said, 'No more rain, kids.' For years in a row we had no rain. It was the worst drought in memory. Crops wilted in the fields. Rivers ran dry. Cattle tore down the thatch off roofs and chased women carrying empty buckets. Baboons invaded households and grabbed live chickens. Animals died in the plains. We had no food to eat. Our shops were bare. Our granaries sneezed dust. We turned to Chaminuka and Nehanda and said, 'But what have we done? How can we have a drought *now*, when we have other problems?' Chaminuka and Nehanda sulked. Chaminuka caressed the knob of his staff and looked away from us, towards the distant hills. Nehanda picked the threads off her cloth and said, 'You know what you did.' We said, 'We don't understand. Please explain,' and she said, 'You are too young to know. One day you will know.' Now we had no water to drink. Our dams filled with sand. Our taps ran dry. We stood in queues in the scorching sun, taking turns to suck the greenish water trickling from rusty taps. We dug wells in our backyards. Our toilets leaked into our wells. We got sick. We went to empty hospitals. There were no beds. There were no medicines. There were no nurses. The nurses had run off to lavish, well-lit hospitals in foreign lands. There were a few doctors who spoke a funny language. Prices doubled every month. There were massive retrenchments. We turned to strikes, stay-aways and go-slows. We printed more and more money.

Rudo did not have much money. She had only seemed to have much money. She did not worship money, really. She was a civil servant, a poor struggling servant, a widow in her early forties, but she was content with what she had. She wanted something more than money, something she could not define, or was not prepared to define. She wanted to share her time, her miseries, herself with somebody else. She did not want my money, really. She wanted something else from me. Or so I thought. But we sometimes talked about money. Money, money, money. Like when I couldn't buy Tariro a jumbo-size pizza because the price had doubled overnight. Like when she showed me her latest salary slip with nothing on it but deductions. Like when she showed me her monthly medical-aid bills. Like when she told me she had to see three specialists every month. Like when she told me, out of the blue, out of the very, very blue, out of the bluest of blues, that she was a chronic manic-depressive. Like when she told me she had taken herself off medication because it was too expensive, and addictive. Like when she told me she had turned to yoga and meditation to get to sleep. Like when she told me she had a brain tumour for which she would have to be operated on outside the country. Like when she told me her Mazda needed a complete overhaul. Like when she showed me papers from the Salary Service Bureau detailing the paltry amounts she would get if she took an early retirement package for health reasons. Like her plans to buy a stand, or rent a stall at a flea market, or even purchase a hammer mill to grind maize if she got that precious package. Like when she asked me if we could take Jean out to comfort her after her miscarriage. I did not know how to help her. I was impotent before her wishes. If she had asked to borrow money I could have considered helping her, very much against my better instincts, I suppose, but she never asked. Not directly anyway. Perhaps the word 'borrow' did not exist in her vocabulary, or had once existed, and long ago expired. Perhaps she had already borrowed the word borrow.

Last Wednesday I was in the petrol queue all day. I phoned the garage and they told me they might have something that day and when I rushed out there I found a kilometre-long stretch of cars waiting. It was six in the morning. I was hungry and unwashed and hastily dressed. The queue snaked round three street corners and at the mouth of the garage it split into four columns of cars. The diesel queue, the trucks and Combis and buses and lorries, wound in from the opposite direction. They had camped for two days in the queue, waiting. There was pandemonium at the garage. The road was blocked. The garage attendant and security men were battling with a rush of blaring cars. A policeman was negotiating with a ring of enraged drivers. This garage usually received petrol every day but for the past few days it had had nothing. Petrol, no diesel; diesel, no petrol. It was always like that. Alternating. If you had one then you didn't have the other. I made a U-turn and parked behind the last car in the queue. The queue was not moving. I did not go to work. It was no use going to work when you did not know if you could get there and how you would come back. Somebody in our lift club had taken my children to school and I just *had* to find the fuel to go and pick them up and bring them back. I got out of the car and talked to other men under the trees. We talked about garages that sold petrol to selected customers at night. We talked about backstreet boys who sold the stuff at ten times the official price. We talked about cars or households that had gone up in flames when unwary hoarders lit up cigarettes or candles in makeshift store rooms. We talked about ailing wives; about children who go to fancy schools and talk with funny accents and refuse to cook for their daddies; about newly elevated company directors who stashed away billions. We talked about mushrooming churches that made fortunes from unsuspecting millions. We talked about the drought. We talked about new farmers who won prizes growing wheat and winter maize. We talked about others who stole irrigation pipes and fencing wire and tried to sell them off. We talked about price freezes. We talked about hoarding. We talked about houses in the townships where one could buy, at five or six times the normal price, unlimited supplies of bread, sugar, maize, mealie-meal, salt and cooking oil without having to join the queue. We talked about queues at the banks, in the supermarkets, in the pubs, at the bus stops, at the mortuaries, at the cemeteries. We talked about people stumbling like zombies, waking up at three in the morning to get to work and getting home at midnight. People turning into alcoholics to survive each and every day. We talked about catastrophes on the highways, of smashed up designer cars, of busloads of students burnt to ashes on the roads, of overturned trucks and mangled trains; the foul breath of unappeased departed souls prowling the air. We talked about men who now deserted their wives for days and slept with their girlfriends on the pretext that they were in the petrol queue. We talked about crime and divorce. We talked about AIDS.

We argued about elections.

'Our case is beyond politics,' said one resident drunk, 'We need some kind of supernatural intervention.'

The woman in the twin-cab behind me heard us and smiled and vaguely nodded us on. She threw her head back over the seat and tried to sleep. It was hot. I bought two pink freezits from a vendor and offered her one and she said 'Thank you' and sucked on it and tried to go back to sleep. I wanted to talk to her, but I don't think she had had breakfast. There were cases of cosmetics in the cab. I wondered if she was a shop owner or a sales lady. Or a border jumper.

At four o'clock Rudo phoned me on my cellphone to ask me where I was. She said she had tried to get me all day but as usual the

*network was jammed. She said she had not phoned me at home because
I had told her not to. The other day when my phone was dead she had
decided to burn up precious juice and driven right up to my gate and
hooted me out to give me a brand new shirt for a Valentine present.
I had reluctantly accepted it and thanked her but told her not to come
to my house again. The gardener and the maid could see her. My
children could see her. Besides, I didn't care a hoot for Valentine's
Day and Christmas and New Year's Day and Independence Day and
the like. I was too old for that. Holidays depressed me. I told her she
must stop leaving messages for me at home, or else. And now she was
saying the doctor's results had come and she would have to be operated
on in three weeks. She was saying her psychiatrist had said she must
go back on anti-depressants. She was asking – what was I doing in
the queue? How long was it? Was I bored? Who was that young girl
at the bakery I had said could keep bread for her? Did I want two
litres of cooking oil? How long was this petrol queue? Was it moving?
Had there been any delivery yet or were we just waiting? Could she
come and keep me company in the queue? Talk to me? Bring me some
beers? Tell me about her retirement package? About her operation?
About the anti-depressants that bloated up her body and made her
numb? About Tariro? Did I think she should send Tariro to boarding
school? Would she then be lonely? Could we talk about Jean's recent
miscarriage? About myself?*

*I told Rudo not to come. I did not want her to come. She was
wearing me down with her miseries. The last thing I wanted was
somebody wearing me down. I didn't like the way she went on about
Nontokozo and the hot-blooded, high-density lasses with five borderline
O-levels and typing certificates who were supposedly dying to serve
me fried lizards' tails to soften my brain. Rudo offered me new
possibilities, but I didn't like the way she was crowding me into the
little corner of her snobbishness and prejudice. By the time the tanker
arrived, at seven in the evening it was too late anyway, and she
would be preparing dinner for Tariro.*

When the tanker arrived people banged out of their cars and scrambled up from the kerbs to gather along the fence of the garage. A young man rode down past the fence and nonchalantly shouted, 'Diesel only! Diesel only!' A hubbub went up. Was it diesel? Was it petrol? Was it both? Surely it must be diesel because the last delivery had been petrol! No, but this green tanker had two compartments, one for diesel and one for petrol! But was it big enough for that? No, it wasn't. Yes, it was! But how was that possible? Didn't the two fuels mix? Oh, but didn't you know the tanker had two divisions inside? Didn't you know the green tankers had divisions inside? All right, but how much were they delivering? Four thousand, five thousand litres? And look at the queue! Two hundred cars at the very least. Would the delivery be enough for all the cars? Would they give full tanks or half, or only twenty litres perhaps? Would they serve until the fuel ran out or would they send the customers away at closing time and tell them to come again tomorrow? Were garages governed by closing times any more? And this garage was lucky, wasn't it? Getting deliveries when others went for weeks without anything. Look, the attendant is dipping his stick into the two tanks and they should be serving within an hour or two. Come, guys. Get into your cars and close off all the gaps. Order, patience, people. We'll *all* get served. Patience please. Gosh, I wish they would issue us tickets so we know who gets served and who doesn't, so those who won't get served don't have to waste their time in the queue. Now look, those stupid Combi drivers are jumping the queue and jamming the entrance and mobbing the policeman! God please no …

I got served at ten to eight – the day's ration of twenty litres, which would last me three days, but it was better than nothing. I threw money at the attendant, swerved away from the pump, thrust my car in front of a blaring bus, waved back the incredulous driver and inched out past the wall of Combis, into the fresh air. When I got to the school, at eight, the kids were waiting, sitting patiently in the dark, clutching their bags under the trees in the deserted yard. No one said a word as we drove home.

Now I know, Rudo.

I have been queuing up all my life.

I have been sleeping in endless queues, yawning in the tired mornings of my dreams; unwashed and hastily dressed, and naked to abuse; hungry for friendship and tolerance and thirsty for intelligence and respect. I have U-turned into lots of queues, many a wrong queue, only to be told at the crammed garages of my fantasies that I am in the wrong lane, or to be turned away. I have idled in snail-paced queues, burning up my precious juice, only to be sent away with a quarter of my fill. I have waved away kindness and trapped myself among the Combis of my own selfishness …

I'm sorry, Rudo …

⚘ Maize ⚘

Memory Chirere

When it began to rain heavily and the wind soughed, she saw it as an excuse to sit in her hut. She was too tired to cross the acres of grass and bushes to get to know her new neighbours a little better.

They had already met in an impromptu way, at the watering place. Through the first greetings and introductory conversations, they had memorised one another's names, and places of origin and even noticed their mannerisms. There is a time for everything, she would say to herself, retiring to bed in her hut, in the middle of her still largely uncultivated acres. She was, nevertheless, satisfied that she had come, beneath her feet was her land, her soil: soft virgin earth where you could dig deeply without ever striking rock.

Here the nights were long and punctuated with shrill insect calls, and one's soul crept into a hole and rested there like a nightjar.

When the door creaked, she thought it was the wind. But, to her surprise, she saw first a boot and then the full frame of a man!

She almost screamed, but the man's dreamy face in the half-light assured her that all was well.

'Caught up, here, in all this,' the man said, as an excuse. 'The rain is coming from every direction and I knew I couldn't go far.'

He looked at her, putting his hands together in greeting, and said 'Please.'

'All right,' she said, 'Take no chances in a storm.'

Reassured, he reached outside and dragged in a small battered suitcase. 'You won't mind,' he said. He had a way of looking that made her think that he was a man who had risen above his problems. He had the dreamy eyes of a newly-born puppy.

'I am on my way back to Madziwa. These people say it is too late in the season to give me some acres. Ah, how I wish I had my own ground.' Then, rather experimentally, 'You were given this portion?'

She only nodded, studying him.

'On your own?' he asked, rather slyly, his eyes half closed. She nodded again. He sank down to the floor, leant against the wall close to the door and looked up at the thatch. He chuckled, exposing great white teeth and said, 'You did it.'

'How could you tell?' she asked.

'A woman's roof, this,' he said, 'but good, nevertheless, and no leaks.

The rain thrummed outside and she thought he looked both harmless and vulnerable.

She saw him alternately yawn and doze off, and heard his bones creak like an old wooden chair. 'You don't mind,' he said, falling gradually and awkwardly to sleep, fidgeting and mumbling.

At dawn, he was still asleep in the same posture. She giggled, lifted his suitcase, and mischievously hid it behind the clay-pots.

She went out with a hoe to dig holes for sowing maize in the soft unploughed soil. The swing of a hoe, quiet thoughts, and the occasional refrain of a work song, the farmer's friend

As the sun rose, she heard him say, 'Thank you for the hospitality. I'd better be off now.' He stood at the edge of the clearing, akimbo, like a boy cooking up a trick. 'Thank you,' he repeated, and she thought he had a special voice for thank yous.

'Easy up,' he said, affectionately, 'at this rate you won't see noon.' He laughed easily and left.

She stood watching his departing figure and wondered if it had all been a dream. It must have been at mid-day when he reappeared, saying, morosely, that he had left his suitcase behind. He went into the hut and came out immediately, cross, telling her that he could not find it and that he would not tolerate any games. Amused, she went into the hut with him, showed him the suitcase and apologised for the inconvenience caused by her little game, adding that they were friends now. He would neither be pacified nor persuaded to sit down to lunch with her.

She followed him, pleading that he accept, at least, a morsel of bread wrapped in khaki paper so that he could eat as he walked. He refused, rudely, and stopping on the path, ordered her home immediately.

She threw the bread into the bushes, sat down and burst into tears. He laughed, fetched a switch from the bush as if bent on thrashing her, but she rose quickly, gathered her skirts and fled homewards.

Maize is a great crop. It sprouts and rises like grass if the soil is rich, moist and warm. Then several weeks afterwards you have to fight the weeds. Farmers say one hoe cannot do it alone, there should be several hoes on a maize field, calling and beckoning at one another. With one hoe, you can only turn and scrape while the weeds watch, calling you names.

He returned one Sunday morning, saying he was selling three brand new hoes that he carried on his shoulders, and would also see a cousin living around here somewhere.

She did not pay much attention to his programme, but kept on weeding.

He put his hoes down, selected one and joined her, uninvited. She only wanted him to say he was sorry about last time but he did not do so. When she was certain that his apology would not come, she retired to the edge of the field and sat down, visibly sulking. But he continued weeding; going down double rows, returning, cutting across the rows in squares. He would not stop and she thought he was parading his skill and she hated him for it because all she wanted was his apology.

She rose and walked to her hut knowing that, despite his zeal with the hoe, he would cast a glance at her retiring figure. Later, he followed, peeped in and found her lying down. 'What is wrong, are you ill?' he asked.

She nodded and closed her eyes. 'Do you even care,' she thought. She rolled over and faced the wall. He picked up her old axe and went out. She heard the sound of chopping wood and she thought how sweet the sound was. He came back with short logs and carefully lit a fire.

In the evening she complained of a headache but he said he was going away and would maybe see her one day. He laughed casually and began to walk away and she hated him with all her might.

She rose, went after him and told him never to come again to her acres.

He said he did not mind, laughed again, lifted his three hoes onto his shoulder and hurried away in the setting sun.

She rushed into her hut and cried for a long time and did not rise to prepare supper.

The following day, she felt cold and dizzy. She thought it was because of the crying. She rebuked herself for having cried about a man, a stranger. When she tried to rise, she slumped down and groaned. She told herself it could not be malaria but just a common cold that would pass, as many other things had passed in her life.

In the afternoon, it rained heavily. When she crawled across the hut and looked out, she reflected that her knee-high maize crop was a garden in the middle of a wilderness. Maize speaks about human presence and settlement.

She lay back thinking that on just such a rainy day, the man had happened across her for the first time. She would have called out his name, if she'd known it. She had a vision of him walking through the storm, his brand new hoes aslant across his shoulders, walking to the end of the world.

Days later, she entered her hut with a bunch of vegetables and found him squatting by the fireside, roasting a piece of meat. She coughed and sat down.

He did not greet her or excuse himself for trespass. She dealt with him as if he had always been with her, only asking, 'Will it take long to roast?'

'It is almost done,' he said in a low voice that made her think he always had a different voice for each statement he uttered. He scooped the meat from the fire, deftly tore it into two pieces and held out a piece to her. 'Good when it is hot,' he said. But she did not take it, prompting him to place it carefully on an empty plate next to her, before he left.

At first she thought he only wanted some fresh air, but, later, she knew he had gone away. Her heart sank helplessly with the setting sun.

That night she wished it would rain. Rain helped her create the sweet-sad illusion that he was in the hut with her, snoring by the door, an old suitcase at his feet.

The maize was soon tasselling, rolling up the top leaves and pointing into the sky, where all things come from: blessings, curses, darkness, rain, winds, locusts, friends …

Then, in the patter-putter of a morning drizzle, two men, her neighbours, brought the man in unconscious. 'He said he was from Madziwa and that he is your husband! All we know is he wanders about the new acres.' They deposited him at her door and left.

When he regained strength and speech a day or two later, he said he had suddenly felt dizzy and violently sick and now should he go away again? He was all right. He was rarely ill.

She said that no he should rest. There was no need to wander about, really, when she had acres she could not exhaust by herself.

He did not talk again about going away. When she asked him why he had told her neighbours that he was her husband, he laughed, but later, he looked her straight in the eyes and said, 'Suppose I should try?'

It was her turn to laugh, and he let her be. When she was through, he surprised her by gathering her in his arms and hoisting her up.

'Yes,' she chuckled, as he brought her down and pinned her, playfully, beneath him, on the floor.

❧ Fancy Dress ❧

Alexandra Fuller

My *mother dressed me up* as 'I Never Promised You a Rose Garden'
for a Fancy Dress party at the de Wet's farm. Being a closet-lover of
Barbie dolls, fairy princesses and high-heel shoes, I had been
lobbying hard to attend the fancy dress attired in something pink
and frilly.

But, 'You don't even like dresses,' my mother told me.

'Yes, but how can I dress up as a Rose Garden?' I argued. 'Nobody
can be a Rose Garden.'

'No, no. That's just the point, Alison. You're *not* a Rose Garden.
"I *Never* Promised You A Rose Garden."'

'But why?' I wailed.

'It's your song. It's what was playing on the radio when you were
born.'

'That's even *worser*. How can I dress up as a song?'

'*Worse*,' said my mother, 'that's even *worse*.'

Tears pricked the back of my eyelids but I could not let them
spill. My mother resented tearful children whom she usually treated
with a sharp smack, 'To give you something *real* to cry about.'

'How come Veronica gets to be a princess?'

'Because the tutu that the Viljoens gave us fits her and it doesn't fit you *and* she has long hair.'

Veronica smirked. My hair had recently been chopped to within an inch of its life. Now it stood in uneven bristles.

Mum stripped me down to my brookies. 'Now stand still,' she warned me. She wired a cardboard rose (depicted as wilting and clearly on its way to death) onto my head and then lowered a drum, which had, until moments earlier contained pesticide, onto my shoulders. The drum smelt stinging and deadly. 'Hold onto the drum while I find a way to attach it to you,' Mum said.

I clutched the drum. Veronica ducked behind my mother and mouthed, 'Ha! Ha!'

'Veronica's teasing me!' I wailed.

'Stop that both of you, or I'll give you both a jolly good hiding.'

'No one's going to know what I am,' I protested.

'Yes they will. Look. It's written all over the drum.'

'But I am not supposed to be *Pesticide*,' I said, peering over the edge of my imprisoning outfit at the skull and cross-bones with which it was decorated. 'Nobody will *understand*. How will anyone guess that I am supposed to be *not* a Rose Garden?'

'The clever ones might guess,' said Mum. 'I think it's really very witty.'

I sagged inside my poisonous box. We lived in the Burma Valley, in the far eastern crease of a valley on the very edge of Rhodesia in 1977. Nobody clever lived here. The clever people lived in cities and towns far away from terrorists and landmines. Clever people did not scrape together a living on remote farms in the middle of a War. They lived in real houses that had running water and electricity and some of them even had television.

The horse boy, the cook-a-boy and the nanny had to wrestle me into the back of the Landrover. Only the front half of the vehicle was mine-proofed, and I was in the back half. I pointed this out to

Mum, 'If we go over a landmine, you and Veronica will live and I will get blown to pieces.'

'Oh, stop making a fuss, Alison,' said Mum and after that we couldn't talk until we got to the de Wets because the Landrover shrieked and roared and rattled and, in a general way, contributed to the future loss of hearing of all who rode in her for any length of time.

Strapped into the cardboard pesticide container, I was forced to stand up, knees bent, all the way to the party while Veronica blocked my view out of the front window with her gold-painted crown made of Pronutro cereal boxes and her frothing pink tutu. I seethed and sweated and itched and glared at the back of my mother's head. I even hoped, in a self-pitying way, for a landmine. That would show them. When I was hung up like biltong drying in the sun from all the bushes and trees on the side of the road, then they'd be sorry.

But nothing happened to release me from my mother's over-active imagination. We trundled on without mishap and I was still Alison encased in a pesticide container and Veronica was still smug in her princess outfit.

I had some difficulty getting out of the car at the de Wet's house. Their dogs growled at me and had to be locked away before I could be retrieved from the back of the Landrover by their cook-a-boy, Tickie. I tottered unhappily toward the front lawn where the mothers were sipping tea and the other children were parading in a circle waiting for the winner of the best costume to be announced. The sweat, which had begun to steam up from my armpits and belly, seemed to be having a chemical reaction with the pesticide residue and I was emitting a powerfully polluting odour.

The other children were adorable as elves and pixies and cowboys and soldiers.

'What are you?' they hissed at me.

'Stupid,' I replied. 'Can't you tell? I'm *not* a Rose Garden.'

'What?'

'If you were clever,' I said, fighting back the urge to collapse in a heap of tears, 'you would understand what I was.'

Natalie de Wet won the Fancy Dress competition (dressed as an angel) and Fiona Johns was second (dressed as an actual, blooming, healthy sunflower) and Marc Hyde (as a Red Indian) came third. Prizes were awarded: South African pens and pencils, South African chocolates and South African erasers in the shape of strawberries or oranges that smelt as if they should be eaten. I shrank with disappointment. My sister and I were, of all the children present, least likely to have access to anything from South Africa because my father had said, 'The problem with South Africa is that it's full of bloody Afrikaners,' and had refused to take my sister and me on holiday to Durban-by-the-sea; instead we had to go fishing in Inyanga where there was no chance of running into a bunch of bloody Afrikaners but a reasonably good chance of running into a terrorist ambush.

Sally de Wet, who was the bloody Afrikaner responsible for the fabulous Fancy Dress prizes, emerged from the shadows of the veranda. Her first gin and tonic had given her mouth a wet, lopsided look that I knew (even without *really* knowing it) was sad-sexy and lonely and was a prelude to tears-before-bed. She was a beautiful woman shoved down here among the insects and the heat and with a dearth of attractive men. Which didn't mean she had given up – not like the other women who had resigned themselves to post-baby bulges below the tightening bands of their homemade skirts.

Sally wore a false bun on the top of her head; an arrangement of clip-on brown balls of fake hair that reminded me of a pile of fresh, shiny horseshit. She wore clingy nylon skirts with slits up the thigh and slick-on-skin shirts that gaped showing flat, brown breasts and large purple nipples. She walked in a way that suggested that she could always unhinge her hips, if she liked. It was a walk that repulsed children ('These hips are too busy,' they seemed to say, 'go away and play!') but I saw the husbands watching her slyly from behind blue threads of cigarette smoke. Now she clapped her hand against her thigh and tossed her head so that the horseshit bun threatened to dislodge, 'Okay, children, you can all swim now. Come on, come on. Last one in is a cowardy custard!'

The other children stripped down to their brookies or under-rods and flung themselves into the swimming pool – small, muscled, sun-smoothed bodies as lithe as fish in the pale, haze-filtered afternoon sun. When I, on the other hand, was eventually freed from my fancy dress, my very white skin had erupted in an unattractive pattern of pink welts.

'Alison has leprosy. Ha! Ha!' the other children shrieked. They told me I could not get into the swimming pool with them, 'Because you'll give it to all of us.'

I glanced back at the mothers for help. They were shaded on the veranda into indistinct lumps of indifferent maternity. They had abandoned the tea tray for the cocktail trolley some time ago and their voices were starting to rise with the kind of excitement that meant the kids could bleed to death before we would get their attention again.

'Alison has lep-ro-sy,' the children sang, splashing me.

I slouched away from the pool quickly, past the old frangipani tree where Natalie and I (one victorious afternoon a long time ago) had found a boomslang and past the veranda with its distracted mothers, to the back of the house where the de Wet's nanny was doing the washing. As I approached her, I covered my bare, splotched belly with my hands, so that she would not see my leprosy and send me further into exile (although where could be further into exile than this, I could not imagine).

'Hello, Picannin Madam,' said the nanny when she saw me. She was swishing the de Wet's clothes around in a milky mixture of steaming water and soap in a large bath of peeled enamel overlooking the massive storm drain that separated the house from the tobacco barns. The clothes twisted and spun under her hands as she pounded them against the edge of the bath. She rocked with every thrust, as

I had seen the women do when they pounded mealies or stirred their sadza porridge and the sound was always like a drum, thunka-thunk. Then she stood up on tiptoe and clipped the clothes to the line that stretched past the kitchen to the top of the security fence. The de Wet's old, scabby ridgeback was lying under the dripping clothes with his eyes half-closed, feeling the plip, plip, plip of the warm water on his sore-crusted back.

Mum had said, 'Bloody Afrikaners never take care of their dogs. They're worse than the *munts* half the time.'

'White *munts*,' said Dad. 'That's all they are. Bloody Afrikaners – white *munts*.' Once Dad had got us all thrown out of a hotel in Salisbury for calling the Greek manager a Mediterranean *munt*. So I guessed, although I couldn't be sure, that the only way to escape being a *munt* was to be like our family. Pukka British with inherited silver for the servants to steal and with old prints of horses chasing foxes on the walls (even though the prints had long ago lost the glass from their frames and had been stained by rain-through-the-roof and rat pee).

'Where's Tickie? Where's the garden boy?' I asked.

The nanny straightened up and arched her back against the ache of her labor (when she wiped the sweat from her nose, she left a crooked mustache of bubbles across her lip). 'Tickie is inside,' she said, 'the garden boy has knocked off for the day.'

'Good.' I slunk down on my haunches and wrapped my arms around my knees.

'Do you want for something from them, picannin Madam?'

I scowled up at the nanny and shook my head. I had been afraid that, without my pesticide-container cover, Tickie or the garden boy would see my small, flat breasts. Mosquito bites, we called them, when they were flat like this with hard, aching centers. I had been told by Natalie de Wet that even the slightest glance of a girl's breasts, however flat, might incite the 'Affies' to dreadful, barbaric acts too gruesome to detail. I wondered how the Affies managed to contain themselves with Sally de Wet around since she was always on the verge of slithering out of her clothes altogether, let alone revealing a passing glimpse of bare boobies. It must take up all their energy, I thought. No wonder they were so lazy and had to be shouted at all the time, 'Stop loafing, you boys!'

The nanny smiled at me, 'What is your name?'

Instead of answering, I stared carelessly off toward the barns and hummed to myself until she went back to her laundry. Immediately, I regretted the loss of her attention although I tried to distance myself from my need for her. I watched ants scuttle across the patted-damp red earth with tiny morsels of white soap in their mandibles, their antennae waving in gestures of panic as if there had been a dreadful ant emergency somewhere nearby. I could hear the other children shouting and splashing in the pool from the front of the house. When I thought that *they* were not having to entertain themselves watching ants, the end of my nose grew heavy and tickling with threatening tears and a sob bubbled up from the bottom of my throat and burped out of me before I could stop it.

'Ah Madam,' the maid shook the spare water off her hands and arms and came to me. She crouched down in front of me and her arms went over my legs, slithering with wet and soap. 'What is the matter?' she asked. Her breath was fresh and green with the stalks of grass she chewed and her hair smelt of Vaseline.

I longed, in my anger and resentment, to shove her away from me. To slap her or kick her or to say, 'Don't touch me.' Instead I said, 'Look,' and I uncurled myself to show her my welts.

'Ah, *ndine tsitsi*, picannin Madam,'* said the maid.

'Speak English!' I shouted.

The maid said, without losing her soft sing-songing voice, 'Sorry, sorry. I am sorry for you, Madam.' She picked me up from the armpits and dangled me out in front inspecting my belly. 'What has happened to you?'

---

* Ah, I have a good heart, little Madam.

'Some poisonous *muti*,' I said, feeling in her powerful hands like a rag doll, 'it got onto my skin.'

'Ah, ah, ah. Why?'

I was crying hard now, in the face of this sympathetic ear. The maid dropped me back on the earth and she gave my stomach an experimental pat.

'Owie,' I shrieked, although the touch had been soothing to my itchy skin.

'Why did they put some *muti* on you to do this? Who would do this?'

'My mother did it.'

The maid laughed to show her disbelief.

'She did, I promise.'

'Then we must wash it off,' said the maid although she still looked at me in a crooked way to show that she knew I was lying. 'Step up in the bath. Look, nice warm water for you.' Before I could argue, the maid had plunged me into the bath, empty now of de Wet laundry, but scummy and thick with soap. She sloshed water up my back and neck. 'Washing back,' she sang, 'washing belly, washing feet – they not be smelly. Washing face, and washing nose, washing bottom, washing toes. Wash all over, make a wish,' and giving me a friendly spank on the stomach, 'like a slap on the belly with a big, wet fish.' I looked up at the wide, blue sky above the maid's head and laughed and squirmed in her hands so that she might be tempted to slap my belly again.

At that moment Sally de Wet appeared from the kitchen with her horse-*kaka* hair and her wide-swinging hips and her gin-wet lips and she said, in her bloody Afrikaans voice, 'What the hell do you think you're doing in my washing?'

And I said, 'The nanny put me in here.'

The nanny let go of me, as if I had unexpectedly bitten her, and backed away from the bath where I floated, bobbing up in the soapy white water like a massive slithering cork. For a dreadful few seconds Sally de Wet glared from the maid to me and back again to the maid, as if deciding upon whom to unleash the full force of her fury. She settled on the maid.

'What the hell do you think you're doing?' she screamed. 'I could fire you! I could fire you! Why did you put that child in with my washing? *Sis*, man! *Sis*! Don't you have any sense? Hey? Where's your sense? Now the clothes will be dirty again.'

The maid's mouth grew sullen.

I said, 'But Mrs. De Wet, the washing is all done. Look, it's hanging up.'

'My God, child,' said Mrs. De Wet, snatching at my greasy arm, 'you come with me and put some clothes on. I don't know what your mother will say. My God. What if Tickie had seen you? Hey, hey? Or the boys at the tobacco barns. Think of it? What would they think?' Then she lowered her voice and clutched both my shoulders and turned me towards her. Now her mouth, warm and sour with gin, was very close to my nose, 'They're not like us, you understand? You understand? You don't just bath out here in the open where any Affie can see you.' She shook her head, 'You Poms have no idea, do you?'

I could see over Sally de Wet's shoulder to the maid. I tried to smile an apology to her, but my mouth was too confused to make any shape. Besides, the maid had closed her face to me. Sally de Wet tugged me harshly by the hand, 'Come with me,' she said and although she did not say where we were going, I knew it was to the place of far, *far* exile. From now on, I would be beyond the reach of the other children who were sure to find out about my unorthodox bath, and beyond the reach of my mother who would never forgive me for humiliating her, and beyond the reach of my sister who would say, 'Why can't you just be normal?' and beyond the reach of the de Wet's nanny who would never risk helping me again. Now I was on my own and when I knew this I stuck out my worm-swollen belly with it's welted skin and I tugged disobediently against Sally de Wet's hand.

I said, 'My Dad says you're a bloody Afrikaner,' and then I waited for the sting of the slap that I knew was going to come.

Years later, I recognised that moment as the first truly African thing I ever did. It was the thing that made me change from a Pom to a *munt*. It was the moment when they started to say about me, 'What a waste of white skin.'

❧ The Wooden Bridge ❧

Wonder Guchu

I *heard footsteps* – three or four pairs – behind me. Breaking into a trot, I ran round a corner and stood, alert.

The road was deserted. The night was still. A few neon lights flooded the dark streets with an assortment of colours. Street-lights, some choked with dead insects, flickered on and off, casting eerie shapes on the pavement and the grey walls of the buildings.

A lone guard paced up and down the veranda of a furniture shop – a ghost in dreamland. A car without lights drove past. In the distant locations, dogs wailed. All around me, the night kept on, pressing hard, advancing with the precision of a serial killer.

I leant closely into the shadows, waiting, listening. Then, after making sure that there were no footsteps echoing through the darkness, I stepped out carefully and sprinted down the empty street, past the sleeping guards whose legs protruded onto the pavements. I crossed 3rd Street and ran past 4th. Halfway between 5th and 6th, the footsteps caught up with me.

I could feel the sweat on my back. I ran faster and shot past a shopping mall. Then the Post Office shadows welcomed me into their wide-open arms. I slid into their darkness, and held my breath, waiting; listening.

After a while, I heard the silence: dark and unbroken. The night was turning, spinning. I felt the darkness, saw its jagged figures streaking across the street, and disappearing. The shadows of tall buildings seemed grotesquely shaped into dinosaurs, waiting to snap me into pieces the moment I ventured out. I shrank from these dreadful creatures.

A metal bin clattered onto the hard pavement nearby. I let out a sharp yelp, and then swallowed quickly, as if trying to draw the noise back. But it tore through the still air, triggering more sounds and a sense of shuffling feet. A warm wet trickle coursed down my legs.

I listened for the footsteps. I heard nothing coming. I ran towards 7th Street; fled past 8th. When I was about to cross 9th, a sound rang out ahead.

I stood transfixed. The footsteps also froze. They were trying to confuse me, make me relax. I changed direction and tried to walk steadily along Nyika Yedu Avenue towards the wooden bridge. A cat scuttled across the avenue ahead. I trembled but I kept on going, my damp trousers chafing my crutch.

The footbridge is an extension of the avenue. It has been there as long as I can remember. We played on it when we were young. Enjoyable were the endless trains that snaked below as we stood on the wooden slats. The iron rails rattled and the planks tickled the soles of our feet as the many carriages thudded past towards the station behind the gum plantation.

I was in Grade 6 when a man was found hung on the rails – naked, and stabbed several times. He roasted in the sun for half the day like the Christ they used to teach us about at Sunday school. The trains, meantime, went on chugging past the bridge, rattling the rails and, no doubt, tickling his palms too.

The stream of people from Squatterville 13 did not falter on their way to the city. All day long, they poured into the Mupedzanhamo area, walking past the slowly grilling body. A small crowd would gather from time to time to observe the dead man.

Since it was our first occasion to come near a dead body, we crept over to the bridge in the afternoon, just before the police came to collect it, and in defiance of our parents' advice.

The man hung still, his head limp; dry blood, browned by the sun, caked his face. His eyes had rolled backwards. A torn shirt clung to his bloodied back. It flapped in the wind like a plastic bag trapped on a fence. The stab wounds, showing crimson flesh, attracted flies. His toes seemed to grope for the ground far below.

We were taking in all these details when a man from Squatterville 13 shooed us away.

The dead man's identity was never established.

But long after the body had been removed, stories about who had murdered him did the rounds. Only one took root. Its theme was that his girlfriend had hired thugs to deal with him – why, was an ending never told.

A week later, we went to watch the trains steaming along under the bridge. We saw rusty blood stains on the rails. It was also around then that people who used this route at night spoke about seeing a man falling from the bridge onto the rails below. It became a kind of a folk tale, an urban myth. Even today, mothers who want to frighten their children tell them about the ghost of the man who was found hanging on the footbridge.

When I approached the bridge that night, I felt warm. Between me and Squatterville 13 lay the cemetery. I knew that once I walked past it, I would be free. The houses and streets would swallow me. Of course, at night one could not see the settlement: it lay, unreachable, tucked somewhere under the armpit of night.

My feet echoed on the surface of the bridge as I walked gingerly across it. The old billboard, which once carried an advertisement of a man eating sadza, was now just a silhouette. We used to throw stones at it. The picture of the man eating sadza was our target. The competition was to see who hit him first.

I had almost crossed the footbridge when I heard the footsteps behind me, hurrying to catch me up. I quickened my pace. Now I felt there were four or five pairs of feet echoing over the bridge. I felt their presence closing in on me.

I stopped and leaned over the cold railing staring into the darkness. The twin lines far below shone like the eyes of a cornered cat. I thought about the bloodstains on the bridge rails, of the many trains that had snaked their way to the station behind the gum plantation, of the man whom nobody knew, and of the many feet which had walked over the bridge.

A warm trickle of fluid coursed down my legs. It was not a shame any more, but relief.

❧ When Samora Died ❧

Annie Holmes

Lomagundi Road

From the back seat of the car, Beth watches Maria's familiar hands on the wheel as she drives, the back of her neck, her arms tanned golden, the very particular shape of her shoulders. Her fingers know the softness of Maria's skin, like stroking a bird. How extraordinary to be so close but forbidden to touch her, to have lost the easy physical permission of lovers.

It's a dry October, the parched season, electric with anticipation, building up for the great crashing lightning storms to come. The grassland is dry and yellow to the wavering horizon, but musasa trees have sent out new leaves in vegetable trust that rain will follow.

Together today in the yellow Mini after weeks apart, they are playing the host couple, showing Maria's sister Gina the country, laughing about the signs along the Great Dyke Pass, perfect lesbian photo ops – 'Great Dyke Butchery' and 'Great Dyke Car Repairs' – about post-colonial British beverages – weak coffee, strong tea – the precise opposite of the Italian sisters' taste.

Gina wants to know how life has changed in the six years since Independence, and Beth tries to explain how history tipped over, as the small parochial colony she'd grown up in had transformed itself into an African-ruled and supposedly socialist nation. She describes the government inviting Bob Marley to sing at the Independence celebrations, and her parents launching a Zambian poet's new anthology in the garden, drummers on the lawn beside the pool, strings of lights.

How personal that history had felt, how synchronous with her own dreams. Not nearly enough change, they agreed in seminars and around kitchen tables, and not nearly fast enough. But once, driving in town on a rainy afternoon past her old, formerly whites-only high school, Beth had seen two teenage girls, one black and one white, wearing the same uniform that she'd worn herself, dancing in front of the school gates, their heads thrown back, laughing as the rain drenched them.

Chinhoyi Caves

Just where the road begins to lift from the wide cultivated plains up into the pass, they stop to show Gina the caves, climbing out of the car into the heat, and scrunching over the stone-strewn dirt road in their takkies.

The cave entrance feels like a portal into myth. Rough gravelly sounds cease, the air is suddenly still and, when Beth leans against boulders for balance in the murky light, the stone is cool against her hand. The three women walk silently down the steep steps between heaps of boulders. The cavern opens wider and wider as they are drawn down towards the light, towards the eerie turquoise of the Sleeping Pool, lit from hundreds of feet above where a sinkhole opens to the sky. Beyond the pool, the cavern twists on into bat-screeching darkness.

Gina is gratifyingly stunned, and Beth and Maria smile at each other, a flash of accord. Maybe now, Beth allows herself to hope, following Maria's khaki shorts and blue vest down the steps, maybe out here, we'll be all right. Perhaps this is how grown-up relationships are: one learns to breathe until betrayal and ache subside.

At the water's edge, wet-suited divers are testing their oxygen tanks. No diver has ever reached the bottom of the Sleeping Pool, one of them explains to Gina, although they go hundreds of feet down into its ballooning belly. 'When I look up from deep underwater,' he says, 'I can see the sky above, with the sinkhole framing it. And the weird thing is it seems like somehow the clouds and the birds and the sunshine are all contained under the surface of the water.' Gina nods.

Over their heads, in the dry heat above the lip of the sinkhole, musasa seedpods twist and explode loudly. They crawl back into the sweaty little car, and drive westward up and over the Great Dyke Pass and through farmland, acres of dry mealie fields and acacia woodlands. A hundred kilometres further on, the road reaches the edge of the savannah highveld and falls away dramatically into the vast flat heat-shimmering Zambezi Valley. From the escarpment, they can see the dirt road stretching into the ash-grey basin of the national park, punctuated with baobabs.

National Gallery, Harare

Six weeks before this trip, Beth had watched Maria and an apparently irresistible young photographer visiting from Sweden as they twinkled at each other through an interminable exhibition opening. St Peter's Kubatana marimba band played 'Tie a Yellow Ribbon' in the courtyard and then annual awards were presented under hard, hot TV lights. Beth slipped away from the crowd, out onto the steps below, leaned against the wall in the dusk with a plastic cup of acidic wine. She watched children play in the sculpture park, hiding and seeking and shrieking around the monolithic grey and green stone pieces: birds that morphed into fish, women with lizards in their hair, astronaut moon-faces with hooded eyes.

She knew that Maria would leave with the photographer. Their non-monogamy pact, in action for the first time.

If the situation had been reversed, Maria would have come to claim her, but when Beth imagined herself crossing the gallery's parquet floor to say – as truthfully she longed to say – 'You can't do this. I've changed my mind,' she pictured herself as a 1960s housewife with a hairdo and a handbag that matched her shoes. There was no way she wanted to be loved and cleaved to by proclamation. What she had wanted, she now realised, was to keep the doors open in order to be chosen daily.

She turned back to look at the crowd at the far end of the gallery. Distance and TV lights encapsulated the audience, their faces raised sunflower-like to the ceremony on the ramp above. She was suddenly an exile from that intense bright life. She glanced over women from a village craft co-op, ambassadors' wives and a group of rasta sculptors, and then saw Maria's sleek black head bent towards the Swede's, laughing. Who could resist Maria laughing?

'A more reactionary country than we're led to believe,' Beth remarked abruptly to a young woman standing near her, a woman she barely knew. 'Sweden, I mean. In fact, I begin to have doubts about all of Scandinavia. Oh I know, I know,' as the woman made to disagree, 'they may appear to be progressive, those people, but they're ignorant, they interfere, they just don't care what trouble they're stirring up.'

When Maria headed in her direction later that evening, Beth looked at her lover as though she was a stranger, maybe another species. She'd been running scenarios on her inner screen – rage, reconciliation, reunion – but they all evaporated on contact with actual Maria, smiling, unrepentant but slightly wary on the steps beside her.

'Horrible wine,' Beth commented blandly, to her own surprise.

Clearly, they were not going to fall instantly back into each other's arms. Some powerful force field kept them a good metre apart, and the air had thickened, making movement sludgy. Maria proffered another cup of wine, slowly and deliberately, as if she were demonstrating for an audience.

'I've drunk far too much of it,' Maria said. She laughed. 'I feel like I might pass out.'

Delight seemed to bubble up in her, barely contained.

'So,' Beth asked, still flat-toned, taking the cup Maria offered, 'are you coming home with me tonight?'

'No,' Maria said and looked firmly into Beth's eyes. 'You know I'm not staying. You know I have another plan.' It was one of Maria's finest attributes (one among many, Beth thought sadly), this idealism, as fierce on the politics of personal love as on the freedom of nations.

Beth sighed and looked out at the sculpture. 'I don't think I can do this,' she said softly, almost into her cup.

'Beth. We've talked about this, we agreed …' Maria didn't ask, there was no query in her voice, only a dare: don't let me down.

Mana Pools

The yellow Mini feels even more like a bright city plaything once they are down in the searing heat of the valley, where the graded road throws small boulders up in their tracks as they roar along. Beth is driving when one of the stones strikes something crucial in the undercarriage and a rear wheel begins to thump ominously. They cannot stop there in the late afternoon, out in the park, no human beings for miles, tree trunks recently ravaged by hungry elephant, so they press on.

At last, after handing the Mini over to a parks mechanic who says he'll do what he can, they set off for an evening wilderness walk, uncrimping their limbs, alert to distant howls and cries above the sunset birdcalls.

A Landrover approaches, swirling up a rust dirt wake as it brakes beside them. 'Hallo there!' the driver calls out. 'I'm Cliff,' he proffers his hand for them to shake. He wears a John Deere tractor cap above a sun-ruddied face, and behind him in the open back of the Landrover are a group of men, one woman and several cooler boxes.

'So,' Cliff enquires, 'would you girls like to join us on a game drive tomorrow morning?'

Beth wants to say, 'Very kind thank you but we're fine,' but Maria and Gina respond enthusiastically.

'And then maybe some canoeing in the afternoon?' This is the clincher. Canoes! Maria is delighted.

They are not to worry about a thing, Cliff insists: he and the guys will come by at dawn to collect them. The Landrover drives away and the women head back to their lodge.

They take their pick of the six beds on the open veranda upstairs, each under its own mosquito net, with a view over the wide, reed-lined Zambezi on its way to Mozambique and the Indian Ocean. The lodge sits on the banks of an inlet, with the main river beyond an island. Far away, on the other shore, Zambian hills reflect the sunset.

As they unpack, they hear a loud splash. An elephant has waded off the nearby island and is making its way across to them. Then another, then another. They loom up out of the river and lumber silently across the grass to eat seedpods from the acacia albida tree growing right next to the lodge.

When Gina goes to take a shower, Beth and Maria continue to stand quietly side by side on the veranda, looking down on elephant rumps. After so long apart, it's Maria's proximity that preoccupies her.

All day, Beth has been bright and social, to preserve Gina's once-in-a-lifetime holiday. And now the night air is soft on her skin, the photographer is back in Sweden, and Maria has chosen the bed next to hers.

'Shall we push our beds together?' Beth asks.

Maria is silent. Then she says, 'I don't feel anything for you any more. I wish I did, I was hoping I would, but,' coldly, distantly, 'I don't.' and she walks away.

In the future, when Beth looks back on all of this, she will see the topography of dunes, while in the moment she sees only sand. History twists like a musasa pod and explodes; dreams tarnish;

airplanes crash into mountains. At the time, she feels hopelessly passive, but later she will know that she was fighting hard.

Cicadas shrill with the darkness. The night is loud, as nights are in the bush, with crickets piping, the distant cackle of hyenas and a roar that is probably a lion. After she blows out her candle, Beth lies listening to elephant breathing a few feet below, the grassy sound of their trunks nuzzling out the seedpods, the rasp and huffle of hide rubbing against rough tree bark.

Vundu Camp

Cliff and his friends open beers in the back of the Landrover at 7 a.m. and call out 'Rhino on the right' and hand round binoculars and speculate about recent kills below some circling vultures. Beth pulls her hat down as low as it will go and steadies herself against the back of the cab, leaning into the wind, ducking branches as the Landrover clatters along the hard-ridged narrow track. She wouldn't have liked Cliff's bunch at the best of times but on this game drive she loathes them fiercely, sentenced as she is to six more days in the constant distant presence of her former girlfriend, and being for all of today a prisoner of Cliff and his cooler box full of beers. They won't hear of the girls going back, absolutely not! It's time for breakfast and then canoeing on the river.

Gina is fascinated by the fishing camp: miles from the other lodges, with bedroom huts and a rough kitchen and an open-sided eating shelter. Every few days, Cliff explains nonchalantly, a lorry drives hundreds of kilometres to deliver freezers full of steak and beer and supplies for his guests. He introduces them: a chap from the British embassy, Mike – a Rhodie ex-soldier with the shakes – and a woman named Wendy who giggles a lot. There is even a bar with rows of spirits along the shelves – Cliff indicates with a sweep of his arm the wide range of his stock. 'It's a luxury kingdom,' Gina murmurs, half horrified, half amused.

Cliff calls out breezy instructions to the workers he's brought with him. 'Scrambled eggs on toast for seven people, Solomon, and don't forget to sprinkle some parsley.' He gestures grandly to the picnic table and plastic chairs. 'Breakfast, everyone.'

And what does Gina do back in Italy? Cliff wants to know, as Solomon serves glasses of orange juice. 'Well, I work for an organisation that serves other organisations,' she explains, her English words curling up at the edges. 'So, that means with trade unions, women's organisations, networks for new immigrants, third-world support groups. Like that.'

Cliff and his friends grin. Beth can feel them relish the baiting to come. Cliff raises his eyebrows at Gina. 'And I suppose you organise homos too?' he asks.

'No, no,' Gina assures him, matter-of-factly, buttering toast, oblivious to the pejorative, 'the homos have very strong organisations of their own.'

Beth stares miserably down at her scrambled eggs, feeling like an unwilling antenna for everyone's subtext. On the plastic-webbed camping chair next to her, jittery Mike snorts through his nose, thrilled as a small boy listening to grown-ups talking smutty.

Just then, a safari company's Landrover pulls up and its young driver leaps to the ground and lopes over to the thatched half-walled shelter where they are eating. A classic Rhodie man of the bush, Beth thinks, in his well-worn khakis. His veldskoens pad softly on the soil.

'Howzit?' he greets Cliff. He doesn't come in, but leans on the half-wall and asks, 'So did you guys hear? They took out Samora last night.'

Beth watches him closely. He and Cliff exchange half-grins. The white midday sunlight throbs and time moves very slowly.

Cliff gets out a small short-wave radio and they all pull their chairs closer to the table to listen, even Beth. Through crackle and static, she hears the BBC confirm that the Mozambican president and thirty-three others died when their plane crashed into a mountain the night before, Sunday, 19 October 1986.

The metal chair legs scrape on toast crumbs and grit on the concrete floor as Beth stands up, her vest clinging sweatily to her back. Everyone else is squinting at the tour guide silhouetted against the bleached glare – white river sand, white dust on scrubby bushes and thorn trees, metallic Landrover glint.

'Probably his own people, hey?' the tour guide suggests.

Beth cannot listen to him any longer. No one notices her stumble out into the blistering sunlight and across paving stones to the white-washed concrete-walled bathroom.

In years to come, Beth will listen calmly while some acquaintance proposes that the radio signal that called the pilot towards the mountain might have come from Maputo itself. People she respects will hypothesise that some Mozambican factions might have wanted to be rid of Machel because he was holding to an outdated socialist path. An impossible idealist. 'Picture all the marginal small-fry countries as tightrope walkers on the taut line between East and West,' someone will insist. 'When the line goes slack, they tumble.' All the same, way in the future, the evidence from the wreckage will support her own gut reaction that day.

From the bathroom, she hears Cliff explaining to Gina in the particular patient tone of a realist to a well-meaning idiot 'what these people will do to their own kind.'

Where is Maria? Why is she silent? Why doesn't she speak up?

'Oh please!' Beth shouts from the bathroom door. The group in the shelter turn in surprise. Solomon suspends his work, looks over at her from outside the kitchen hut. 'The South Africans did it,' Beth shouts, her voice raw in her throat. She is glaring directly at Maria. 'You know that! You know that!'

Zambezi River

How do they get through the rest of that endless day in Vundu Camp, the day after Samora died? Solomon clears the plates. Minutes creak by and finally hours have passed and it is cool enough to go on the river.

Cliff announces that he is really the only one with experience in canoes. Beth mutters that Maria and Gina are both excellent canoeists. Cliff glares at her. What he wants, he says, is a man in every boat, and begins making assignments.

He puts Wendy into the bow of the first boat, Mike in the stern, and, as if in punishment, makes Beth the third in the two-person canoe, sitting on the bottom instead of a seat, allocated an ineffectual stump of a paddle. They slide along at water level. Infuriated by Wendy's dainty and girlish paddling, Beth tries to demonstrate a sporty dyke proficiency that she doesn't in fact possess. At the back of their canoe, twitchy Mike paddles half-heartedly but cannot steer. They drift repeatedly into sandbanks and snag on weeds.

The Zambezi glitters with terror and splendour. A distant group of hippos sends an advance guard to check out the canoes. A buffalo, the most dangerous beast in the park, keeps time with them in a lazy brittle-legged canter along the nearby shore. Crocodiles slide down the banks and, probably, under the canoe. The sentinel hippo's red eyes move on a level with Beth's as she squats on the floor of the inept craft. Now his great grey bulk rises and he unhinges his terrifying yaw of a boat-sized mouth wide in warning. And then, he plunges, waves streaming from his underwater progress in their direction.

The Revolutionary: a brief encounter

Derek Huggins

It *was winter* and the middle of the night. The sky was clear and it was cold. The lights in the offices of the criminal investigation department in the small provincial town still burned bright while outside the robots changed colours to empty streets and avenues.

The man sat on a chair in the middle of a small office at the end of a gloomy corridor. He was a big, tall man of middle age. His brown face was strongly featured and handsome. He had a high forehead and above the slight recession at his brow, a good head of hair. A blanket that he pinioned to his chest with one hand, was draped around his shoulders and the drapes hung down to the floor. Beneath the blanket he was naked except for his underpants. Yet he was an imposing figure. A man accused of being a terrorist. He had been driving a car that had been stopped at a road-block on a main road in an outlying district, and two machine-guns had been discovered in the boot. He had been arrested, cautioned, and detained. His clothing had been confiscated, labelled, and put into plastic bags for forensic examination. His fingerprints had been taken and he was waiting to be charged.

Greg Stanyon, the young detective, sat on a chair behind a desk opposite his charge and wondered what to say. He pushed the old Remington typewriter to one side and idly straightened the yellow-jacketed dockets that lay in the desk divider. He had relieved a colleague and his job, for an hour or more, was to keep the man awake, to get him to talk, and to obtain whatever information he could, while his senior officers made further enquiries and prepared the charge sheet. It was not what he had imagined himself doing, when as a boy of eighteen from the Kentish downs, he had applied for a post as a policeman in the colonies, and had been wooed by a photograph of a trooper on horseback in the African bush.

'Why do you do it?' he asked suddenly.

'Do what?' said the man. His voice was deep and resonant. He spoke English with a cultured accent.

'Smuggle guns.' The big man shrugged.

'I do not have to talk to you,' he said in an authoritative voice.

'No. You don't have to say a thing. Yet the facts are clear. You were caught in possession of machine-guns. Arms of war. You are still under caution. Anything you say I might write down and use against you, in evidence. But we have been thrown together for a while. I have to ensure that you do not try to escape or hurt yourself. So we might as well pass the time talking.'

'I would rather sleep.'

'I would rather you talked. I cannot sleep when I have to keep you company. And I don't want to sit and look at you and say nothing. Let's talk. Talk about anything: your wife, your children, your work, your *musha*, your cattle. It's just a moment in time. There will be a lot of time for thinking and sleeping.' The man looked at Stanyon sharply and sighed.

'It was necessary for the progress of the revolution.'

'What revolution?'

'Don't tell me you don't know which revolution?'

'You tell me.'

'The People's Revolution. The revolution that is coming. It is only the dawn, now. But the people will rise and there will be a revolution here.'

'Without you?'

'I will go to prison. It does not matter about me. I am only one. But the revolution will not stop. The revolution is certain.'

'And what will be the outcome of your so-called revolution?'

'The people will win in the end. Many will die. Many will be imprisoned. But in the end the people will win. There will be freedom from the yoke of colonialism. There will be one man one vote. There will be independence for the black man in his own country. They will take their land back from the white man. And they will control their own destiny.'

'High ideals. Where did you learn … to be a revolutionary?'

'I studied at university here, and overseas. Political science, and economics. I have read much. Lenin, Mao, Grivas, Che …

'Che?'

'Guevara … Do you not know him?

'The Cuban?'

'Yes. He is a great revolutionary. What do you think of him?'

Stanyon shrugged. 'I don't know enough about him to judge. But I see you are influenced by him?'

'Of course. He gives me courage in the struggle.'

'And you? How long have you been committed … to the struggle?'

'I have been a member of the nationalist cause since its inception. I am a nationalist. I believe in the nationalist cause. I am an activist. I have struggled and fought for it. Many others are struggling for it.'

Stanyon felt a twinge of unease but he sought not to show it. He hadn't come to Southern Rhodesia to be caught up in a conflict. He'd come to escape from the bleakness of England. Much as he loved the lie of the land, the folds of the valleys and the downs, the woods, the fields, the meadows, his home patch had seemed so small, and lacking in excitement. Like his own grandfather's brothers, who at the turn of the century, had sailed for South Africa and Australia, he wanted adventure, a new life, as well as to do something useful. It was Africa that had pulled at him ... Cetshwayo, Chaka Zulu and Mzilikazi of whom, as a boy, he had read and had seen depicted in engravings in old encyclopaedia. He collected himself. There was a job to do.

'Of which party or faction are you a member?'

'That is immaterial. It does not matter which party or which faction, or if they fight against each other in the power struggle. They all belong to the same principle of the nationalist cause. And, in the end, the nationalists will win. It is destined. The whites are very few despite their immigration policies. You cannot contain us forever. You are outnumbered. Oh, I have nothing against you individually ... personally. It is the principles of truth and justice, democracy and freedom that must prevail in the end. I would hope there is room for you in the new order. We shall need all the skills of all the people to succeed. There is room for all people. But there must be change. Without a change of heart and attitude amongst the whites there will be continued conflict. There will be a war. The war is coming.'

The talk of war made Stanyon sigh inwardly. Born under Battle of Britain skies, his earliest memories were of the sirens, crashed fighter aircraft, and 'doodle bugs' flaring across the night sky, of German prisoners of war who lived in a camp in the woods and made wicker baskets to barter with the village folk for packets of cigarettes, and himself begging 'Got any gum, Chum' of the American soldiers as they marched along the roads before the invasion of France. He could not remember his father, who had gone to soldier in the war, and only came home when he was five. But these circumstances were different. How would one justify being involved in such a conflict as this?

'Hence you being caught in possession of machine-guns.'

'Yes. I cannot deny that I was in possession of the guns.'

'Where did you get them?'

'I am not going to tell you.'

'Smuggled across the border from Zambia?' The big man remained quiet.

'Who passed them on to you? Black man, white man …?'

'I am not going to tell you.'

'You're going to take all the blame?'

'Yes.'

'For the cause.'

'Yes. For me, there is no option.'

'Yes, there is. You could tell me the names of your contacts and accomplices.'

'I cannot do that.'

'If you are co-operative and assist us in our inquiries, you will stand a chance of receiving a lesser sentence.'

'Still I cannot do that.'

'You're a brave man.'

'No. I am not a brave man. But it is necessary. The leaders must also suffer for the cause as an example to the people.'

'The people will soon forget, even if they know.'

'Perhaps. But my fellow comrades will not forget me. The revolution will remember me.'

'The guns. What were you going to do with them?'

'On or off the record.'

'Off the record.'

'On your word.'

'On my word.'

'They were, of course, to be used for the revolution. I shall not tell you, no matter what you might say to me ... do to me ... for whom they were destined. But, yes, for the revolution. To begin the revolution. To make an attack on an installation. To demonstrate our coming might. To send a signal of the coming struggle. To make the people aware. To send a shiver of fright through the whites. To make them think again. To make them seek a peaceful solution.'

'You make it sound so simple.'

'It is simple. Change, and majority rule, is the way forward for everybody.'

'One man, one vote.'

'Yes.'

'One man, one vote, one time. You won't get a chance to vote again.'

'No. No. You are wrong. There will be democracy. Democratic principals will be put in place. There will be equality and freedom for all.'

'Maybe. Yet what you contemplate ... what you intend to do to create change ... by making war ... will bring death and injury to many, and damage to property. That is wrong. That is unlawful. My job is the protection of life and property ... anybody's life and anybody's property ... plus the detection of crime and the apprehension of criminals.'

'That is what you say. But who is making the laws. The colonists. There need be laws but not such repressive laws. We are oppressed and repressed. Listen to the will of the people and be prepared to make changes to accommodate the will of the people and their leaders.'

'Your leaders, your politicians, you nationalists. You incite the people to revolt. You have your meetings and rallies in the cities. You urge the people to demonstrate and revolt, and they throw stones, and smash and loot, all in the name of freedom. Your agents go to the rural areas and hold meetings in the bush in the middle of the night. You incite the villagers to burn schools, fill dips, cut telephone lines and cattle fences, hamstring animals, slash tobacco … and God knows what else.' Stanyon felt his anger and his voice rising. He had been on numerous patrols in the districts investigating such politically inspired acts. He sought to control himself and lowered his voice.

'And all in the name of freedom. Sons of the soil, rise up! And the people get caught in the middle and suffer. Because it is their schools that the arsonists burn down. And the dips, which are rendered useless, are for their cattle. How can you justify all of this? And the intimidation, and violence, and murder of any of your people who oppose you? Don't try to tell me that it doesn't happen because I know it does. We have to pick up the bodies.'

'It is the fault of the white politicians. Your politicians. They follow the will of their people to stay in power. They do not accept change as an answer.'

'The white electorate?'

'Yes. They will not accept change as an answer. Is that not so?'

'Who's questioning who?'

The big man laughed aloud.

'Tell me what you think.'

'I don't know what to think. I can't speak for the politicians, or for the white electorate. What I will say is that I have never met anybody like you before. I never met a revolutionary before. You are an unusual man. I can understand how you feel … the frustration. But the whites fear change. They do not trust you nationalists. And you are wrong to resort to the gun. You should be patient and work towards a peaceful solution. If you pick up the gun and begin shooting and killing, the security forces will react, and hunt you down, and find you, and render you harmless and put you in prison. And if you start shooting at us, we shall be forced to shoot back. You talk about a coming war … well, I hope for everybody's sake, that it doesn't happen.'

'Our parties are banned, our leaders are detained, our operatives are imprisoned. Our meetings are banned. Our people's homes are raided in the early hours. What are we to do? What would you do? We are impatient for our freedom. We have tried talking, but your leaders do not want to listen. If you are a man you fight. We have no other resort but to the gun.'

'Is that a just cause?'

'It is. There is no other way.'

Stanyon felt for his cigarettes and proffered them to the big man.

'No, thank you. I don't smoke.'

Stanyon lit a cigarette. A train whistled. Stanyon knew it was the Salisbury to Bulawayo overnight arriving at the station and discharging its fatigued and sleepy passengers for their walk home. He though about what had been said. He knew he would not report on the exchange. There was no point. It would be regarded as nationalist rhetoric and would not be understood in the manner and the context in which it had happened. It had been honest and confidential.

And it would make no difference. It was the first time there had been such an arrest for possession of arms of war. Inevitably, it sent a strong signal about a new phase in the nationalist struggle. There was urgency and excitement within the department. Stanyon knew that the big man would be convicted and that he was doomed to imprisonment. The big man knew it too. The evidence was overwhelming. He had been forced to brazen out a police road-block that he had suddenly come upon. There would be the evidence of the policemen, who had stopped him and found the guns. He did not deny possession. The weapons were machine-guns of Second World War vintage and of Russian origin: long-barreled, with wooden stock and a round drum to contain the belt and bullets – they were in immaculate condition, and smothered in grease. Even if his fingerprints were not found on the weapons, there was the likelihood that the forensic scientists would find traces of grease on his clothes. He would be charged and then remanded in custody in the maximum-security wing of the prison while awaiting trial, and while further enquiries were made about him and his accomplices. Stanyon wondered what sentence would be handed down, if he were found guilty. He did not have the act to hand. At best it would probably be ten years, a long time. The big man's hope must be that his revolution succeed and provide him with an early release.

'What you say perturbs me. Your talk of war. You are an intelligent, well-educated man. You appear a good man. Yet you are running around the countryside with machine-guns in the back of your car. It is a waste of your life. Does that not worry you?'

'Yes, of course. I will go to prison. I will miss my wife and family. But I will study. And when the revolution is over I will play my part in the new order.'

'You are so sure of yourself.'

'I have to be. Or else I would not be a nationalist.'

'Well. I wish you good luck in the prison'.

'And you too. I hope you will survive the coming war. Think about what I have said and you will see that it is impossible for it to be otherwise.'

'Yes. I will think about what you have said, but I am not convinced you are right … that there must be war. Time will tell.'

'You will find out that I am right.'

'Perhaps.'

'Now, I want to sleep. You do not mind?'

'No. Carry on.'

The big man lowered his chin to his chest and slept immediately. Stanyon lit another cigarette and watched him, wrapped in his blanket, snoring gently, with his bare feet on the floor. The train whistled again. It was the express setting out on its next journey. Stanyon doodled on his notepad, drawing squares that joined each other with circles and held triangles within them. As they extended across the page, he thought about what the big man had said. He did not want to contemplate a war but it was possible that if the politicians did not solve the problem, there would be one. What he would do if there were a war, he did not know. Time would tell. Certainly, the situation was becoming worse. The incidents of politically inspired violence and civil disobedience were increasing and exacting a toll on lives, the economy, and the manpower of the police who had contend with them. And he had not found out anything factual for the investigation. No names of contacts, no accomplices, not where the guns had come from, nor where they were to go, or how and where they were to be used. Yet the man interested him. His conviction had surprised and impressed him. He had, after all, been frank and candid – even too voluble and reckless for his own good. Stanyon appreciated his trust.

The telephone on the desk rang. The big man blinked his eyes open and looked startled. Stanyon picked up the receiver.

'No. Nothing much.' Stanyon said. The man looked intently at him.

'Yes. Very well,' was all Stanyon said before he put the receiver down.

'The Inspector is ready for you now. He is going to charge you and invite you to make a statement. They are sending for you now.'

'I shall not tell him anything.'

'As you wish.'

Stanyon stood up, then picking up his notepad and pencil, put them in his briefcase. He was going home to bed. There came a knock at the door and an African detective came in.

'Let's go,' he said. The big man got up, and holding the blanket clear of his feet, shuffled to the door.

'Good luck,' said Stanyon.

The big man looked at him and as he went out 'Think about what I told you.'

Stanyon nodded his assent and said,

'A revolutionary to the end.'

* * * * *

Stanyon never learned what happened to the revolutionary. He never saw him again, nor heard or read about him, and never came across his name, either in the war that followed, or the post-independence aftermath. About thirty-five years after the brief encounter, when driving in the northern suburbs of the capital, he came across a road named similarly to that of the revolutionary and he remembered him, and wondered what had happened to him, and if the road was really named after him. He hoped he was still alive, and well in old age, but imagined that if the road really were named after him, he had died. If so, he hoped it had been outside of prison walls and in a free Zimbabwe.

❧ The Ugly Reflection in the Mirror ❧

Alexander Kanengoni

Last week I had an extraordinary discussion with a white commercial farmer who happens to be my neighbour in Centenary, where I have recently been resettled. I have spoken with white commercial farmers several times before but there has always been this profound problem: right from the outset, the farmers always assumed a domineering attitude. You saw it in the elevated look in their eyes; you saw it in the arrogant twitch at the corner of their lips; you saw it in the way they wanted to control the discussion, reducing you to a mere listener. The most exasperating thing was their indifference, as they put you through the humiliation, as if this was the only way there was to deal with blacks. That was how I had known it to be with the white commercial farmers. Perhaps it was my imagination. Perhaps I was seeing things that were not there.

But that day, as we stood in the middle of my twenty-acre field of beans that he had helped me to plant, the man looked away into the distance and said there was nothing in the country as close to the hearts of the people as the land. It was like a bomb from the blue and it caught me completely by surprise. In all of our previous discussions, we had talked about so many other things: how he helped communal farmers from Musana and Masembura to grow paprika; how, as a result, he had been issued with an EPZ certificate to enable him to export paprika to Spain; how the future of the country's agriculture lay more and more with irrigation, given the increasingly unpredictable seasons – but never the sensitive issue of the land, the heart of Zimbabwe's politics. It was deliberate on my part, and I could see it was also the same with him. We were afraid the issue might explode in our faces.

I lit a cigarette. What was old Fleming up to, talking to me about the land?

He continued looking into the distance. Above us, dark and low clouds coming in from the west piled slowly, threatening a deluge.

'My friends don't talk with me any more,' he said, and laughed carelessly. I remained silent and he shot a quick glance at me. He continued, as if talking to himself, 'Because I tell them no matter who comes to power, if he doesn't resolve the land issue, the people will chase him out of office.' He laughed again, but there was resignation in the thin voice. Something in my mind snapped. We had never gone this far before. He breathed in heavily.

A long pause.

'For God's sake say something! Anything!' He looked at me angrily, but I said nothing because I did not have anything to say. He had caught me by complete surprise. Then he pointed his frail hand at a huge mupangara tree at the edge of the field and said that was where the farm ended.

'I told the people from the department of land when they came to demarcate this half of the farm to make plots for you people, but they didn't listen. Their peg misses that tree by several metres into the Crown Land.'

Crown Land? Did he say Crown Land? Besides having an undyingly attachment to the land, the old man was also still living in the past. All Crown Land had become state land in 1980.

'My grandparents came here at the turn of the last century and got this place.'

Something inside me began to rise; before I knew it, I said, 'In Chivhu where I was born, they pushed us away in the early sixties to make room for the farms. I lost my black puppy called Machena in the evictions. It was very painful.' I was surprised by the calmness in my own voice.

He looked at me quickly and his eyes lost all expression. 'That is the past that now haunts us.'

'It shouldn't have come to this, though,' I said, suddenly feeling pity for him, but he reacted angrily.

'How am I expected to have helped avoid this confrontation when Tony Blair disowns that past? Is Rhodes not part of the history of the British Empire? They can call me what they want but I tell them to their faces that this is a war we will never win.'

Silence. I was completely unprepared for this discussion in the middle of my sugar-bean field with Mr Fleming. And in the sky above, the rain clouds kept piling.

'Down there,' he said suddenly, pointing toward the vlei, 'it's all *katondo* – deep, heavy, red soils that can grow any crop. You are lucky.'

I sighed.

He continued pointing over the depression and I saw that his eyes had become glazed and that his hand was trembling.

'If you plan it well and the season is good, you'll never go wrong. You are farming.' Was he talking to me or to himself?

'And by the way, the crop is clean, too,' he added, pointing at the beans all around us. 'This is quite a surprise … pardon what I mean …' He patted me on the shoulder.

Of course I knew what he meant. He was being brutally honest. The only blacks they really knew were their farm labourers, their cooks and their nannies. All of the others had to fit into those stereotypes. That was why he was surprised.

As he shuffled away towards his Land Rover parked at the edge of the field, I looked at him and noticed that he walked with a slight limp. And then I also noticed the stoop in his old frame and I thought, My God, how like my late father he looks.

He turned to me from the distance. 'They say you are a war veteran?'

I shook my head helplessly and walked away, smiling to myself. The Land Rover roared and sped off. And then heavy drops of rain began to hit the ground and I continued walking across the field. We had never come this far before.

❧ Mea Culpa ❧

Rory Kilalea

It first reared its head *when he was very young.*

He took his mother's yellow satin gown out of the wardrobe and began dancing. Smells of an old 'dress-up trunk', a sudden rush of perfume in the folds, gold lights as it swished around, crushed smells, yellow satin smells, memory smells. A cool slip of cloth against the skin smell, the sound of a Kodak 8 mm, mother watching, dad filming with wide butcher's fingers pressing the camera, the smell of beer on his breath, recording the dance.

It was just a dance. That was all.

A young uncircumcised boy dancing in his mother's dress, innocent joy as 1950's parents watched their boy parade sexuality, swapping love for performance.

He next danced in his sister's pink nylon pinafore.

Until his father's laughter.

Dad lifted the nylon skirt and wondered why this little girl had a pink worm in his panties. That was the moment when Luke noticed his Dad's green eyes, and watched rain trickling down the sad small Bulawayo windowpane.

Bulawayo, a small town in colonial Africa, dominated by English working class hopefuls for a better life away from 'home', where greyness, post-war rations and unemployment reached out to guide them to the sunny lands of Rhodesia.

It was then that Luke felt the first shudder of fear. The real terror of not knowing. Or rather, of knowing that if they knew, he would lose their love. And it was in Bulawayo, where peculiarities were not the stuff of the 1950s, where togetherness and starting afresh, were the rules.

Catholics would call it the loss of innocence. The time for eating the apple in the Garden, of his mother telling him, that queers go mad because …

Because God did not make man to do such things to each other.

Because of wrong places …

Because it often led to spinal problems …

Because of the smell of eau-de-cologne when his mother kissed him goodnight and his brother turned over in his calm blue-eyed sleep, and his sister's curls gurgled at him. Reveries of no expectations.

Or the sound of his mother folding the newspaper as she pencilled the crossword waiting for his daddy. Or it could have been the silence, urging on waves of private thoughts, of wishing for a place where he could be alone and work it all out, and the frustration that he did not know what to work out anyway.

Of hands over ears when his father rolled in drunk and he heard a fist crunch into flesh and strangled mother's cries.

'Dear God, Love, don't hit me! Holy Mother Mary God! Forgive him …'

The sound of her head hitting the smooth red polished concrete floor. Of pretending that the floor was too shiny, and she had slipped. Of a blue, bruised eye the next day as she hugged Luke and told him that his father was the most romantic man she had ever known, and that she could love no other.

Of nightmares. He had just reached the ceiling on a wobbling tower of chairs in the safe room of his mind, and as he opened the trap-door, hordes of devils fell upon him.

Mea Culpa.

He could not get away. They were there all over his room. No longer a private place.

Mea Culpa.

Luke shot up in bed sweating. The blue tin clock glared at him. Luminous green numbers. The smell of stale man stained on his sheet, crystallised on his skin. The bed felt clammy and his feet were cold.

He walked over to the window and peered stupidly through the blinds, trying to sense anything else but the frantic beating of his heart, the smell of sin, the dirt feeling of his mind.

The blinds of every student room were Government Issue green, but at night they cast blue-black lines across the room, making it appear something more than it was. More than just a room. It had been his home for one of the most important years of his life.

His first year at university.

Luke shuddered.

The car park was grey. Two o'clock in the morning lonely, three Hillmans and one classic green MG, in need of repair. Under the single neon light the sports car looked black. Like the lines of shadow across his white skin. He traced the shadows over his ribs. His skin looked nearly blue, like the neon.

'You OK?'

A warm breath came up behind him. Luke wheeled around, turned away. He'd forgotten his nakedness.

He nodded, stopped his lips from saying, 'No'. A hand touched his shoulder and turned him around.

'You've never done it before have you?'

A father voice. Nothing hidden voice. Soft voice. Threat to his privacy voice.

Devils tumbled out of the ceiling.

Like a memory.

The priest took his glasses off, as if direct eye contact would make it easier.

'You've never done anything to yourself?' he intoned, like the beginning of 'Hail Mary, Full of Grace', while his hands played, stepping over the beads of the rosary. Luke's throat tightened, but his tie felt too tight, his eyes felt see-through, as if the priest could read his secret thoughts. He knelt on the floor, and felt like a child. He did not want to tell the truth, but he did not want to sin more than he had already.

He wanted to go back to junior school and kneel in front of the grotto of the Virgin Mary and push Jesus thorns through his flesh to show his passion, his total love, and his sacrifice for her. The blood was nothing compared to her pain, her suffering for her Son. The pain of those thorns was comforting; it had a beginning and an end. It did not feel like a priest asking him if he played with himself. It was not right – how could the priest know how much he wanted to, how much he wanted other people to. How could anyone know such secrets?

He did not want to be different. He did not want anyone to know how he had pretended that his foreskin was too tight so that he could be circumcised, just so that he could look like his brothers: the other boys.

'Don't worry, just show the doctor!' His mother's voice seemed to laugh at him, and he felt guilty that he should be so shy.

'It must come off.'

And then the smell of the gas in the hospital, the smell of the nurses, so clean. The bile which rushed at him when he woke up from the anaesthetic, and the sudden pain which he was not warned about. The hands, the bandages, the smell of disinfectant. The smell of loss while everyone examined his privacy.

Just so that he would be disguised, at least for a while.

'Don't you know what love is?'

A hand whispered over him, playing in the shadows, like the speculation that God lives in the eternal present – that everything that we know is not past or future to Him, it is Now.

The hands were Now. And the touch of that hand in his mind brought him fear. Luke had strayed into the unknown, and he did not want it.

And he lusted after it.

And he felt guilty.

Like another lifetime.

'Are you ready to confess?' Luke stared at the priest's eyes, without looking directly at them. The open eye gaze makes priests think you will only tell the truth.

His father's eyes were pale green, brown flecks with gold lights, and when Luke looked at him, just off centre, his whole face looked like a green meadow.

A smiling meadow in which he could never play.

'My son, do you masturbate?' The sin existed. He'd said it – the old priest had admitted the sin. The Mary grotto was far away.

But it did not sound exciting when he said it.

It didn't sound like the surges of joy when the lights were out, deliberate sin where no one could see your failure. The rush of awful blood to sinful places, to places that were more exciting and warm in the dark.

Now it sounded cold.

Luke cleared his throat.

For two years at school Luke thought he wanted to be a priest, that he would serve God, that he would pay for his secrets.

'You must have had thoughts, surely?' suggested the priest. Luke felt the floor begin to hurt his knees. He could not admit to looking at other boys in the changing rooms, could not admit to using his school ruler to compare his growth, did not want to remember the shock when his father suddenly peered under the skirt of a pink nylon pinafore on that dress-up day.

Priests are the ones who can stop the devils coming out of the ceiling. And the devils were close.

If Luke confessed, it would no longer be a secret. And the secrets had become part of him.

'We have said mass for your vocation,' smiled the priest. 'You should confess to Almighty God now, before He makes any decision for you.'

Luke felt himself falling through space, the trap-door was open, devils tumbling down on him, laughing at him, urging passion, defying it to rise again. He could not close the trap-door in time. He had to confess.

'Yes, I have, father,' he whispered, and the priest smiled his absolution, almost gratefully, even before Luke had finished his sentence. Luke wondered if the priest had known all the time. Dark exultant heat suddenly filled him. A freedom of love, almost of the sin itself.

And then, suddenly, he stood up, forgetting to recite the mantra of thanks to the priest.

'I have no vocation,' Luke said, and left the priest telling empty beads. Luke ran along the school corridor. He breathed out, shame and relief, and as he rode his bicycle home, he did not know whether a priest could ever again stop the devils falling.

'It wasn't enough?' A black gentle hand, warmth over his heart. Spatulate fingers with pink tips and perfect half-moon nails. Straightforward, no-judgement nails.

'Are you scared?' he whispered. 'Or don't you care?' Luke shifted.

Young.

Whitenaked in front of an olderblack man.

Also naked.

'I don't ...' Luke began shivering, shaking in the dark.

Like the garden-boy, who pulled out Mum's flowers and Dad lashed him with his belt.

Flowers from a dry garden bed. The boy crouched against the wall, trembling. The shadows were sharp, as he watched his father's arm rising, then disappearing in the black.

Then, afterwards, the boy said, 'Thank you, Baas' to his father.

Because he had pulled out Mum's flowers.

'Thank you, Baas.'

The neon shadows arched over, partly hid the black man's body as it closed in on Luke. Luke wanted to run away, to cast away the black hand reaching for his.

'Don't be scared,' the black hand brushed over him, through the shadows, 'Don't be frightened.'

The hand reached around his, rough and tender. Touching hands.

Blue volts shot across his mind, screaming a sin.

Wanting.

And the secrets had become part of him …

A rough whisper deep in his ear. Smells came and went, passion and disgust, and then suddenly the smell of stale semen. Luke's stomach lurched – that his sin, his mortal sin, had finally been committed. That now it was done, what would be next, what could finally stop him?

His self-loathing, the relentless blame he could never escape, threatened to smother him. The black shame deepened within him, the sin was part of him. He was wrapped up in, had become, 'The Sin'.

Luke turned away from the black man, sat again on the bed.

The devils had now gone inside.

'Guilt?' The black hand touched him again. That was all. But Luke knew. He should have felt love, but he felt only the expectation of love, that was all. Underneath that, there was nothing.

The hand felt strong on his shoulder. Almost fatherly.

'You enjoyed tonight, didn't you?' Luke looked up at Munya's face – it wasn't the face of sin or lust, it was a face he had loved.

Black as sin.

And he hated himself for knowing it.

'There is no need to be ashamed.'

But he was ashamed. Because he also felt released, relieved. No thorns in his grotto had warned him.

'But it feels wrong.'

Luke stared, first at the bed, then back to the car park. As if he was trying to find an answer. From the symmetry of the shadows in his dark student's room, to the lonely MG in the car park, to the shadows hiding the year on his calendar.

'It didn't appear that way a few hours ago.' Munya's voice was low, disappointed. He began to pull on his shirt.

Luke wanted to say 'Munya … where does it go?' He wanted Munya to tell him, to guide him, just as he had for the last year. And then Luke realised what a teenager he was. He tried to laugh, to ward off the weakness he felt rising, then collapsing, deep inside himself. He grunted, somewhere between a laugh and a cough.

'You find me funny?' Munya sounded different, not naked.

Luke did not want Munya to feel the shame he felt, he wanted him to be happy, to feel that they were still the same friends they had once been. That this had been a strange moment where their affection had become physical, too tangible.

Where they had touched the hardness, the softness of each other's bodies. It had made a difference.

'No Munya … it's just …' For a moment Luke thought that they could pretend. But there were other telltale lies. Signs and smells, which anyone would know. There were two men alone in a room at dark dawn, talking like lovers.

Naked.

He did not want to be different. He did not want anyone to know.

Munya lifted up his arm to slide on the sleeve of his white shirt. The light danced blue-green off his chest and wrapped around into the valley of his armpit. Glancing colours as his body moved privately in and out of the light.

Luke had to break the silence.

'There are some parts of a man that don't dance in time to the music.' Luke immediately regretted his foolishness. Again he felt the weakness, the dread sucking away, threatening to rob him of his soul.

Just so that he would be disguised, at least for a while.

Munya's face was impassive. The warmth in his voice had faded, his voice distant.

'Luke, this isn't a game to me.'

His body was perfect, the browns, the ochres, and the dark shadows. Luke thought of the curiosity both of them had in each other. Bodies of different colours, of such exquisite beauty, that he thought he would never be able to understand … or love like this again. The brown-pink of Munya's skin not touched by the sun, the blue-pink of his. The blue-black of Munya's lips, the grey-pink of his, the blue eyes, the brown eyes, dark nipples, soft nipples. Hard muscles, soft muscles, and the slow unravelling as they realised what they were doing.

And the tenderness of that knowing.

The secret knowledge that both of them were making love. Luke had never known such physical joy.

He could not close the trap-door in time.

Luke watched Munya's face dancing in the blind shadows as he searched for his shoes under the bed. They both felt stilted; caught each other's glances, looked away. Munya dressed his body again with organisation.

'Nearly time to go …'

What had happened to the easy intimacy when they went into the black township to listen to Reverend Joseph Dube lecturing on liberation theology? Of arguments about war, when the word of Jesus was for peace?

Laughing Hamlet in a black township. And how they had loved Reverend Dube's gentle lecture, and his patient understanding of white students in Africa trying to justify their position in a black country.

'Join the Struggle,' Joseph Dube had said to Luke. And Luke wanted to; he wanted a cause with which he could justify the garden boy's 'Thank you, Baas' to his father. He wanted to belong to something, to someone, in a way that would reach down deep inside. He wanted, ached for a black friend.

And this naked man with whom he had shared his body, this friend Munya, had helped him through the battle.

The oddness of a British white and black University in Rhodesian Africa.

The aloneness of being a white boy with long hair in a men's residence of rugby-playing farmers' sons. Rugger-buggers who upturned the furniture of a room if they thought you were a liberal. Or broke your face with their fists.

Munya had guided Luke through their racism, introduced him to seething Marxism, even spies reporting for the white government.

And always the undercurrent, the black distrust of the white boy, the boy who felt he should not be held to blame because of his skin colour. Sometimes, at the bar, Luke would say there was no black or no white, only grey. And Munya and the comrades would laugh at his naiveté.

And then Luke felt as if he was cheating, as if he were again an outsider.

But he was in a world that few white Rhodesians would ever know. Doors which Munya had opened, with hours of cheap wine and lofty thoughts; from the spirituality of Yeats, to fierce arguments over Zefferelli's Romeo and Juliet, to long joints of Mozambican green marijuana, and hours of laughter flat on their backs on the lawns of the University common. Of vast hangovers, and quiet times, when Munya spoke of his youth, of dusty walks through the bush to school. That Munya thought he too should have been a priest, but the mission fathers had talked him out of it. Black men needed other priests for the Revolution. They needed someone to teach the young, to help them forget the fear of the leopard in the bush, the silence of the African night, the comfort of a smoke smell in a mud hut. They needed someone to take garden boys and turn them into politicians.

So Munya went for education. Perhaps that is how he could help the revolution. Or avoid it. And he had never shared his doubts with anyone except this white boy.

Munya told Luke his deepest secrets, revealed innocence beneath colour, a safe confessional.

At night Luke lay in his bed and thought of the contentment, the one-ness with this black man – an intimacy that he had never known. It was like leaning against the skin of the large fig tree on the farm, alone, far away from his parents, or those who would make judgements.

But Luke was frightened – Munya seemed so much like a surprise gift, that if he looked at it too closely, it would be taken away.

Like a dead bird which he found near his fig tree on the farm.

Beautiful but dead.

'I must go …' Munya was dressed. Luke watched him rub his hand through his curls. Watched him turn towards him.

He knew the penance would have to come.

'Luke …' A pause in which the dawn light in the room stopped.

'What we did is not in my culture …'

'No … nor mine,' said Luke.

'If they ever find out...'

'It … was because we were drinking?' asked Luke, trying to beg some normality into his room.

'They will call you '*ngotshane*' – a queer …'

'Even worse … the rugger buggers …'

Munya smiled.

'They don't like blacks either!'

Older now.

Until his father's laughter. Dad lifted the nylon skirt and wondered why this little girl had a pink worm in her panties.

Luke grabbed a towel, hiding himself, and flicked on the kettle to make some tea. The noise of the kettle, the everyday sounds, drew Luke to a real place.

Fear.

They had gone to a place where the whites and the blacks would not understand; which even they could not understand.

'How will you get out of here without anyone seeing you?' said Luke.

Munya laughed. Deep laugh. Warm laugh.

Luke shook his head. His arms trailed off, unsure what to do. Felt as if he was being cornered.

'Munya, please ... it's not a joke. It's dangerous. If anyone finds out that you were here, then both of us ...'

Hands flailing, knotting the towel even tighter around him.

'Are you scared?' he whispered. 'Or don't you care?'

Munya switched off the kettle, spooned some dried milk into the mugs, heaped sugar into the white powder and mixed it all up. Then a black tea-bag, and boiling water poured over the steam.

Deliberate, like sin.

The sun was beginning to rise now. Luke did not feel cold anymore. The steam from the kettle formed a mist over the mirror.

Silence.

'So ... what are you thinking?' said Luke.

'That you need some tea!' smiled Munya. 'Here – I put plenty of sugar in it!'

Luke cradled the cup in his hands.

They were now having tea.

Shadows and sunlight.

'This is very strange,' Luke blurted out. 'Black man. White man … after they …'

Another silence as Munya slurped his tea.

Luke hated the sound of his lips sucking in the tea with a hissed breath, as if he was drinking it out of a tin cup in the black compound on a farm.

'Have you done your essay?' Again the veil of normal conversation slipped over the room.

Luke thought of the essay on Marlowe, the terrible death of Edward because he had a catamite, a man-lover. He cleared his throat.

Death. Because he had loved a man. Had kept a man as his mistress. A red-hot poker death. A screaming death. A nearly invisible death.

The sun stared through the blinds. Munya riffled through the papers on Luke's desk, silhouetted against the prison bar shadows.

Pause.

A rejected voice.

'Did I lose you?' Munya sounded young.

Too young.

Luke wanted Munya to be in charge. To allow him to lead him out of this labyrinth.

But it was somehow different now.

Then Munya laughed again. A hollow laugh, loud in the mourning light shafting through the green blinds.

Of hands over ears when his father rolled in drunk and he heard a fist thump into flesh and his mother's cries.

'You know, if I was a freedom fighter I would say that you perverted me. A white man ruining the morals of the black man.'

Luke would have laughed at the irony. But this morning, it was not funny.

'Munya! It has got nothing to do with that. You and I are …'

' Friends? Are we? Were we not excited just because we broke the rules?'

The memory of a priest who had named the sin.

Falling off his tongue in a way which made the sin cold. Deeper.

Luke's tea tasted sour. Not enough sugar.

As he slipped on his shirt, he dropped his towel. He hurriedly fumbled with his underwear, tripped as he pushed his feet into the briefs. Embarrassed, he slapped the elastic against his belly, and watched dry flakes flutter down to the ground.

Dried memories.

Penance memories. Luke wanted to go back to the grotto. Something to understand. The pain of the Jesus thorns at least was comforting. It had a beginning and an end.

'Reverend Dube loves men too, Luke.' The sentence hung over Munya's teacup.

'He also loves *ngotshane* …'

The Reverend asking him to join the Struggle. Surely he didn't mean?

Luke paced around the room. He was angry. He wanted to be alone to work it out. Had Munya been playing with him?

Munya was still. Too quiet.

Too intimate.

'I love you, Luke.'

And the touch of that hand in his mind brought him fear. Luke had strayed into the unknown, and he did not want it.

And he lusted after it.

And he felt guilty.

'You must leave, Munya ...'

'Last night was like a prayer for me.'

Munya's shoulders were hunched against the window. Leaning as if he wanted to break through.

'We made love.'

'You have to leave now, Munya.' Luke's voice was tight.

He felt a pain he did not know, was not warned about.

Munya sat on the desk, covering the Marlowe essay, slowly lifted his eyes to Luke,

'Is the novelty over so soon?'

Another pause.

Red hot poker death. Almost invisible death.

'Is that why you look angry?'

Luke forced away the memory, still wanted it to swallow him. Tenderness, smells, touches they had shared over the night.

'Or is it my colour?'

Luke felt a growing pain rise up from the pit of his being. He pushed Munya across the room. Munya looked shocked, backed towards the bed. A betrayed bed.

'Munya! You started it ...not me ...'

'Ah ... Black man gets blame.' The sun struck Munya in the eyes and he looked very sad.

'Munya stop it!!' Luke grabbed Munya's sleeve.

'Don't touch me now, Luke …'

'Why? Why are you talking like this?' Luke shouted.

He felt the thrill, the dirt of the sin seeping through him again as he grabbed Munya. Ravaging him with hope, then sudden shame.

'I am not an *ngotshane*, Munya. I am not queer! I am not!' Luke lurched towards Munya, trying to cover the dread, that threatened to smother him.

'I want … only … us.' Munya's face looked crumpled.

Munya had told Luke his secrets, showed the innocence beneath colour. Wishing they had crossed a divide together. That it had worked.

Luke suddenly panicked. Together with someone. Not having freedom to be an outsider.

He could smell the loss while everyone examined his privacy. No longer the safety of before.

'Munya … It … is wrong!'

'Because it has been done?' Munya's brown eyes were veiled now. Father's eyes. Troubled eyes.

A smiling meadow in which he could never play.

'Black man and white man together is wrong?'

Like a dead bird which he found near his fig tree on the farm.

Munya wheeled around. Almost angry.

'And who was the willing victim, my friend?'

Luke clenched his fists.

A dark exultant heat filled him. The freedom, almost of the sin itself.

'Stop it, Munya!'

He would not be trapped by this man. Like his mother. Like his father.

Of a blue bruised eye, and she told him that his father was the most romantic man she had ever known, that she could love no other.

Munya moved towards Luke. Slowly. Deliberately.

Luke felt sweetness evaporate from the room. No longer would they be able to laugh, be able to touch, to make it all better.

Falling through space, the trap-door was open, devils tumbling down on him, laughing at him. He could not close the trap-door in time.

And then Munya kissed Luke.

Tenderly.

It was then that Luke felt the first shudder of fear. The real terror of not knowing.

Glancing intimacy.

Luke did not draw back … Shadows reached across the room. He longed to make things the way they were.

He tried to lift his hands to push Munya away. But he could not …

The world slowed down, little specks of dust floating in the morning light. Luke closed his eyes, so he would not, could not see. And then he knew he wanted to hit Munya. He wanted to kill the memory.

Fist crunching the beautiful brown skin. Venting hatred so intimate that he would enjoy the contact.

Swapping love for performance, using their confessions, their laughter, to hit him again.

And again.

The shadows were sharp, as he saw his father's arm rising and then disappearing in the black.

And then watch, as the man crumpled to the floor.

Destroyed.

The sound of her head hitting the smooth red polished concrete floor. Of pretending that the floor was too shiny, and she had slipped, stupidly.

Luke forced himself to draw back from the familiar smell of the man who had been part of him.

The echo of the violence subsided and Luke stood, watched this black man in his room. A yawning chasm stretched between them like a Judas kiss.

Munya shook his head and then looked straight into Luke's eyes.

'Thank you, Baas,' was all he said.

He opened the door.

Without looking back, he left.

🐦 The Grim Reaper's Car 🐦

Nevanji Madanhire

My *fingers are itchy*. It must be the rats. I didn't wash my hands last night after supper; mother didn't notice. I wonder why? Mother has always said that if I didn't wash my hands after supper the rats would nibble at them all night. There are so many rats in our house. I see them every day, coming from under the cardboard box that contains our clothes. There is also a hole in the corner of our house. I saw them last night, darting in and out of it. All rushing towards my fingers. They were big. One was the size of a cat. It darted towards me, its whiskers long and sharp like a porcupine's quills. Its mouth was sharp too, with protruding teeth. They were long and sharp just like father's *okapi*. I couldn't scream or move away when its slimy tongue licked my fingers. It must be the witches that froze my muscles because why, otherwise, couldn't I scream?

But father should do something about the holes through which the rats come into our house. He only says the house is too old to be repaired. He accuses the colonialists for having built such houses for black people. But I think if only he could buy a bag of cement he could make a few bricks and plug the holes with them. Our house is no different from the next one, or from the hundreds of others that make up this place called Tafara.

Tafara. It means happiness. They say the place was given the name because so many years ago, before even my father's father was born, black people did not have houses to live in. I think they lived in shacks at mines or around the towns where they worked. Those who were lucky and worked for white people as cooks lived behind the white people's homes. They were lucky because they were also given food by the whites. So the story goes something like this: the whites saw that their suburbs were getting crowded so they decided to build a home for their workers. And when these houses were built and given to the workers, the workers were very pleased, hence they called this place Tafara. But that's many years ago.

They say in fact, in books, the place was originally called Single Quarters. That means the men who lived here were not allowed to bring their wives. So the houses are very small. It's only one room really but recently we were allowed to extend them. Mother added a small kitchenette but she does not cook in it any longer. It has become the children's bedroom. So she does all the cooking outside, in a shack made of plastic. But that is okay. Everyone has a similar structure in their yard. It has no windows, so when mother is cooking in it we children would be playing outside because, as she puts it, 'The air in here is not enough for all of us to breathe.'

But when it rains, as it is doing these days, she cooks in the house because it does not rain in the house.

I am not going to school today. It's because of the fever. Mother says I have got a fever. She says it's hot on my forehead but I don't see what's wrong with a little warmth because I am cold. But the rats. Why doesn't father trap them, or buy some of that stuff they say kills them. The tin even says 'Keep Out of Reach of Children'. If it can kill children surely it can kill rats. Father insists that there is nothing he can do about the rats. He says they have always been part of the house. Always, that is, since he was a child himself.

I think the rats come from the fields. Yes, they come from the fields because that is where we grow maize and rats love maize. Now that everyone has harvested their maize the rats follow us to our homes and eat the maize, or if they cannot find any they eat the mealie-meal. So we can't win. We harvest our maize so the rats cannot eat it but they follow us to our homes and eat our harvest.

They are not really fields. Just patches of land that the municipality has not decided how to use. We are not even allowed to grow crops on the patches of land. In fact there is a sign that says: 'Growing crops here is illegal. All crops will be destroyed.' Sometimes they destroy the crops but most times they don't, especially during the council elections which come every two years.

In rural areas they build grain stores away from the houses so the rats remain there. Only in rural areas they do not call them rats. They call them mice. They hunt them and eat them. They say they are delicious. I tried one and vomited so much mother had to give me a solution of sugar and salt. But she enjoyed them. She said that in her childhood she used to trap them in the fields.

We haven't been going to the rural areas recently. Father hates the place. He says it reminds him of poverty and witchcraft, but mother says it is because he failed to build even a hut because of laziness so he is ashamed because all other men of his age have decent homes. I don't blame father. I hate the place too. I think it's better to be poor in the town than to be poor in the rural areas. I don't know why.

Could father have been a child once? Without the beard? Without the ginger hair? Without the veins that stand out on his hands? With a set of clean white teeth and two white eyes? I think he is afraid of the rats himself. As scared as I am when they come nibbling at my fingers in my sleep. Because why for example did he open his *okapi* when we heard a noise behind the cardboard box the other day? It was only rats! But his eyes popped out like those of a rat that has been kicked against the wall and is dying.

Today is Wednesday. There will be an assembly at school today; I will miss that because we sing the national anthem on Wednesdays. God Bless our land which we won through the blood of our gallant fighters. Father says he was one of the gallant fighters but I don't believe it because he is so afraid of the rats. Scared of them as they come to nibble at his fingers. But father always cleans his hands after supper. And I will miss the assembly. The headmaster addresses pupils every Wednesday.

'Good morning, school,' says he.

'Good morning, Sir,' say we.

'How are you?' says he.

'Very well thank you and how are you,' we say.

I had a fever last Wednesday and my jersey was wet because of the drizzle.

I think I am oversleeping. And I haven't gone to the toilet yet. People must go to the toilet first thing every morning. Mother says the morning wee cleans away the demons of the night. But mine is hot, it must be because of the fever. Yesterday I nearly cried because of it. I am afraid I might cry. My stool, too, was hot yesterday, and watery and yellowish. It must be the demons.

Mother has gone to the market to sell tomatoes. She never puts tomatoes in our vegetables. She says they are all for sale. I wonder why she doesn't sell salted nuts. Amai Pupu does. They sell very fast. At the market people say they sell fast because she soaks them in her child's wee before frying them. They sell at a dollar per handful. Mother should do the same. She should use Tati's wee, or mine. But mine is so hot and yellowish I think customers would get the smell. Young kids' wee does not smell. If she doesn't want to sell the nuts herself, I will do so on my own.

The idea of me selling nuts is not bad. One dollar per measure. I would not know what to do with that money. I would buy myself a white dress like Pupu's, with lace all over, and a pair of black stilettos. Then, maybe, I would go to church. I would also buy mother a similar dress and similar shoes. For father I would buy a packet of decent cigarettes. American Toasted Milds. Then I would save a dollar a day.

Three hundred and sixty five and a quarter dollars per year!

The other day we went into town. Mother said we were going to see a doctor. But when we came out of the doctor's he had done nothing to me. No injection, which was a relief.

No pills either. Mother said the doctor was too expensive.

But, outside the doctor's was a beautiful shop. I did some window-shopping. I liked the TVs. We sometimes watch TV next door. The other day we saw the president. It was on Independence Day. The president fought for freedom, not father. If father is right that he too fought for freedom why doesn't he wear a black suit, a white shirt and red tie? I can imagine our president holding a big gun; like Rambo's. We saw Rambo at the community hall last month. I think Rambo was just imitating our president, for how could he shoot so many people if he was not imitating our president?

The TVs were expensive. The smallest one cost $150,000. But if I sell nuts and save a dollar a day, we can still buy it. I won't give up until we buy the TV. Then we would see our president from our own house. I wish I could see him one day holding the big gun as he used to do when he shot all the white settlers.

I am a born-free. That means, when I was born, the president had already killed all the settlers.

Oh, it's still Wednesday. I slept and then I thought it was the following day. I woke because of the dream. There was a big black car, it stopped by and a man looked out through the window and said: 'Let the children come to me.' It was our president but why didn't he have eyes in his sockets? And I didn't like the look of his smile. It was too … toothy.

I have missed assembly. I should have seen all the Misses today in their colourful dresses. They dress best on Wednesdays. I don't know why. But I like Miss Ndoro's hair. She puts rollers in it every night and when she removes them in the morning the hair falls back in waves. I won't need rollers when I grow up. My hair is soft and wavy. I mean since the beginning of the year. I think I am growing up. And I am in Grade 5. Next year I will be in Grade 6. And then I will be in Grade 7.

I think I should go to the toilet now.

Mother hasn't returned from the market yet. I am not hungry but I haven't eaten anything since morning. Anyway this is not the first time I have felt that way. Mother forces me to eat when she comes back from the market but the more I force the food down my throat the more I feel like throwing it up. I think I am not hungry.

Father has not come back either. I don't know where he is. I don't know how he spends his days.

Tati is slung on mother's back and enjoying himself. I don't think he ever feels hungry because as soon as he begins to cry mother puts her breast into his mouth and he tugs at it with his hands and begins to suckle. Sometimes it's as if he is chewing the breast. I think it's made of rubber because Tati's teeth are sharp.

It's time to take my Cafenols. A few years ago mother used to give me the pink sweet ones. Now she says I am grown up, so I have to take the white bitter ones … they are bitter. Mother buys them in piles. They are always in packets of three. One, three times a day. At first I used to just close my eyes and swallow them down with water. Now they stick on my tongue. No matter how much I try to flick them to the back of my mouth they stick on my tongue and begin to melt. They are bitter. I tried another trick. I dissolved them in water and tried to gulp the solution down. It was terrible. I tried to wrap them in a morsel of sadza and swallow them, but they still stuck in my throat. Now when mother is away I just don't bother. I just throw them down the toilet. But when she is here … Oh. They say the tongue is what tastes stuff. I have never been able to avoid the tongue. I wish she would give me those pink sweet ones. I can't be that old, can I?

Mother must be coming any time now. This is about the time she prepares the evening meal. I think it's a trick. She does not want to cook the afternoon meal and the evening meal. She cooks sometime between the time she is supposed to cook the afternoon meal and the evening meal. It looks like everyone down the street has followed her example. Or, is it that she has copied everyone else's example? So mother is coming in any time now to prepare our lupper. I think the word lupper is known only in our street.

But I don't think I will have lupper tonight.

Father normally comes home a little later than mother. I think it's also a trick. He knows his meal will be ready and mother would have brought some money from the market. After eating he always asks for money from mother. She always says she does not have any. I don't believe her because the basket in which she carries the tomatoes and the vegetables will be empty, or almost empty. Then how can she say she does not have money? She does not look good with those black eyes.

But why can't father get a job? Pupu's father works. If father really fought and chased away the white settlers he should get a good job. The white settlers had good jobs, so we are told. I don't think father chased away the settlers because, otherwise, he would have a job.

Mother has just walked in. Long time back I would have run to her and taken her basket from her or at least carried little Tati. Now I don't have the power in my joints to do that. Mother understands. But she is always angry when she comes in. I can hear it in her voice.

'Have you taken your pills?' she asks with fire in her voice.

'Yes, mother,' I say, hoping they have dissolved thoroughly in the toilet bowl.

'If you lie to me and you have not taken those pills you will die,' she says.

She walks towards me and feels my forehead.

'Still hot,' she says. 'You are not going to school again tomorrow.'

Tomorrow is sports day. I will miss sports. I am good at high jump. I compete for my house. My house is called Tembwe. The others are Mugagawu, Mboroma and Chimoyo. Father says they are the names of great places. I don't believe him because in Geography the only great places are Great Zimbabwe, the Victoria Falls, Matopos and the Hwange National Park.

I would like to go to the Victoria Falls one day to see the angels flying to heaven.

Mother has lit the paraffin stove. I can smell the paraffin. It makes me feel dizzy. I can smell it in the food when we eat it. I can also smell it in my clothes and in the blankets. It makes me dizzy. Why can't we buy an electric stove that does not have the smell of paraffin? Why can't we buy anything?

Mother is going to cook dried kapenta again. I hate it. I think she should cut away the heads first before cooking. I think it's in their eyes that the smell comes from. And they stare at you so much as you eat them. I close my eyes whenever I bring them to my mouth.

She won't put tomatoes in the kapenta. She says all the tomatoes are for sale. The onions too, and the vegetables. She does not add anything because the kapenta is salted already. I think that is why she alone loves kapenta.

Father doesn't seem to like kapenta either. He is always cursing saying he wishes the war would come back. He says they used to eat nothing but chicken during the war. But where did he get the chicken in the bush? I think he will be lying. That is why I don't think he fought the war.

Mother wants to bathe me but the water is cold. She says she won't warm it because we will run out of paraffin and paraffin is so expensive these days. I hate cold water. I think my fever comes out of it. She says bathing is healthy and cold water is best for sick people. I don't believe it. I can't refuse to take the bath because she will become angry and slap me. I will wrap myself in the blanket afterwards and sleep. I wish they could give me an extra blanket.

I failed to eat the kapenta. Anyway, I am not hungry.

Father has already walked out. He did not eat too. He cursed and cursed.

'Can't there ever be just a piece of meat for the father of the house?' he said as he slammed the door shut.

'Do you want me to go and whore?' mother shouted after him when she was sure he would not hear her.

What is to whore? When I told her the other day that I needed another blanket she said, 'Do you want me to go and whore?'

I didn't have the bath after all. Mother said it would kill me because the water was too cold. But she boiled a cupful of water on the stove. She said that would not waste that much paraffin. She then soaked my towel in the hot water and dry-cleaned me. That's what she called it. She did the same with Tati. She herself had a proper bath with cold water.

I am all wrapped up in my blanket now but I am dizzy because of the paraffin. I can smell it everywhere. Mother is singing a lullaby for Tati. I think the song is funny.

I had good luck today

I picked a button on the road

etcetera

It is funny, the song, I mean.

I am sleepy. I think the lullaby is for me too.

I am cold. I think mother will give me an extra blanket.

I had dozed off. That man in the big black car came again and said: 'Let the children come to me.' He smiled. All those big white teeth and empty sockets. No eyes. But was it our president? I think so, but I am not sure this time. If I go into that big car, what happens?

Mother will give me an extra blanket. It looked warm in that big black car.

Father is holding a gun. He is shouting, saying he is fighting for freedom. Mother does not listen. She looks aside but father holds her shoulder and says: 'Can't you see I am fighting for freedom.'

The gun is only Pupu's toy and shoots water. Of course he is not fighting for freedom; he just wants mother to give him some money so he can go and buy a scud. He shoots at mother, with water.

Tati crouches by the vegetable bed. His belly is full. It is big but nothing comes out of it. I think mother should give him fresh milk. I once drank fresh milk myself and I was able to go to the toilet. If I get into that big black car will Tati know? I think it's warm in the car. Father has bought himself a scud. He is calling me saying: 'Let the children come to me.' Of course no children like the smell of a scud. I won't come to you, father.

I am tired. I have been walking so long. But where am I going? I should be at school by now but this road is endless. I have been walking and walking. Perhaps I should go back home. Mother said I should not go to school today. I will rest.

I can hear sirens in the distance. It must be the president. The big black car is coming. I will just stand by and wave. I love the president. He set us free. I am a born-free.

The first motor-bike has passed, its siren blaring away. Then the next. Then the next. Then the black car. It stops. The president has stopped for me. But will Tati know? Will anybody know that I have gone with the president? The president opens up his arms; and smiles and beckons at me saying: 'Let the children come to me.' He smiles his toothy smile. His eyes are deep in their sockets. I am going. It's warm in the big black car. But will Tati know?

❧ The Sins of the Fathers ☙

Charles Mungoshi

Everyone *had gone* and they were now alone, Rondo Rwafa and his father, the ex-minister. Unknown to the father, the son – who'd never handled a gun before – had one in the inside pocket of his jacket. By the end of the day he would shoot – or not shoot – his father.

They were sitting at the dying fire under the green marquee stretched out over a corner of the big yard of Rondo's house in Borrowdale. Metal and bamboo chairs were ranged haphazardly round the huge fire that had been kept going for almost a week now.

Rondo hadn't been there when the accident occurred but his mind had been repeatedly going over what he imagined could have happened that day. He could see his father-in-law, Basil Mzamane, singing his song to the two girls, the one that he had been singing earlier that day to him, Rondo. Just as he had joined in to accompany the old man – Mutukudzi was also one of his favourite musicians – he could hear his children singing, 'Todini?… Senzeni?… What shall we do?' He imagined a lot of laughter in the car, the old man so involved in singing and the joy of being with his grand-daughters that he forgot to pay attention to what was on the road. As he thought it through again, Rondo still couldn't let his children see what was going to happen to them in the next few seconds. Only the old man saw it – too late – and his *'Maiwe-e zvangu!'* didn't register on the children's minds. Or so Rondo preferred – wanted – to think. He couldn't bear to imagine what would have gone through the children's minds if they had seen *it* coming towards them. Probably – *it is just possible* – that they did see it, but couldn't understand what it meant. It is also possible that they might even have cheered the behemoth coming towards them, towering above them. The sight of it moving inexorably – so Rondo wanted to think – might just have made them unaware of its destiny. So, after all, they just might have died happily – or, at least, obliviously. Rondo was trying to erase the pain, trying to come to terms with it as it coursed through him again and again.

He was sitting on the same sofa he had sat on for the past week, chin lodged in the heart-shaped cup of his hands. He had only left the sofa at the insistence of his workmate, Caston, who, under the pretext of buying groceries for the mourners, was really trying to take Rondo's mind off things a bit. For the whole week he had been hearing the low continuous buzz of murmuring voices, broken now and again by the keening and wailing of some female new-arrivals, as the mourners came in and went out of the tent; sitting with them, the bereaved family, or leaving to attend to some urgent personal business, but always coming back again later to keep them company, to mourn with them. Of course, Rondo was not unaware that all these people came for different reasons: some out of the genuine awareness of neighbourly goodwill, some out of respect and some – well, you could see it in the way they stared into the cameras as they shook hands with the old man, the ex-minister, Rondo's father. These photos would open doors in the future. People would be remembered. Rondo had seen the crowds milling all over the place. He had heard their voices, low and consoling, but sometimes also, loud and laughing, seemingly having forgotten why they were gathered at this house. (These loud voices seemed more honest than the low ones.) And then he heard all the voices as one, a strong hushed roar – wild beasts on the rampage? A distant river in flood? Only it was July, height of the cold dry season. Some voices had found lodging in his mind and he had heard – and understood – that they were all talking of what had happened in his home. It was not natural, they were saying. And then there were the songs. The haunting songs that the women had sung all night, every night, throughout the whole week, and that were now echoing back to him as he sat there across the fire from his father.

They sat like that for some time in silence. Rondo started, as if waking from a deep sleep. He was certain that something had roused him, touched him physically, but he couldn't immediately tell what it was. He looked up. He turned his head right and left. He was surprised to find that his father was now sitting beside him, on the sofa. The thought that his father had changed places without his being aware of it, scared him. He also noticed that his father's hand was resting on his knee. Despite the fire and the general warmth in the seat, Rondo felt the coldness of that hand through the thick material of his jeans as if shards of ice had been deposited on his flesh.

'Your grief will pass away like dew in the morning sun. One day you will be grateful, glad that this has happened now and not later. You will remember me and thank me.'

'*Why*, Father?' Rondo's mind was elsewhere. His voice sounded strange to him. They were not talking about the same thing.

'You will hear people talking. They will try to give you all sorts of advice. It's lies. Don't listen to them,' his father was saying, but Rondo found himself straining his ears, only to hear a silence settling down inside him, heavy as a huge stone, in that space which his children's voices would have filled. He felt his father's fingernails digging into the flesh of his knee as if he were trying to make him understand something that he couldn't say in words.

Rondo's eyes fixed on his father's. He saw, in the older man's eyes, the glow of the dying fire. A little flame flared up, flickered and died. Slowly, almost contemptuously, Rondo removed his father's hand from his knee. His father's eyes opened a little wider, in surprise, then quickly he gave a little sad laugh, 'Nothing lives for ever. You are still young. You can have other children.' Without another word, the old man rose and shuffled towards the house. Rondo heard him coughing horribly; then the cough was abruptly cut off as the door to the main building banged shut behind him.

As his father entered the lit area in the veranda, Rondo had thought his shoulders looked narrower and droopier than he had remembered them. With more intensity, the thought which had begun to visit him with almost daily frequency since the accident, came once more: *I mist have been afraid of just a shadow*. His wife, Selina, might have been right after all. To admit that she might have been right, that she could possibly be right, was not a pleasant thought for him to entertain: *You are always in the shadow of your father*. She'd even gone as far as saying: *I could do better in your pants*.

In the shadow of my father, he reflected again, as his thoughts grew clearer. *Exactly what am I doing to myself?* His mind moved on to his colleagues in the journalistic fraternity and their attitude towards him. While they didn't exactly laugh at him to his face, they certainly didn't take him seriously. They might have wanted to, but Rondo was one of those people who at any gathering, inadvertently became a laughing stock. And the worst of it was that Rondo, feeling defenceless, would join in their laughter, as if to say: *Well, if you see me as a fool, I'll be one*. In short, everyone seems to be telling Rondo to 'Grow up. Get a life,' and yet …

There was the scrape and squeak of a door opening. Rondo looked up and back at the house. Silhouetted in the doorway, with the light behind her, so that he couldn't see her face, stood his wife, Selina. They looked at each other like that for a long moment and then Rondo turned his gaze back into the fire. He realised he was expecting to hear again the squeak and scrape of the door, to tell him that his wife had gone back into the house. He didn't feel he could endure company at the moment.

Then he heard the snap of a twig very close to him and he looked around. It was Selina. He restrained himself from shouting at her – which would have surprised her. He hadn't heard her footsteps as she approached him across the thick lawn. This thought, combined with the earlier one of his father changing places, alarmed him as he realised the possibility of many things, things to do with life and death, that were happening *to him* without his being aware of them. But this thought quickly melted away when he felt – gratefully – the warmth of Selina's hand on his frozen shoulder. He could smell the wool of the blankets she'd risen from, recent sleep still lingering on her. Without looking at her, he raised his hand and laid it on top of hers on his shoulder. Then, her fingers cracking as he squeezed them in his, he was trying to say something to her that couldn't be said by word of mouth. And also trying to get from her something which was more than body warmth. He let his head rest against her belly, his skull just nudging the underside of her breast.

'You haven't slept a wink for the whole week,' Selina said in a very low voice, as she crouched by the fire, knocking several pieces of wood together into a blaze.

'I feel as if I have been asleep all my life,' he said, at the same time wondering whether she understood what he meant. He sank his fingers into her dreadlocks.

'I finally managed to sleep last night – thanks to your mother.'

Selina was silent for a moment, then she went on, 'All night, every day, we sat side by side. Then last night – I suppose she saw me nodding off, and she just took my head and put it on her lap. I hadn't realised how exhausted I was. And how I needed a mother to hold me just like that.' Another silence. Then, unexpectedly, 'A great woman, your mother.'

Because he was thankful or confused – Rondo said, 'And my father?'

Selina tensed: 'What do you mean?'

'Oh, nothing.' Now he was – as always – on the defensive. Of course he didn't mean *'nothing'*. What he really wanted to know was what his wife really thought about his father. So far, she hadn't said anything at all about anything, not since the accident in which her own father and their – his and her – own children had perished. It exasperated him that she always seemed to hold herself above everybody else, as if passing judgement on them – and him – weaker mortals. Subconsciously, what irked him, was that she hadn't said anything – good, bad or indifferent – nothing that would, at least, indicate a direction for him to take. Although he might have not known it throughout their life together, he now seemed to have an inkling that she had always made all the decisions. (A fact which had been quickly commented – and acted – on by his father.) Now, how he was to handle his father largely depended on what she, Selina, said about the old man. But now she was behaving as if she … Rondo wondered if she *knew*. He could never tell with his wife. Or, possibly, his own mother could have told her – they were inseparable, his wife and his mother. The two of them also knew how to get information. Rondo had always been surprised – he would burst into his, or his mother's, house with what he thought was something neither of them would have heard. But the thing about them was that they wouldn't embarrass you by letting you know the 'news' was old hat. They would look kindly at you and from that look you would know that they had been hiding the information from you for the past month – or even a year. They preferred not to offer 'news'.

'Very strange', Rondo said to Selina.

'What?'

'This accident.'

Selina stiffened. Then she turned her head slowly away from the fire and looked at him. She stood up, took both his hands in hers, and gently pulled him up, 'Come on. You need rest. Let's get you some sleep and then I will prepare you a big breakfast. I can't remember when I last cooked you something since we started employing a housemaid. Come on. I don't want to lose you as well.'

'Lose me?'

'To the maid.' But she suddenly let go of his hands as if she had remembered something else she would rather forget. She put her face into her hands and gave one big heave of the shoulders.

Rondo put his arm round those shoulders.

'I think I'll accompany Papa's body to Bulawayo tomorrow,' she said after she had stopped crying.

'We will go together.'

'No.'

'Why? Are you blaming ...'

'No No No Noooo!' She didn't quite scream, but she put her hand to Rondo's mouth and then rushed off across the lawn and into the house, crashing the door shut behind her.

He looked after her at the closed door, feeling the way she'd gone. She'd realised he'd been about to say something, he thought. Something that hurt only him – but would later filter out to those near him. She was always telling him that he apologised too much. It was a form of selfishness, she said. But he had been brought up in a different world: she had been brought up by people with 'long hearts' – people who forgave others – all this he understood now – and he? Rondo remembered telling Selina about his first disappointment – and the first sermon from his father, who was then – he didn't know in those days of political troubles – but, of course, his mother knew. Anyway, an uncle had given Rondo an old guitar. He was only four then. His father had come home – in Old Canaan, Highfield, then – and found him strumming away tunelessly on the instrument. His father had broken the strings and thrown the whole contraption into the fire, saying, 'No Mick Jaggers or John Whites in *my* house! Scum! They have no sense of responsibility, those people. Flowers of the sun. Playing and singing on trains with no destination in mind. Railway followers. Tch. Tch. Tch. Rolling Stones. No son of Rwafa has ever been a rolling stone ....'

He had been only a child – and he didn't have any idea who Mick Jagger or John White were. But he had remembered the fear that had been planted in him then. (He'd peed in his shorts – he'd told Selina!)

And he had told her all this because he loved her and he was about to lose her because his father, a full-blown *bhuru rokwaNyashanu*, would not let the Rwafa family be demeaned by an effeminate son who wanted to marry into an ingnominious *muDzviti* family. And he would have lost *her* if she hadn't stood by him – she, her father and his own mother. The flames of that burning guitar had gutted all the courage out of him.

It had always brought tears to his eyes to see his mother and wife together – while his father frowned – and even spat – at the relationship. And throughout, Rondo didn't know what was behind all this – tension – in their relationships. Once, his mother tried to simplify it for him: 'Your father is Zezuru-Karanga and, once-upon-a-time, they were raided by the maDzviti-Ndebele. Well, in those days or even in these days, if you have a war, you have a war. It does bad things to people's minds. So they will always remember the pain of the scars rather than the relief of the healing. Your father, *mwanangu*, is one bombed-out battlefield of scars. And his deepest scar is that he cannot forgive: not just his enemies. You. Me. Anyone.'

It hadn't meant anything to him then, but it had been easier to accept than, 'Well, my son, give me a grandson, to whom I can leave all this.' *All this* was, Rondo thought, his cars, houses and money. And his *charisma* – because, though he might have been afraid of him, Rondo really thought that his father, his *Daddy* , was the greatest. In his nightmares, Rondo would have done anything for him.

But after the ignominy of marrying a muNdevere, there was the further ignominy of having a grand-daughter with Ndevere blood as first in the family. And then a second grand-daughter. After all this, there was nothing that could have appeased Mr Rwafa, the ex-minister, Rondo's father. It was as if his son Rondo had been written out, written off, disappeared.

But the problem was that Rondo was an only son, and an only child.

As an only son, a lot of things were done for Rondo by his father, of which the young man was not aware. And because he was not aware he did not show his father enough gratitude, or respect. Rondo's father was, therefore, a very disappointed man. At times so disappointed that his wife had to do a lot of humiliating things to cool him down. She might have enjoyed their affluence as one of the members of the small ruling elite in a newly-independent government, but Mrs Rwafa had very deep fears about the future of her only child. His father loved himself so much, he was prepared to destroy his son in his endeavour to have – a duplicate? an heir? Mr Rwafa, as Minister of Security, seemed to have pursued his duties so zealously that he hadn't been able to distinguish Party from family. And people had suffered. Especially Rondo, to the extent that never, throughout his life, had he been able to answer any one of his father's questions. He had developed a stammer. His mother could have told him that lots of people developed a stammer whenever his father asked them questions. It had taken Rondo a very long time to realise what his father's job was, although he knew that he was somewhere high-up-there. And Rondo's mother was caught in between the sensitivity of her husband's job and the sensitivity of her son's nature. In a way, each of them lived locked in their separate cages.

Rondo always thought his father must be right; he was too diminished to think otherwise, and he was afraid for his mother whenever she had to oppose the old man. He loved – or thought he loved – his father, but the topic was too charged to consider deeply. Maybe he loved him because he always did everything for him? His mother did a lot too – the more intimate things like underwear and peanut butter – but his father was out and up there with Batman and Superman. Yet he couldn't tell in exactly what sense. And Selina? It seemed the first time she came into their house she had understood the whole situation: Rondo's father had asked, 'Who are her people?'

and the moment Rondo told him, his father had walked out. He had stayed out of sight for the whole day, yet Selina later told him it was the most enjoyable day she had ever had in her life. From day one, Selina had – so it seemed to Rondo – taken to his mother like her own, or like an old friend.

Rondo loves both his mother and his wife but now he is wondering whether they, too, are not laughing at him. Like his colleagues at work.

Rondo Rwafa knows very well that he is not a brilliant journalist. In fact, he couldn't even remember how the job had come about. One morning his father came into his room and said, 'Slob, wake up. Time you earned your own keep.'

'Slob.' His father's language exactly. None of the words he used to address Rondo had any respect in them. It seemed that there wouldn't ever be anything that his son could ever get right. And Rondo suspected that in her less I-love-you moments, Selina saw him in this same light: less-than-me. Only his mother seemed to see him as whole.

So, Rondo had found himself at the *Clarion*, the city's daily paper, among people who seemed to start laughing at him the moment they set eyes on him. Yet – yet – they held him in a kind of awe. He had been presented to the office by no other than Rwafa himself. They flocked round him. They asked for favours – which, of course, they got (although at times it meant a few uncomfortable minutes in his father's office at home). Yes, his colleagues laughed at him, he knew, but – now, he didn't know – could it be malicious? He gave them money – advances – at the thin times of the month, and not a few had used his name to get something or other from finance houses, credit stores, legal firms and so on. But – was it possible that all the time they had been laughing at him?

Recent events were driving Rondo's thoughts down avenues he was not accustomed to. More than mere recent events were making Rondo see something else in events that he'd always taken for granted.

Of his workmates, Rondo could say Caston Shoko was the closest to him, although not quite a friend. Caston wasn't very popular with the rest of the fraternity because he behaved as if he knew all the answers. Maybe, because of this, he saw the company of Rondo as the lesser of the two evils. Anyway, Cas loved to talk and drink and Rondo had lots of money and a guileless face.

A long, long time back, Caston had asked Rondo: 'Do you know what your father does?' Rondo had shrugged the question off. A second (or another) time, Caston had asked again, 'Have you ever wondered about the Second Street accidents?' And again, Rondo had shrugged his shoulders.

'Do you even know what they are?' Caston asked.

'No. What are they?'

Caston had laughed: Rondo would always be a naive clown.

Rondo had laughed because he didn't know and he didn't think it mattered. Now, after this accident, thinking things over, Rondo had a better idea of what Caston had often tried to tell him. And Caston more than confirmed it when, on one of their several trips in the past week to buy food and firewood for the mourners, he said, 'This is your story. It would be a betrayal if we wrote it up, since it involves a colleague.'

Silence. Then, looking at Rondo, he said slowly and conclusively, 'This is a typical Second Street accident.'

Rondo stared at Caston like a trapped animal. He felt terror, and in that moment accepted that he had always refused to think about why his father left the house in the morning and what he did before he returned in the evenings – or the following week, for that matter.

Caston observed his friend quietly. There would never have been a good moment ... He put his hand on Rondo's shoulder. 'You can't be a child forever, Rondo.'

They walked slowly to the car, and drove back to Borrowdale in silence. Caston stopped the vehicle. Rondo sat motionless in the passenger seat; his friend looked at him for a moment, and said quietly, 'We're home, Rondo.'

Then, as Caston began unpacking the goods from the boot, he said, 'In case, you need it, there's a gun in the glove locker. It's loaded.'

Rondo had not been used to living his life from deductive or logical thinking but now, the accumulation of events and the history behind them had made him so numb, he was almost a zombie. And Caston wouldn't leave him alone.

According to Caston, this whole story had to be seen from the point of view of Rondo's father.

'What happened at the birthday party?' Caston had asked.

Rondo couldn't see anything wrong with the party except that two old men, his father and father-in-law, had made speeches that seemed to have turned sour. His mind seemed at times, to have an amazing way of getting rid of the details of an experience.

'No,' Caston had said. 'Only one old man made a speech. And that broke up the party, didn't it Rondo? Don't you remember that?'

And Rondo remembered. He even remembered other incidents that Caston didn't know anything about. Rondo recalled what had happened at the birthday party, but a day before the party, there had been – a quarrel? A misunderstanding? – between his father and father-in-law. There had always been a tension between the two men but the episode at the party had rendered it dramatic.

Although he thought he loved his own father, Rondo had always sensed that if he had to choose, he would pick out his father-in-law as his father. It was just a feeling, not defined, not absolute. Nothing about his father-in-law's demeanour showed that he was a very successful businessman and the MP of a constituency in northern Matabeleland. When he was with his father-in-law, Rondo always felt that the space around him had expanded. He didn't know exactly how to put it but he felt he could – and he would be allowed to – do anything he wanted. Only on very rare occasions had Mr Mzamane mentioned his differences with Rondo's father, and even then he would conclude, 'Of course, he is free to think as he likes.'

So, at one point in their married life, Selina suggested that they invite every relative and friend for a joint birthday celebration for their daughters, Yuna, six, and Rhoda, five. Mr Mzamane had married again after Selina's mother had died and Selina didn't yet feel comfortable with her stepmother. So, in the invitation to her father she had alluded to this. She knew that her father would understand, and he did, he came alone. He also came a few days before the celebrations as he had business to conduct in Harare.

Mr Rwafa – surprisingly – drove to Rondo's home to see Mr Mzamane on the morning after his arrival. He seemed quite cheerful, which was also very unusual in Rondo and Selina's house, but more especially in the presence of Basil Mzamane. Not least because the bill for the couple's wedding celebrations had been met by Mr Mzamane. The larger part of the expenses anyway: Rondo's mother had helped too, in tears at times, because her husband had told her, '*Who* did you say is wedding?' and had conveniently left town 'on State business' for two weeks. Selina couldn't believe that this was just a courtesy call, a friendly gesture towards her father. However, the ostensible purpose of this surprising visit wasn't kept secret for long. As with other high-ranking officials in the ruling party, Rondo's father had had his eye on a certain farm in the Ruwa area. which was presently owned by a white man, a Mr Quayle. Rondo had driven to the farm on several occasions because he had a natural love for the outdoors: the trees, the hills, the open vistas. On the first occasion, he had gone out to the farm with his father; subsequently, Selina had accompanied him. She seemed to like the Quayles too.

Indeed they seemed very nice people. Each time he visited the farm they presented him with some of their farm produce: milk, honey, apples – whatever was in season. They had to force the bounty on him since he was too shy and embarrassed to receive gifts from people.

Rondo learned, from Mr Quayle, that the relationship between him and his father 'went years back … when we worked together in a bookshop in town … but its now mostly sustained by our passion for duck-shooting.'

Rondo hadn't bothered to find out anything more from his father about this relationship. He didn't even speculate on the possibilities that it could go beyond just duck-shooting.

'Ever shot duck, Mr Mzamane?' Rondo's father asked Rondo's father-in-law that day before the birthday celebrations.

'No, why?'

'Because I'd like you to watch some duck-shooting today. Sad you can't shoot yourself. It would have been more fun.'

'One can always learn,' Mr Mzamane said.

'Isn't it a bit late in the day for you?'

Mr Basil Mzamane had laughed his uproarious laugh and said something that had made Rondo laugh as well. But Mr Rwafa seemed to disapprove. He was a man who laughed little.

They drove out towards Ruwa in Mr Rwafa's Pajero. Rondo had wanted to sit alone in the back, to give the two elderly men a chance to talk – same-age-boys stuff, but Mr Mzamane had declined to do so saying, 'I suffer from vertigo.' Rondo had had to sit in front with his father, wondering what vertigo had to do with anything.

At the Mabvuku turn-off they found an open truck parked by the roadside. It was full of youths singing *chimurenga* songs and waving ugly-looking clubs. Some even had bows and arrows and spears.

Immediately they passed the truck, it fell in, right behind their own car.

'Your duck-shooting posse?' Mr Mzamane asked.

Rondo laughed. He hadn't thought about it at all.

'Damn right,' Mr Rwafa had replied and Rondo stopped laughing at the chilly tone of his father's voice.

'They must be pretty good marksmen to hit flying ducks with those clubs.'

'Not at all. We hunt *sitting* ducks.'

Mr Mzamane gave another of his uproarious laughs, saying, 'That's pretty good. I must tell this to Radhebhe.'

There was no more talk in the car but, looking behind him, Rondo wondered whether his father hadn't been telling the truth after all. The truck was still behind them. When they stopped for some drinks at Ruwa, it stopped at some distance on the road ahead. And it fell in behind them again when they passed it.

As they turned off the main Mutare road to the farm, the truck also turned off.

'Now, tell me. Is this just coincidence or what?' Mr Mzamane seemed a little dark – with fear or just worry?

Rondo's father didn't bother to answer. Rondo didn't even think that there might be something ominous about the truck trailing behind them with its load of club-wielding, slogan-chanting youths. He was pre-occupied by the sudden beauty of the land they were driving through. He did, however, wonder briefly whether the boys in the truck saw the same things that he saw in the countryside. If they saw anything, their minds probably wouldn't register it or were fermenting with thoughts of what they were going to do wherever they were going.

As they drew closer to the farm, the singing – chanting almost – grew louder, more intense, menacing. It was no longer just ordinary singing. There was something elemental in it, the naked, unashamed raw lust for blood. Not that Rondo didn't like the singing. He had been brought up on these songs, although in peacetime the words would be different. And he found himself wishing that the youths were using peacetime words.

Right now, right here where they were just leaving an area of bush – musasa, mutondo, mususu and an assortment of wild fruit trees – and coming into the open of the valley towards the river, the land provided a breathtaking view of its immensity. Across the river lay some low granite hills, with dark forests and mountains in the blue distance. It was just after midday, yet something affected the atmosphere so that the heat seemed subdued and the air acquired the dark colour of old memories. Rondo thought: any moment a duiker will disturb the tall grass and dash across the road. And more from a forgotten or unknown memory rather than a remembered reality, his nostrils were filled with the smell of fresh water.

Soon, they were rolling down to the stream – with very little water in its bed – and crossed a narrow concrete-and-stone bridge into the scrub on a low hill. They kept on driving up, then round a bend in the road, almost a blind turn, and there they came upon a jeep, stalled to the side of the road. Its hood was open and a white woman was bent under it, looking into the engine. She looked up as Rondo and company came to a noisy, dusty halt beside her car. The lorry with the chanting youths pulled up behind Mr Rwafa's car. The woman stood, frozen, her dirty hands gripping a greasy spanner.

There was a moment of silence as the woman looked at the men in both vehicles and the men looked back at her. For a few painful moments, neither side seemed to know what to do with the other. Then the woman brought down the hood of the jeep with a loud bang, moved quickly to the open door of the jeep, reached in and pulled out a rifle.

The youths in the truck jumped out at that moment and advanced towards her. Rondo hadn't heard the sound of the door open nor Mr Mzamane getting out but suddenly there he was, standing with his hands raised, the woman behind him and the mob before him.

They all froze. Mr Mzamane spoke in a calm, fatherly voice: 'Let us all remember we are human. This lady probably needs our help. Even so, if there is something you had planned to do, I don't want to be a witness to it, because I am not part of your plans. I am a stranger to this part of the country. Is this how you treat visitors in your homes? Would you like me to tell the people where I come from that this is how you treat people here?'

There was a stunned silence, and a slight tremor of knobkerries being lowered by a degree or two.

Then an impatient voice rang, 'Chef? Who is this man?'

All eyes turned on the young man. That was when Rondo realised that his father had sneaked out of the car and disappeared.

Quickly, Mr Mzamane assessed the situation and said, 'You see? He gave me word that today is cancelled. Go home. He is going to contact you. I am his Bulawayo comrade. We are in the same work, same rank.'

For no reason that Rondo could see at all, the men lowered their clubs and got back onto the truck grumbling. They drove off.

'Thank you,' the woman said, but she continued to clutch her rifle. And that was when Rondo recognised her.

'What seems to be the trouble with the car?' Mr Mzamane asked.

'It just seized.'

Rondo felt that he should have done something to help, and because he hadn't, he kept his head very low out of embarrassment.

Mr Mzamane opened the hood of the jeep and fiddled with the engine and said, 'Try her, let's see'.

The car started on the first kick.

The woman thanked Mr Mzamane profusely. She gave him her name. Mr Mzamane said it didn't matter. She asked if they had time so they could drive to the farm, it wasn't far, for a cup of tea. Mr Mzamane joked, saying that they had to hurry and catch up with the singing boys in the truck before they got up to some other mischief. The woman thanked him again and said that if in future he was ever in that area, he should drop in for a cup of tea. Or he could make an appointment with her husband for duck-shooting. She gave a small laugh, thanked him again and drove off.

Less than two minutes after the woman had driven off, Rondo's father appeared from behind a bush. He didn't say a thing. He got behind the wheel and they drove back the way they had come.

About thirty minutes of total silence in the car seemed unbearable to Rondo. Also he felt terribly oppressed and morally bound to say what was bothering him. One of those very rare occasions when fear of his father was less than the pain inside him.

'That was Mrs Quayle back there,' Rondo said.

'Is she your mother?' his father snapped.

'Do you know her?' Mr Mzamane asked.

Rondo looked furtively at his father. Mr Rwafa concentrated on his driving.

'I am asking *you*, Rondo', Mr Mzamane said.

'We often drive to the farm. Father sometimes …'

'Traitor,' Mr Rwafa spat the word out under his breath.

'Shoots duck with Mr Quayle?' Mr Mzamane offered, laughing. 'Nothing to worry about, Rondo. They – or at least she – seem good neighbourly. You heard her invite me to tea? I am sure you too have had tea with her or them?'

When neither Rondo nor his father answered, Mr Mzamane told Rondo that he had to grow up and see people as they were, as individuals. He talked of how some are good and some are bad and how sad it was that the majority of people seemed keen on seeing only the bad in people. He told the story of a white farmer in the Manhize Mountains who was – well, not exactly a spirit medium, but who believed in *vadzimu*. Whether he believed or not, Mr Mzamane said, was not the point. But it seemed to help his prospects. The story behind the story is that his grandfather settled in the area of the Pazho people, thus taking possession of their sacred pool, Kapa. Not only did the sacred pool come under his farm, the ancestral graves, the forests, the beehives – everything that had given the Pazho sustenance, was on his farm. Well, might is right, a fact of life. But three years after Kakuyu – that's the name the locals gave this settler – three years after settling on the farm, he couldn't prosper. Every year several head of his cattle died from an unknown disease. Baboons, wild pigs and birds played havoc with his grain crops.

'He was thinking of selling the farm and calling it quits when the headman of the Pazho people told him what to do. You see, although Kakuyu now owned what had been these people's ancient land, he allowed them to make use of the sacred pool and pray to their ancestors. So, the headman thought, why not help him as well? So, he asked him to buy a *retso*, the black-and-white cloth of *vadzimu*. He told him what to do with it every morning at the sacred pool. He told him the words to say. And that he had to leave a handful of grain from the land.

'The man had a bumper harvest the following season. Only one cow died, and that could easily have been from old age. That man was the grandfather of the farm's present owner. The Pazho people enter and leave the farm as they like to attend to the graves of their ancestors, pray at Kapa, set up beehives, mousetraps, birdtraps, termite traps ...'

'Shut up, traitor!' Mr Rwafa shouted, his voice icy, and he rammed his foot on the brakes of the Pajero.

'There is more to the story than ...'

'If you respect me ...' then he started the car and they were off again.

Rondo wouldn't have tried to see what lay behind this incident if Caston hadn't asked him to remember what happened at the birthday party. And what had happened at the party?

It had turned out be a great party, at least at the beginning. No one paid attention, at first, to the two elderly men, the politicians, who were quite conspicuous by their keeping as far apart as possible. If you didn't know the score, or didn't look closely, you wouldn't notice the tension behind their tight smiles and loud laughs, as they seemed to compete in entertaining the groups of children and young parents that formed and dissolved around them. Basil Mzamane could have won the contest easily if he hadn't been too aware of being 'away from home'. At one point, Mr Rwafa managed to raise some eyebrows when he referred to Mr Mzamane as 'The Honourable MP'. There seemed, at least to an innocent ear, no innuendo of sarcasm or irony in his voice. A number of people were so moved that they observed a few seconds of silence. It was an unusual admission from Mr Rwafa and it revealed a rare chink in his armour, people thought. There was a noticeable relaxation all round after this. Selina and Rondo even allowed themselves to think that this was what they had wanted all along. A moment like this with their parents, all their parents; Selina felt the party had served its purpose.

But then, out of the blue, someone – Rondo couldn't later remember who it was – probably one of the dreadlocked crop of reporters – said, 'Mr Minister' (they still called Mr Rwafa 'Mr Minister' in deference to his past glory – and, well, his age), 'Why don't you tell the children a story, Sir?' 'Yes!' another one shouted. 'We haven't heard you tell us about what you did in the liberation struggle.'

Someone should really have stopped the whole thing at this point but nobody did; and Rondo later remembered having the feeling that he used to have as a boy, when he embarked on something that he knew was not allowed to do, and yet the very thought that it was not allowed, fuelled his action.

It was quite a peaceful scene: the children chasing each other and screaming and squirting water into each other's faces and firing crackers; Rondo and his friends minding the braai, standing around and joking glasses of beer in hand; and the women in their own corner of the garden – it looked as if nothing could possibly disturb the equilibrium of things. But then someone had asked that question – and already it was too late to do anything about it, when Mr Rwafa raised his voice and said, 'Are you sure you really want to hear about that?' 'Yes!' Quite a number of voices shouted back. No one noticed Basil Mzamane wandering quietly away, pretending to be admiring the plants in Rondo's garden.

Mr Rwafa made all the children sit cross-legged at his feet. Rondo and his friends made themselves comfortable in sofas, legs crossed, beers in hand, forming a protective outer circle around their children.

Mr Rwafa talked of betrayals. He talked of traditional enemies of the people since time immemorial. Enemies of the state. Enemies of the clan, of the family. Looters and cattle thieves. Personal enemies. People who spat in the faces of their own people. Child thieves. Baby snatchers. He talked of his waking up to his mission. He talked without any shame of his personal prowess. Of his achievements. The obstacles he had to overcome to get where he was. 'The obstacles were nothing,' he said. The main thing for them to remember was that, 'No son of the Rwafa family would ever play second fiddle to anyone's lead. A Rwafa's place is always up there, at the top, out there, right in front of the crowd. No one who carries Rwafa's blood should carry anybody's pisspot!' He raved on, foam flecking the corners of his mouth, his eyes an incandescent red. His voice rose higher, hurt – terribly, terribly hurt – by effeminate, spineless sons of the family who marry into the families of their enemies, poisoning the pure blood of the Rwafa clan.

Rondo couldn't look at his father. Guests started leaving, silently, one after the other, grabbing their children by the hand and hurrying them to their cars where they summoned their wives. Rondo was rooted to his seat, an untouched drink in his hand, unable to look up or to wave goodbye as his father carried on and on like one possessed. At some point, his father had rapped the ground so hard with his favourite hard-wood walking stick that it snapped cleanly in two. His father had looked at the broken, ornamented stick, a gift from admirers in Mozambique, as if it were the death of a well-loved heir and only child. He had wiped bitter sweat off his brow.

Rondo listened to his father, sensing that something terrible was happening, or had already happened, but unable to tell exactly what. Everyone had gone and only he and his children remained. Rondo looked at the children, six and five years old. He looked at their open-mouthed, wide-eyed innocence as the old man rambled on: 'They need to be smoked out, flushed out, blasted out of their hiding places, the impostors!'

Remembering all this, Rondo had been reminded of another incident that he had almost forgotten. He wondered how he could have done so.

It was the day he had helped himself to some ripe mangoes from the neighbour's garden. He hadn't seen anything wrong in that but the neighbour had come upon him, pulled him down by the leg and given him a thorough thrashing with a green peach switch. And when his mother heard him howling, she had come running out and lifting her skirts in the man's face, she called him a child-murderer. The man went on shouting 'Whore!' and called Rondo, 'Woman's child'. And then his father had come into the neighbour's yard with his thick elephant-hide belt and without even bothering to find out what the matter was, proceeded to thrash Rondo. Even after all these years, the sight of his mother dragging herself on her knees from one man to the other, back and forth, begging them, clapping her hands to spare her only son, her only child, that alone gave him a very uncomfortable feeling, and he just didn't want to remember. He had never told anyone about it, not even his wife. At that early age, he was only eight, although he didn't have the words, he must have understood what *powerlessness* meant. Yet his mother had always insisted, 'Your father really loves you. He just doesn't know how to show it.'

It was that same feeling at the birthday party. Rondo remembered. After the party, things couldn't be expected to remain the same. There was a tension in the air. Mr Mzamane tried to joke a bit but gave it up, saying he had to sleep early for the long drive to Bulawayo the following day.

That was when he had asked if Rondo and Selina could let his two beautiful grand-daughters accompany him. It had been a long time since he had given them a real treat. Rondo and Selina had said they saw nothing wrong in that. But Rondo also remembered a seemingly insignificant thing that had happened soon after they had given their consent.

Rondo's mother had asked, 'Did anyone of you see where my husband went?'

People had laughed. Remembering it later, Rondo was not sure that this should have been ignored.

Rondo stood up from the fire in the marquee and walked to the guest room that his father had been using throughout the week. He didn't knock. He found his father reading a magazine, sitting on a sofa.

'What took you so long?' his father asked without taking his eyes off the paper. Rondo didn't answer. He pulled a folded piece of paper out of his pocket and handed it to his father.

After reading it, his father looked up and said, 'Did you ask one of your more intelligent friends to write this for you?'

Rondo didn't answer. It was all he could do to stand there, unblinking. His father hadn't asked him to sit down.

'I wouldn't have believed that you had it in you,' his father laughed harshly. But his laughter caught in his throat when a gun appeared in Rondo's hand. But something was wrong. Rondo had the butt of the gun pointing at his father, as if he was offering it to him.

His father's eyes opened wider still and a great flood of sadness washed through him. He looked wearily into the face of his one and only son. He searched all over his face for a foothold of manhood, for a handhold of hope, 'So, the whole thing is your idea then?' He took the gun out of Rondo's hand and pointed it at his head.

Rondo could have been a rock for all that he felt. It wasn't courage. Just numbness. Stupidity, his workmates or friends would have said. He understood them now. Somewhere inside him, a deep wish emerged that his father should shoot him. That would simplify matters. He would be taking care of things as he had always taken care of the things of his life.

'I haven't used a gun before,' Rondo said calmly. 'I thought you'd do this thing better than me. After all, this is the story of your life.'

Slowly, his father put the gun on the floor, reached inside his jacket and took out his own service pistol. Rondo watched all this as if it were happening on the screen. Then, unexpectedly, his father hissed, 'You two get out of here and shut the door!'

Rondo obeyed and as he turned, he saw Selina in the doorway – with a gun. She didn't resist when Rondo pushed her gently out closing the door softly behind them.

The sound came as a soft muffled plop.

But Rondo was looking at the gun in Selina's hand. She read his thoughts, and said, 'Your mother gave it to me.'

Rondo bent his head in silence.

❧ Mermaid out of the Rain ❧

Stanley Mupfudza

The newspapers called the long week of heavy rainfall 'Seven days of Noah's rain'. No one could remember a time when so much rain had fallen in the city. I, on the other hand, will always remember that week for another reason. It was then that she came to me.

I found her huddled on my doorstep.

She had wrapped herself in newspapers in a futile attempt to protect herself from the downpour. 'Come in,' I said, as if I was in the habit of finding strange women on my doorstep. She looked at me warily. I walked into my single room and left the door open for her to follow. After a long while she walked in out of the rain.

I gave her my girlfriend's clothes to wear. My girlfriend, Maggie, was a journalist. She was currently away on assignment. She did not exactly live at my place but occasionally slept over, and so she kept some of her clothes there. The woman was slightly taller than Maggie but the clothes would serve their purpose.

She gulped down the food I gave her. I silently tipped more food onto her plate from mine, ignoring her half-hearted protests. She ate with gusto – it was obvious she had not had a decent meal in ages. Once, when she thought I was not looking, I caught her staring at me in wonder.

She had no voice. She could not tell me her story. The texture of her life remained hidden in her silence. She slept on my bed while I braved the floor. When my landlady found out that I was living with a strange woman, she was furious. She thought I was living with a whore and was cheating on Maggie. It was ironic really, for, to the best of my knowledge, despite her being member of her church's 'Gracious Women' club, her Pastor administered more than just prayer when he paid her special visits.

So, I paid her no heed.

When Maggie returned, there was fire in her eyes. There were nuclear missiles on her tongue. Their fallout scalded my ears, turning my heart into a Hiroshima of anguished love.

'Who's she?'

'I don't know.'

'You can't be serious, Muchemwa.'

She always called me by my full name when she was angry with me.

'I honestly don't know who she is.'

'You mean you're sharing a single room with a complete stranger?'

I nodded.

'A woman, Muchemwa! Am I expected to believe this is all innocent goodwill?'

'It's the truth, Maggie. I found her on the doorstep, cold, wet and hungry. I decided to help her.'

'Why?'

'She needed help. I could offer it.'

'You're not Pharaoh's daughter, Muchemwa, going about saving some lost souls in the river – or rain. And I'm not some naïve school girl you can ...'

'I'm telling you the truth, Maggie. There is nothing between me and this woman. I just felt sorry for her.'

'You just felt sorry for her! If she had been a man, would you have felt sorry for her? If I found a man on my doorstep and I took him in how would you feel?'

I said nothing.

'I go away for a few days and I find you shacked up with this …' Her lips could not form the word in her mind.

'It's not like that at all.'

'What's it like then, tell me?'

With what idiom shall I speak of the dark things that walk her dreams? With what words shall my tongue paint pictures of her screams? How can I tell you, Maggie, of the anguish I feel because I cannot slay the dragons of her invisible nightmares? In the light of day, all I see are the shadows of her pain in the depths of her eyes. The only thing I am doing is offering her the sanctuary of my single room. There are secret wounds bleeding inside her. I know not their source. She sheds silent tears in the dark when she thinks me asleep. I wish I had the key to the dome of her silence, for her silence is not peace, Maggie.

Maggie chose not to understand. She took her clothes, except the ones the woman wore, and left. Words stood between us, and understanding. They were the tools of her trade but they drove us apart. I could not explain my need to heal this woman's private pain. Her unseen scars haunted me. Her terrible loneliness frightened me. Sadly, I watched Maggie walk out of my life.

As I walked back to my room, I had a feeling that someone was watching me. I looked over my shoulder and saw someone hastily draw the curtains across one of the windows in the main house. I remembered that it was the landlady's fifteen-year-old daughter's room. The last time I had seen her she had looked worried and dejected. At the time, I thought nothing of it.

After the seventh day, the rain stopped. The sky, though, remained gloomy and overcast. On the day that the rain stopped, the neighbourhood dogs ran through the streets, tearing away with some bloody rags. Everyone was incensed. Rumours spread quickly. Before we knew it, they weren't rags but a foetus. And the question was asked: who could have done such a terrible deed? No one thought that it could have been their own daughters or sisters. No, *they* were too well brought up to do such a thing. It had to be that whore that I was living with. My landlady was at the centre of the allegations.

Ours is a neighbourhood where people have moved up in the world. We're a cut above the high-densities we've escaped. We made the news, the other day, when we refused a name that associated us too closely with a nearby ghetto. Heaven knows, we might be near one, but we are definitely no longer *of* the ghetto. Imagine our horror when the city council offered us a Shona name, of all things, instead ... Talk about a decline in standards! We protect our integrity, our territory, our move up in the world. This is why we have my landlady, for example, and dogs. Dogs to bark, dogs to frighten away thieves that might steal our hard-earned possessions or beggars that might bring the area into disrepute. But the dogs that we keep are not pets, they don't have names or bells on their collars, or get taken for walks. And many of us consider buying them dog food, or bones, a luxury we can ill afford – they are not human after all. So the most enterprising among them scavenge – besides, to feed them would make them dormant, lazy, and they would not protect us.

So they move around at night, barking, scavenging, and foraging into dustbins, leaving a scatter of litter all over our beloved neighbourhood. Ours was a righteous neighbourhood, full of righteous people like my landlady. So when it was said that the dogs had found a foetus, the remains of a foetus, it was hard to believe. In fact it was logically impossible. But the sordid, rotting, unlikely news travelled round the area like wildfire: whatever it was, was a threat to our virtue, our moral uprightness. It was a cancer that threatened to devour the sacrifices we had made to get where we were, it tarnished our reputation with the threat of immorality. It threatened our traditional virtues, it was worse than the dogs turning up an old condom from the Pastor's bin …

They labelled the woman who had come to me out of the rain a witch. I found them milling around outside our yard. Some had stones, hoes and axes.

'Death to the witch!' they chanted.

'Death to the witch lover,' they added when they saw me. I pushed my way through the mob. I was more concerned about her safety than mine. Finally, I made it to my room. She unlocked the door and let me in. The fear in her eyes had intensified. When she saw me her eyes widened in alarm. I was bewildered. Then I felt her gentle hands touch my head. She showed me the blood. Someone must have struck me with a stone or something as I walked through the crowd, but I had felt nothing.

She washed my wound and dressed it with so much tenderness that I cried. I, who had failed to silence her cries all these nights, found myself being comforted by her. She rocked me in her arms. I did not know who she was, or what she had gone through. However, despite her own personal demons, and the nightmare that awaited her outside, she found it in her to give me tenderness. That night a gentle drizzle fell upon the earth. There was a threat of thunder, with lightning streaking across the face of the sky, but the rains that fell were gentle.

I should not have gone to work the following day. Nevertheless, she shooed me away. She was going to be safe, she gestured. Foolishly, I did as she wished. Now, it is said the landlady unlocked the gate for the mob. They broke my door down. Some of my property was stolen but I do not care for it. I grieve for her whom they drove away from my house as if she were an animal.

Because she had lost her voice somewhere in the mists of her past, she did not utter a word. The women beat her. The men stoned her. The children jeered at her. She did not attempt to run away. It was almost as if she had grown weary of flight. She died on her way to the hospital in the police car that came to rescue her. She had lost a lot of blood. There is a stain on the road, just outside my landlady's gate, which will not wash away, no matter how heavy the rains are. It remains there.

> *I fear to close my eyes at night for I hear her screams in the darkness. Her blood drip-drips in the silence of the dark. However, the times I do sleep, she comes to me with a smile on her face, her speaking voice restored, and she soothes my pain.*
>
> *'It's not your burden,' she says to me.*
>
> *However, I carry it all the same. I have given up the gift of speech.*

... and then the landlady's pretty daughter knocked on my door. She was ashen-faced and tearful. I have something to tell you, she said. She sat down on the same chair that the woman they killed sat on that day that she came to me. She stared at the floor for a long time, her tears rolling down like Noah's rain. I didn't know what to say or do. I sat there and simply let her cry it out, whatever it was that had brought her to my room.

Sure, we had exchanged niceties whenever we met, and before the incident with the woman they killed, I had been her English language private tutor – lessons which were conducted in their lounge with her mother frequently disturbing us, by coming in and out, ostensibly to look for something she never seemed to find, but really to check if I was not violating her daughter's honour. So, as far as her mother was concerned, my room was way out of bounds. But here she was. Finally, with a heavy sigh, she said,

'Teacher, I'm sorry about what they did to your friend.'

'You don't have to be ... don't worry about it. I know you're different from those who did it.'

'Am I really?'

'Of course you are. You are still young ... innocent.'

She burst out laughing and I was taken aback. It was a dry mirthless laugh that sounded ancient, and filled with despair.

'They were mine, you know … those rags the dogs found.'

'What?'

'The pastor, he told me to get rid of it …'

And I knew right then that at the end of the month I would be packing my bags and going back to the high-density where appearances weren't everything, and rumours were our entertainment.

ॐ Mukoma Amos ॐ

Chiedza Musengezi

Nobody sits under the mango tree in our homestead. Mukoma Amos waits there for me to join him every day after school. He is easy to find, like a snail that leaves a silver trail in its path. There is a crisscross of tracks in the sandy clean-swept yard, his movements since morning. I pick the one that clearly shows his palm prints between the near straight-line left behind when he drags his feet along. No, it is not just his feet. He drags along the entire lower half of his body, his thighs, legs and feet. People say my cousin is 'dead or useless from the waist down'. It is true that his thighs and legs are lifeless. They resemble sticks with cotton-wool-soft flesh. They grow lengthwise and do not fill out with live tissue. The fresh tracks lead me behind his mother's kitchen, a brick rondavel. I find him slumped against one of the big stones that support the raised platform on which the granary is built. Beside him is a small heap of stones. Is he preparing for a fight? I move closer and I see his shoulders rise and fall to match his hard, fast breathing. He strangles sobs in his throat. He is angry. His eyes look hurt, his mouth, he is on the verge of tears. I touch his shoulder to calm him. He stiffens, shrugging off my hand. I must leave him alone. But how can I?

'What is the matter?' I ask.

He is unreachable. He does not turn his head to look at me. I
drop my bag of books next to him. I walk away towards my mother's
house, skirting the pumpkin vine that sprouted on its own accord
near the rubbish pit. Unpruned, it has grown into a wild luxuriance
and is now refuge to the hens' chicks. They hide in it when a hawk
eyes them from the air. I climb the anthill behind the guava tree.
From here I can scan the entire village. It is calm and restful. There
is no sign of what has disturbed Mukoma Amos. In the village
carpenter's homestead stand the two brick rondavels for his two
wives and a two bed-roomed brick house with a galvanized iron
roof. I stand on the tips of my toes to see beyond. My eyes follow
the worn path that leads to the homestead of the village builder,
who has annoyed my mother because he wants my elder sister for a
second wife. Only when I turn round to face south, and my eyes
sweep past Mbuya VaGudza's falling roofs encircled with the
overgrown evergreen hedge, do I see three little figures running
towards the village head's homestead. The headman's daughters
have hurt *mukoma* again. They do it from time to time, stopping by
on their way from school to humiliate and prod at him with their
song. I climb down the anthill. 'I'll strike their stupid heads with
these,' he says fingering a stone. He mimics their song.

'*Nyoka yaDriver, Nyoka yaDriver*
Ona muhwezva weNyoka yaDriver.

'Calling me a snake. Likening my tracks to a snake path. Am I a
snake?'

I do not think he expects an answer. The village headman's
daughters are untouchable and they know it. Their father owns the
land our parents work. He alone assigns land and only he takes it
away. Whenever my mother brews beer for sale or for working the
fields she reserves a pot for him. Mukoma's threats to get at his
daughters are not empty. I have seen him settle scores with some of
the village children. He lures them with the many toys he makes in

his solitude. When they are relaxed he grabs one by the angle and no amount of wriggling and struggling breaks his powerful grip. I pull out my old reader from my school bag. I hand it to him with a promise to come back and practise reading and writing after lunch. I am in the final year of primary school, Standard 6. I am thirteen. Mukoma is sixteen. He does not go to school. I hope to go to secondary school next year.

A story circulates in the village about why Mukoma Amos is 'dead from the waist down'. It is said that it is on account of his mother's character, a woman of flaming passions and an insatiable love of sex. The older 'respectable' women in the village would nod their heads together disapprovingly. 'And God has punished her. Look at that poor child.' Behind her back, they called her Murazvu — the flame. I always thought it was because she was a strong woman with a hot temper, impatient with fools and gossips, and only later did I realise that the nickname suggested different fires.

She is tall, washed and scrubbed, her skin shines with Vaseline. She wears good-fitting floral cotton dresses that her husband, Babamunini Driver, buys from Power Store where he drives a lorry. She is loud-voiced and talks freely. She does not walk serenely like my mother but leaps out to grab the things she enjoys. Everyone in our family looks up to her to break in the young oxen for the plough. She works her fields and vegetable garden, and her kitchen is never short of food. It was at one of my mother's beer gatherings that a man took the lid off the secret story. My mother brews regularly to raise money for my school fees. This man, who was drunk and boisterous, came up to Murazvu who was singing away. He accused her of willfully crippling her son. The real reason why Amos is crippled, he said, was that for the time Murazvu breast-fed him, she did not abstain from having sex with her husband. She was impatient for baby Amos to turn two, when she could wean him from the breast. The story ends with Murazvu shouting any insult that came to her lips as she thumped him.

My mother is annoyed that I now know the story. She reproaches me for showing an interest in what she calls 'wrong things'.

'*Wangwarisa*,' she says. She thinks I am getting too clever for my own good.

'What if you know the truth, will it make your cousin rise and walk?'

I regret asking her.

'It is not true. Amos was ill and the hospital could not help. It was too late. He should have had an injection to prevent the illness much earlier. That's all.'

I risk another question, since there is no anger in her voice.

'What disease was it?'

'Polio.'

Clearly her mind is on her clay, she has no interest in taking more questions. She wants it smooth and soft. She stamps it, stopping now and again to pick out stones and lumps.

I have never heard of the word before. I wonder if he once walked. And if so, how did the disease attack him? Did he wake up one morning to find that his legs had given up on him? Or did the disease set in gradually and painfully until his legs grew thin and soft, losing feeling and movement? The questions have to wait. My mother bites her lower lip in irritation before she sends me off to the cattle pasture to look for dry cowdung pats. She uses them to fire her clay pots. When she makes pots she hates distractions. She wants quiet and time alone in which to concentrate. She has all the ones she has made recently out on the kitchen floor. They all have round 'stomachs', as she calls them, of varying sizes that taper into different necks; short, long, wide, narrow, upright and tilted. The small serving bowls are without necks. She polishes them with the small smooth pebble that she picks in the riverbed. She rolls it with enough pressure in her hand to leave the surface with a high polish that she gets with the aid of her spittle. It makes them watertight and gives them a neat appearance. She places the polished pots outside, with their mouths facing the sun so that they can drink in the gentle heat of the late afternoon before she takes them into the heat of midday sun to dry out completely. Then, they are ready for firing. Her pots sell as well as her beer. Village women cast envious eyes at them whenever they walk into our yard. They prefer her clay pots to the enamel pots from Mr Power's store, which heat up too fast and burn food. And they complain that the tin cans cannot keep the drinking water cool. They place orders for sadza pots, relish pots, small serving bowls, water pots, beer pots, storage pots. They pay in cash or kind. Those without money fill the pot of their choice with the rapoko that she uses to brew beer. She is a widow and well-known for making money. My father died when I was a baby and my mother, brother, sisters and I all live under the protective wing of Babamunini Driver.

* * * * *

When I come back from lunch Mukoma Amos is calm. I find him leafing through my old first grade chiKaranga speller. The first ten pages of the book have a colour picture of a person and a word underneath it. The people stand upright with their legs together. Their faces are expressionless, neither happy nor sad. Only their sex is distinct. A man wears a white shirt and a blue pair of trousers and a pair of shoes. Underneath the picture is the word *baba*. The woman has a blue headscarf and a stripy dress and below is the word *mai*. I say each word out loud and *mukoma* repeats after me just like we do at school. He repeats after me.

'*Baba, mai, vana*. (Father, mother, children).

But what about them?' he asks.

'Nothing.' I say

My cousin expects a story. He is disappointed that learning is uninteresting.

He yearns to learn: his eagerness exhausts me sometimes. I tell him that we need to practise writing. I smooth the ground and test the depth of the sand with my forefinger. We need more sand for our letters to show up clearly. I get an old dish and scoop sand from where the pots are scrubbed and washed. I smooth the surface before taking his right forefinger into my hand. It feels like my mother's wet clay. He is ready to be guided. I can turn it whichever way I want it to go. I apply a little pressure near the ball of his finger to make a straight line and the smooth half circle to make 'b's. I do it twice more. I let go his finger for him to try on his own. He makes the straight line with confidence but he hesitates on the half-circle. He places it on the left of the line to make a d. I erase it and ask him to try again. This time he puts it on the upper end of the line to make a P. Differences between b, p and d are too subtle for him to distinguish. We practise with concentration but progress is slow. I stop with the promise that we will write his name next time.

'How about English?' he asks.

I promise to teach him 'My name is Amos. My father's name is Driver,' tomorrow.

* * * * *

I leave my mother absorbed in her pots when I ask Amos to come and help me gather dry cowdung pats.

'Is she about to fire her pots?'

He does not sound keen but I look at him with pleading eyes. He agrees to come along but not before he knows where we are going to find them.

'Across the road where we graze cattle.'

I point in the direction of the cattle pens where the old fields lie fallow, having been farmed to exhaustion. They are sandy and the grass grows short. Big trees are few and far between but bush begins to grow here and there. The fields have been abandoned to allow the land to heal. I hold Amos up by his feet. They feel cold and limp in my hands. He gets on his strong hands and crawls across the road. We head towards the only treed spot where the muhacha trees grow closely to form an unbroken canopy at the top. Here the ground is littered with cowdung pats in various stages of dryness. Cattle shield themselves from the afternoon heat in the shade. They chew cud with their heads up and eyes closed, occasionally swishing their tails or twitching a muscle to shudder off flies. We skirt the fresh green and wet cow dung and look for the pats that are baked rock-dry and lift easily from the ground. We gather the pats into small heaps until we have enough to fire the pots. We leave them for collection later with my mother. I ask him about the polio, the disease that my mother said attacked him. He has never heard of the word. His parents do not discuss his condition with him.

* * * * *

In the quiet early morning the ring of the school bell travels across the land to reach the villages in the neighbourhood. The bell is an old ploughshare suspended from the branch of a tree that grows on the top of an anthill, the only rise in the schoolyard. Every morning around five o'clock, from Monday to Friday, a young man strikes the gong with a piece of heavy metal, quickly and repeatedly. The sound reverberates throughout our land. When I hear it, it is time to get up, wash and go to school. If I pull my blanket over my head and lie under it for longer, I will be late for school. I risk being struck on the knuckles or fingertips with a wooden stick ten to twenty times. I detest it, so I am rarely late for school.

I like my teacher. Every one of us in our class does. He found his way to our hearts through his missing teeth. His toothless front gums make him like a five-year-old, harmless and vulnerable. The class shows that it feels protective towards him by not causing any trouble. When he talks there is a thsss, thsss sound in each word: booksthsss, cupsthsss, eyesthsss. We understand him without difficulty. We subtract the thss from his word endings and we end up with normal speech.

For our English lesson he gives the topic, 'My Favourite Relation'. He explains the words before we start.

'Favouritethss meansthss thathss youthss likethss somethingthss verythss muchthss. Whathss isthss yourthss favouritethss foodthss?'

His question turns the classroom into a forest of hands. Nobody is without a favourite food. They range from rice and chicken to wild fruit: matohwe and mazhanje. The word is well understood. Next, he explains relation which means your brother, sister, aunt, uncle, all the people you have kinship with. He asks the class to give more examples. We give grandmother, grandfather, niece, and nephew. He raises his left hand and brings the forefinger of his right hand to his lips stemming the flow of our examples.

'Allthss rightthss!' He says with a clap of the hands.

He instructs us to take out our English composition exercise books, choose a favourite relation and write. He reminds us to explain why we like the relation we choose.

I write about my cousin, Mukoma Amos. Words flow through my pen on to paper effortlessly. I know my cousin well, my playmate and trusted friend. I describe how he looks and how excited we got when we discovered that he could flex his big toe. We expected the feeble movement in his big toes to get stronger and spread through his lower body until his legs could stand. I tell how when we are totally and completely alone I sometimes hold down his feet and encourage him to get up. With his strong palms firmly planted on the ground he heaves his body only to slump back as he fails to transfer the weight to his feet. I do not leave out how clever he is with his hands. He makes toys with bits of old wire and the fruit of the sausage tree: a span of oxen pulling a plough, a lorry like the one his father drives. I end my composition with how we practise reading and writing and how much my cousin longs to come to school with me if only he could walk. When the teacher gives back my book the next day there is no mark. An unusual comment at the bottom of my work reads, 'See me.' My heart hammers against my chest. I do not know what I did wrong. I expect the worst, the wooden stick on my knuckles or an afternoon of weeding in the teacher's field. I wipe my sweaty palms against my uniformed thighs as I wait to be summoned.

'Sofiathss!'

He calls out my name but not in a cold warning voice. I kneel before the teacher with my book in hand. He asks if the story is true. I nod. He says my cousin may be able to get some help at this address and he writes it down: 'Jairos Jiri, Nguboyenja Township, Bulawayo.'

As soon as I get home I share the news with Amos who does not show any excitement.

'Do you think my father will like it?'

He has doubts but I trust Babamunini Driver. I keep the piece of paper in the safest place I can find, between the covers of my arithmetic book. When *babamunini* arrives on Friday I give it to him. He promises to find out. I cannot tell from the tone of his voice or the expression on his face if he will follow it through.

When he arrives the following week he is driving Mr Power's lorry with his bicycle in the back. Amos has been admitted to the Jairos Jiri School for the disabled. There is a flurry of activity. My uncle cleans the lorry and arranges pillows on the passenger seat to try out sitting positions. When he is satisfied with the arrangement he rolls himself a cigarette. He coughs and blows out a cloud of smoke. He clears his throat and flicks out his tongue to throw out a ball of phlegm. He holds the cigarette between his lips. He unbuttons his overalls heading towards the bath shelter where he takes his bath sitting in the big iron metal basin of warm water. We hear liquid sounds from within: sloshes and splashes, like a big fish in a small pond. Amos's clothes flap on the washing line. Murazvu feels them with the back and then the front of her hand for dryness. Sometimes she pats both her cheeks with the collar of his shirt or the hem of his shorts to feel any lingering moisture in the layered material. She irons them before packing them in a small suitcase.

Afterwards she busies herself with cooking. She is outside her kitchen. With her billowing skirts tucked between her thighs she is bent over a slaughtered chicken, plucking and throwing feathers into a rubbish pit that is close to filling up with fire ashes, dead leaves, left-over sadza and broken clay pots. The smell of singeing feathers fills her kitchen as she dips the chicken in and out of flames. This way she gets rid of the tiny feathers that she cannot pick by hand. She cooks rice and chicken, some of which she packs in a bowl so that father and son can eat on the long journey to Bulawayo.

My uncle emerges out of the bath shelter in a change of clothes but not completely dressed. He guides his leather belt through the loops of his navy blue trousers, draws it tightly around his waist and fastens it. He tucks in his shirt-tail and sits down to clean his shoes. With Amos in the passenger seat and *babamunini* behind the wheel, the lorry is reversed out of the yard into the road. He shifts the gear stick into first and revs the engine. Dust swirls all round.

'Roll up the window and keep out the dirt.'

Mukoma does as he is told. We exchange glances. A smile lurks on his lips. The lorry recedes into the distance until it becomes a small dot that gradually disappears. It leaves a sad silence behind. Murazvu sighs and tears glisten in her eyes. I glance past her and pretend that I have not seen anything.

'Do you think he'll come back? Walking I mean?'

Her voice is thin and tremulous, she sniffs and snivels. I have never seen her cry. She is a strong woman. I have no answer. I give my homework as an excuse to leave, because I too feel the sting of tears in my eyes. At night I close my eyes and darkness brings me relief. I dream about Amos. He has special shoes on his feet. His legs, now supported with special sticks, hold up his body. He is walking with crutches. I prefer my mind's flights of fancy to the stark reality of day.

🚲 Torn Posters 🚲

Gugu Ndlovu

In 1984 I *was too young* to vote, yet that didn't stop me from performing my patriotic duty with razor-like precision. The early mornings were best for our raids. My small but fierce guerilla squad would trudge through Sanki's lucerne field, the dew dampening our broganes as we closed in on our unsuspecting targets. Crouching as we neared, not to be discovered by the sentinels, we waited. Watching for the right moment to strike. Just seeing 'PAMBERI NE ZANU PF' emblazoned on their bloody posters, we were engulfed by a bitter rage. It rose like bile in our throats erupting as earsplitting war-cries roused us into action, and we ran screaming across the field with weapons raised to encounter the enemy.

We ripped into their flesh, stabbing and tearing at it, slashing their principles, punching holes in their policy. Each blow killing HIM and his fat greedy ministers. We surveyed the scene with arrogance. Damage Report: for me and my comrades, a few scratches, a splinter, scraped knees, an undone ribbon and some grass stains on our uniforms: mummy won't like that. The enemy was another matter – they lay indifferent, confettied at our feet.

Treason is punishable by death. Must hide the evidence! Drag the carcasses, stuff them into the anthills. A place where anything from aborted babies to bewitched panties ... disappeared forever. Swallowed whole by the earth.

This was our contribution to the elections, our duty to our country. How trivial it may have been, it filled us with an ironic sense of pride. Like the comrades we'd seen on TV, we lifted our fists and shouted, '*Amandla awethu!*' for the cameras. For now our mission is far from complete. School is still another two kilometres away, our hands stained with the hopelessness of the mutilated posters, our eyes peeled for more that carry the poisonous message.

* * * * * *

News from distant realities far far away, trickled into our daily conversations. In the villages of Matabeleland: entire homesteads abandoned, pots still on the fires; huts set ablaze with sleeping families inside them; mass graves in abandoned mines; mothers stripped naked and forced to watch their children's throats slit; elderly women beaten, raped, and killed for their blankets. From what we were told, an unsettled group of Ndebele army men whom the government called 'dissidents', were plundering villages and killing their occupants.

'It's Him,' our father would say quietly, lighting a cigarette. 'He's killing us.'

Filling up his and Uncle Dan's glasses with more whisky, we could feel the tension in their bodies and voices. Uncle Dan was planning to leave for the UK. Apparently, these weren't dissidents, but soldiers employed by Him to disguise themselves as dissidents and kill the people of Matabeleland. (Many years later we found out that the army consisting of approximately 20,000 soldiers had been given orders to kill a minimum of 100 Matabele people each. The exact figure of how many were killed is still unknown.)

'That's where they start, the villages, I'm telling you, Georgie, he's coming for us next,' Uncle Dan would say after a couple of glasses.

'I can't run anywhere, Dan. How can you run away from home?

From what's yours?' Daddy would say opening his hands out.

'Would you rather he kill you?' Uncle Dan would ask, concerned at my father's stubbornness.

'Agh man he won't kill me – maybe arrest me, yes.' He would say taking a sip, then he'd turn to Uncle Dan to tell him what he always did. 'Dan, you're not a politician, you're not a soldier, you are a businessman, you know how to make money. So go to England and make money. Me, I'm a politician, this is a chess game. I can watch his moves … he's trying to make us angry at our people's expense, and he's doing a bloody damn good job of it; but as long as I'm alive he won't get his checkmate, maybe he'll get pieces, yes, but never checkmate.' Uncle Dan left for England. Our father stayed and continued his game.

Disguised soldiers' fires continued to light dark Matabele nights as they burnt villages. The cries of women and young girls also filled the night air as their bodies were violated. People's hearts were heavy with grief for their losses. That grief quickly mutated into a dark bitterness, as we all tried to make sense of it. As children, we inherited that bitterness as a predisposition. Only after they came and took our fathers did it become truly ours.

* * * * *

In my dream, a large truck was trying to run me down. There was no one in the driver's seat. I was running, but I couldn't run fast enough. Mummy was standing on a hill calling my name. Her voice was getting closer and closer, and then I fell. Mummy called my name again, I opened my eyes to her concerned face.

'You have to get up, honey,' she said softly. 'It's too early,' I croaked sleepily. 'I know but we have to get up … get your shoes and come,' she said as she moved on towards my sisters' and my cousins' beds.

They came in the morning. Before the sun was up. There were a lot of us living at home then, seven of us kids, an uncle and our parents. My five-year-old brother, who'd been up for at least half an hour, came running into the room. He was holding his Lego spaceship, which he'd made the night before.

'There are huge trucks outside, guys,' he panted excitedly. 'And they've got real soldiers in them, with guns,' he added, obviously still intoxicated after seeing a dozen or more AK 47s. My heart sank to the bottom of the Zambezi River – they'd finally come for father. A cock crowed ...

'Is Daddy here,' I wanted to know urgently. 'Yes, he's outside talking to *them*,' Mum said calmly. 'What do they want?' 'They want to know if we have any weapons, so we have to go and sit outside while they search the house,' my mother said, as she turned to wake up another small sleeping body. I cracked the front door ajar to get a peek of what was going on outside. It looked like an episode of the A-team, an action television series we'd once loved: two-dozen or so armed soldiers, scattered amongst half a dozen army trucks of different shapes, sizes and purpose, burdened our front yard, imprisoning flower beds and small trees, digging large muddy skid marks across the lawn. Under a broken peach tree, in a far corner of the garden, Butho's tricycle lay a mangled mess of metal. I walked out of the door, angry and ready to fight ... I was only twelve, what did I know, but I had attitude.

We sat outside on the veranda as the sun came up, while they pillaged our home using our parents as guides. The dogs had been barking all night. Now, they sat around us panting, licking, sniffing and growling. Arrogant, bloodshot eyes gazed uninhibitedly at my budding breasts. We just smiled politely, even shyly, because we were still in our nightclothes, by far our favourites, Snoopy and Charlie Brown, that our Canadian grandmother had sent last Christmas; but even their cheerful happy cartoon faces couldn't soften the arrogant gaze. At least Thandi and Siphiwe were hidden behind the thick matching flannel pyjamas they had on.

A few cradled their AKs and tried to make friendly conversation, 'Wot grrede rr u en?' 'Wot es yowa nem?' Their English with a heavy Shona accent felt like they were insulting us.

Then they piled back into their trucks and drove off taking Daddy and Uncle with them.

We went back into the house now empty with loss and heavy with sadness. Scattered papers, overturned mattresses, emptied closets, overturned furniture – clothes everywhere ... summoned tears that somehow wouldn't fall but turned into thorns that stuck in our throats.

Butho

Daddy said he's going to buy me a new bike, because the soldiers drove over my old one. Mummy says they are bad. Thandi was in a bad mood again. Because her egg was too soft. Gugu got angry and threw it in the dogs' dish and Mummy shouted because that really was a waste. It's boring when she shouts. These days she's always shouting. I wish Daddy was here, then she wouldn't shout. She needs all the National Geographics in the house so she can take them with her. She's going to see Daddy. He's in jail (whisper). But he didn't do anything bad. Mummy said he said something the bad guys didn't like ... but not cursing, like FUCK or SHIT. Mummy says we aren't allowed to go and see him. Only she's allowed to visit. That's what 'they' (the bad guys) say. Themba and I played 'dissidents' today. He's my best friend. This time they were red ants, we killed them, every single one of them – squashed their heads off and chopped off their legs. They took Themba's Daddy too.

Mummy

After endless letters and meetings about the abuse of our human rights, we finally got the okay for the kids to see George. Only I couldn't take all of them. It's only a small step, but I'm already exhausted, and we still have to get him out.

We took the night train up. The three girls shared the top bunks, which pulled out from a wooden panelled wall. Butho and I had the lower beds, which served as seats when we weren't sleeping.

Honestly! Can you believe that six years later the sheets and blankets still have NRR (National Rhodesian Railways) imprinted on them?

It's as if this government of vultures, holding court in their Victorian robes (with the white wigs), are nostalgic for the colonial era, only this time, they are in the driver's seat, inflicting the pain.

We marvelled at the refined fitments of the compartment – a wash-basin that could also be a side table, ashtrays hidden in the arm rests, reading lights that were noticed in walls once the beds were pulled out. Although they generally didn't work, and probably hadn't since Independence, though they still looked functional to an innocent visitor – an ironic and glorified reminder of our colonial past. As a new country of only six years, most things of the colonial era had reached a stage of mechanical dysfunction but were still left in place. Their empty symbols littered and mostly cluttered our lives.

Thandi

We're on the way to visit Daddy, he's staying at Chikurubi Maximum Security Prison. It's a jail. Mummy says he's been there for thirteen months. That's a very long time. Because I'm in Grade 3 now, and Gugu had to give me her old tracksuit which doesn't fit her anymore. Siphiwe and Thembi couldn't come because they aren't Daddy's children, they had to stay home. Gugu said they put Daddy in jail for constipating against the govament. But I think she's lying, she doesn't know what she's talking about. She wouldn't let me bring my Dada (that's my best blanket) on the train. And I always take it with me, even when we go to see Gogo. She said I'm a big girl now and I don't need it. But I don't think I'm that big. Maybe just a little bit, 'cause I did help make the cake for Daddy. I hope he likes it, I put the icing on, it's chocolate, his favourite.

Mummy

Bloody Hell! Are they lined along the entire track from Bulawayo to Harare? Who can sleep with the eternal sound of singing crickets?

The solid darkness rushes by. Broken only periodically by wisps of homestead-hearths and animal smells. In the day it is flat open grasslands, dotted every now and then with clusters of mud huts.

Ideal land for cattle grazing. Quite evident, as the scent of dung rushes in through the window as we pass by a siding. George would have loved that smell. It would have taken him back to his childhood, to his days as a cattle herder. It bothers me that it is only in these recent years that he has begun to share his boyhood with me. I think he was ashamed. I sense that in time it will be his pride.

* * * * *

The train moved slowly into the bustle of Harare's morning rush hour. Vendors, marketing everything from newspapers, boiled eggs and second-hand books to stolen watches, moved mindfully through the tangled congestion of slow-moving traffic. Money exchanged for goods through open windows. Bicycles wove in and out of the chaos. Like scavengers, the vendors swarmed the train as it inched into the station.

Marion stood near a group of women wearing white, who sung a welcoming hymn to one of our fellow passengers. Living in Matabeleland, I'd never heard Shona sound so beautiful. The clapping and ululation of their song floated in through the windows of the train, welcoming us all. A newspaper billboard on the platform read GOVT CLAMPS DOWN ON MATABELE DISSIDENTS. I could feel the thorns rising inside my chest. I was afraid as we stepped onto the platform. We had arrived in enemy territory: Mashonaland.

'Wow, you guys have grown!' Marion remarked, rubbing the top of my brother's head.

'Look, I built an ammunition demolisher,' he said, shoving his latest Lego contraption in her face. 'It's to kill the dissidents,' he said loud enough to catch the glances of several passers-by. He winced as I jabbed him in the ribs.

'Ow! … Mummy, Mummy,' but she pretended not to hear as she floated deeper into conversation with Marion.

I liked Marion Douglas. She was tall like me. It felt comfortable standing next to someone my height. At twelve I already wore a size eight shoe. My fast growing body felt awkward and disproportionate, especially my feet, which felt like a clown's. Somebody had told me that the size of your feet relates to your height. Maybe … I hoped, maybe, my feet were smaller than hers.

'You guys are going to love my car, especially you, Butho,' she said as we all climbed in. Marion drove a Citroen. It worked on hydraulics. You had to wait until the car rose up before you could drive it. The rumble of the car's engine vibrated through our bodies as we waited silently for it to rise. Like the colonial artifacts, it excited us.

'Cool, just like a spaceship,' my brother said in his loud voice.

My sister quietly sucked her thumb. She was grumpy because I wouldn't let her bring her 'dada'. She's too old for that at seven. It's actually becoming a bit embarrassing.

We smelt of train and needed to bathe, but Mummy didn't want to waste time. Marion drove us straight to Chikurubi. Our sleepy faces betrayed our frightened, racing hearts. We hadn't seen Daddy in over a year. The thought of seeing him frightened us. We had heard that he had been unwell. What did that mean? Could he walk? Was he eating?

* * * * *

A huge grey concrete wall surrounded the prison. We had not expected the trimmed hedges and manicured lawn of an English manor house as we drove through the gates towards the buildings. Older prisoners in brown khaki uniforms and shocking white tackies, silently weeded, trimmed and watered the grand manor garden. Eerily, almost in unison, they momentarily stopped to watch as we drove up the road to the prison buildings. We stared back, earnestly looking for him among them. He wasn't.

At the office they told Marion she wasn't allowed in. 'She eesn't a family member,' they said arrogantly. She had to wait in the car.

We walked, frightened and excited, our arms overflowing with gifts of books, magazines, baked cakes, yogurts, school report cards, cigarettes and bed-sheets.

In the room it was us against them. Twelve or so policemen and the four of us.

Their smiles were not kind, but amused.

'Poot yowa things heeya,' one barked, indicating a table with a baton stick. While they carefully examined our gifts, they spoke amongst themselves in Shona. In the midst of their loud conversation we heard ours and Daddy's names mentioned.

They emptied packets, opened letters, paged through books, and opened yoghurt containers. My sister yelped painfully as one mutilated her beautifully iced cake with a penknife. 'Security purposes,' he said stiffly, shoving it to the side of inspected goods. Thorns threatened. I held her hand tightly.

We stepped through metal detectors and were body-searched, then led to the 'receiving room'. It was a bare room, nothing but a wooden bench and a highly polished red floor.

We waited, fidgeting and shifting.

* * * * *

Are we going to see Daddy now? Are we going to see Daddy now? When are we going to see Daddy? Is he still coming? Are we at the right place? When are we going to see him?

* * * * *

Thandi

Butho drove his toy car on the floor. When he got up the knees of his pants were red from the polish on the floor. I told Mummy, but she ignored me. She was quiet and angry. I was already sad because the policeman chopped up my cake for Daddy. He said it was for security purposes. I don't know what that means, but I cried. Gugu wanted to cry but I think that's why she's angry.

We are waiting for them to bring Daddy. We've been waiting a long time.

* * * * *

We heard footsteps and jangling keys. The door opened, a policeman led him in. For a moment our eyes deceived us, we didn't immediately recognise him. A shrunken older man with white hair and in a brown khaki prison uniform shuffled in. His skin had assumed an unhealthy ashy hue. He had lost a lot of weight and the uniform hung on him. He looked at us and smiled, we recognised him through his eyes, which shone as they always did. We gasped, 'Daddy!' and ran to him.

'How are my savages?' he laughed, opening his arms to receive us. 'Savages' was his pet name for us. After tearful hugs and kisses we sat down, briefly intoxicated with happiness, as he hugged and kissed Mummy.

We spoke over a painful silence, hoping that our stories about school and various family members would stop it. The silence got louder. We soon couldn't hear ourselves, so we raised our voices up a notch to deafen it, but it was no use. Only the silence could be heard, bringing up thorns that cut at our throats. It became so painful that we no longer spoke, we surrendered to the warm relief of tears. We cried for our father, for his absence. We cried for all the fathers they had taken.

'Don't let them see you cry,' Daddy said wiping the tears away. A wing had fallen off of Butho's ammunition demolisher; he sat on the floor unaware of rising thorns and falling tears, trying to fix it as he prepared it for 'war'. We wiped our tears, while the thorns still clawed.

'If they see you cry they will feel they have won over you.' I thought of the torn posters buried under the earth in the bellies of ants. My patriotic duty was not to cry, but to crush the ants that had digested those toxic words. I decided, echoing my fathers' words, that there would be no checkmate while I was alive.

New Mourning

Mary Ndlovu

Noma glued her eyes to the polished concrete floor, trying to shut out the interminable sound of hymn-singing. It had been hammering at her head for the past two days. Grass mats covered the edges of the room, but could not soften the hard floor she sat on.

Her feet touched those of her elderly aunt, even though she was leaning against the opposite wall of the small sitting room. Naka Thembi's face was drawn and thin, a tooth was missing, her skin dry. How did she sit there hour after hour, never complaining, never contributing to the occasional stuttering conversation, just there. She was like a rock – maybe the rock of ages, which they were singing about.

Noma wished she could hide in that cleft rock. She did not want to have to face the reality of what was to come. How could this have happened to her, just when she thought she had escaped? She looked again around the room; her aunt was the oldest and her body the most eroded by life in the village: ploughing, carrying water, bearing and succouring children, and then grandchildren – all the fatherless babies that her daughters had deposited in her care.

Most of the women singing were much younger: neighbours and friends from the church, her cousins and in-laws who stayed in town. Tennis shoes had been left by the door, *zambias* covered their legs, but their T-shirts and blouses revealed their lost battles with poverty – so faded that the logos and slogans were barely legible. Ma Mpofu from across the road had sunken cheeks, which heralded the final stages of 'that disease'.

Noma's reverie jerked to a halt – funeral, yes, that was what she was supposed to be thinking about, not the poverty and illnesses of the neighbours. It was still not real. Her own mother – the broad back to which she had clung as a baby, the flexible neck that had balanced a thousand buckets of water – her whole body broken and her life extinguished by a reckless combi driver. She struggled to bring her mother back to life. She re-arranged the actors in the drama: her mother heard the combi coming and pushed the wheelbarrow out of the road; the combi driver slowed down and stopped just before it hit her: the vehicle just grazed her: her mother was in hospital with a broken leg.

The singing penetrated her thoughts, bringing her back to reality. She abandoned her fruitless attempts to reconstruct the scene of her mother's death, and accepted the finality of what had happened.

Not that she had ever been a very good daughter to her hard-working mother. But then her mother had never been much of a mother either. Noma had sensed from a young age that her mother was somehow inadequate. There were the meaningful looks exchanged between her aunt and uncle when they visited and found her mother not home, 'Oh, I guess we should have stopped by MaDlodlo if we wanted to see her.' Even after they moved home to their paternal grandfather's village after their father died, she had continued to disappear regularly to nearby drinking places while Nokuthula, the eldest, cooked *isisthwala* and dished it with *amasi* for the younger children.

Noma had hated rural life, hated the interminable meals of *amasi*, hated the drudgery of fetching water, the stifling heat of summer, and the icy wind of winter. And especially hated the hopelessness of planting every year, only to have the rains fail. She was even happy when the borehole pump broke down, because the river was closer and she didn't have to carry the buckets so far. Besides, she liked the pungent taste of the river water better. But most of all she hated the way her aunts subtly ridiculed her mother. It confused her, because she also hated the way her mother left her to look after the boys.

Noma didn't know when she had reached the decision to leave. She knew from the age of eleven when they went to stay at home that she had to find a way out of that miserable life; she felt claustrophobic and breathless when she thought of living out her life there. At least the school offered a glimmer of hope. And in the end it became her passport to an urban life. The family was not so poor that they couldn't sell the odd beast for school fees, and so it was that she was sent to stay with Aunt Mabel in Bulawayo where she completed her secondary education and eventually found herself at university. She had escaped, and now she was about to be employed in a research lab, developing medicines. She would marry her doctor boyfriend and never have to think about rural poverty again.

While she was away, Noma had not communicated with her mother very much. She knew she was still struggling with the younger children, none of whom had done as well at school as she had. Thamsanqa, the oldest boy was already in South Africa, but she didn't know what he was doing. It was two years since she had visited her mother; what was the point – they had nothing to talk about. Yes, she knew when she started work she would send some groceries, perhaps even take her youngest sister and send her to school in town. But she hadn't reached this point yet. Why did her mother have to leave her now, before she had a chance to expunge her lingering feelings of guilt for not paying her more attention? Was her grief at losing her mother really grief, or was it guilt for not playing the proper role of a daughter?

The singing suddenly stopped. A preacher from the neighbourhood was shouting about Adam and Eve, and then suddenly jumped to Job and his sufferings. And then everyone in the room was being threatened with the fires of damnation. Noma wasn't sure what the point of it all was. Certainly it didn't help her much in her confused state of mind. But thankfully it was soon over. Then her uncle was making the announcements about the funeral arrangements, and gradually people made their departures.

Somehow Noma made it through the next days. She felt confused; wasn't sure who had come and who had not: she only listened with half an ear while arguments proceeded about the place of burial, speakers, flowers, and on and on. She accompanied her uncle and aunt to select a coffin – not the cheapest, which would seem disrespectful, but the next one on offer. When the time came to view her mother's body, she managed to steel herself, and looked without seeing, while her older sister collapsed sobbing into the arms of their aunt. Somehow she managed to freeze her emotions and go through the customary practices without even thinking. She was useless as a support to her siblings, from whom she had become distanced over the years away, and rejected any comforting shoulder from any one of her aunts.

However, she could not escape the journey home after the burial. Nokuthula had to return quickly to her small children in Gweru, leaving Noma as the eldest available child of her mother to see to the younger children and her mother's house. With reluctance she accepted her aunt's suggestion that she travel home two days after the funeral.

Noma had last seen her mother's house in summer, when the fields were green, the cattle fat, and the river flowing. Now, the land was dry. No crop had been harvested that year, and the grain bin, which her mother had struggled to build with the boys, was empty. The kitchen roof had holes and badly needed repair. A few chickens scratched below their laddered nesting spot. The youngest children had been taken to their grandmother's home just a ten minutes' walk away, leaving the homestead eerily silent when Noma arrived with her aunt.

The two-room brick house built several years earlier looked dilapidated but appeared much the same as the last time she had seen it. Noma put her hand hesitantly on the door latch and pushed. As if mourning her mother's absence, the two small rooms were silent. Noma's eyes took in its meagre contents – a battered trunk in the corner, the bed neatly covered with a colourful blanket sent by her brother from South Africa, the jacket on a nail acting as a hook, an ancient sofa with crocheted covers. Her knees melted and she collapsed onto the sofa. Her stomach turned. How had her mother survived this pitiful existence? Even the faded calendar on the wall mocked her with its cornucopia of fruits and vegetables. She despised her mother for never taking the challenge of achieving something more; but the emotion soon evolved into anger, and finally pity. She seemed to have been denied the rich possibilities of human development. But why hadn't she done something about it herself?

Noma felt her aunt's hand on her shoulder. 'There's work here to be done, my child, no time for grieving now. Here, I'll help you with the wardrobe.' Noma noticed for the first time the photos on the dresser top. A small one of her father standing proudly with a baby in his arms; another of her sister's two small daughters, grinning eagerly at an unknown photographer. Next to the photos stood a jar containing some kernels of maize and a medley of different varieties of pumpkin seeds. A pencil and a candle shared the jar with the seeds. A crocheted doily almost covered a stain on the wooden surface.

Summoning what little strength she had, Noma pulled open the top drawer. It revealed not clothing but papers. She picked up a small blue exercise book labeled 'Home-based care'. On the first page was written in the careful letters of a partly schooled adult:

Patience Ncube August 7 bed bound, sores, washed sores, gave water

Mercy Tshabalala August 10 bed bound, gave water

> Patience Ncube August 15 bed bound, gave water
>
> Sipho Ncube August 15 T.B., gave medicine

And so it continued for three pages. The last entry was on the 23rd September, only two days before she had died.

'Strange,' Noma thought. She didn't know her mother had been a caregiver. But then how would she know – she hadn't visited her for nearly two years, and even then, what conversation had they had?

She put aside the exercise book and picked up a thick bundle of photocopied papers clipped together. The title on the front page read 'Handbook of Early Childhood Education'. The pages were worn with use, underlines, ticked paragraphs, and occasional comments. Tucked in between the pages she found another small exercise book with a list of names – a class register! Noma knew of her mother's role as a pre-school teacher, but she had never taken it seriously. She thought it was just a matter of playing games with children while their mothers were in the fields. But here were sections on 'Child development', 'Child needs', 'Stimulating creativity', 'Teaching morality'. Could her mother have been reading this? Surely not. But there were the dog-eared papers. And then again, tucked in near the back a 'Certificate of Attendance' – 'Early Childhood Education for Pre-School Teachers: Part I'. The date was two years earlier.

Noma looked back into the drawer. What other secrets would it reveal about her mother?

There were some used bus tickets, a passport belonging to her father, an old torn Grade 4 maths textbook which must have been passed from one child to the next, including herself. A small New Testament with a blue cover lay on top of a booklet in Ndebele. Noma pulled out the booklet – and recognised it as a translation of the United Nations Convention on the Elimination of Discrimination Against Women. Her mother – where could she have got that booklet? Why would she be interested in it, and what would she do with it anyway?

As she puzzled over this incongruous matter, a light knock sounded at the door and a voice called '*Qoki*'. A neighbour put her head around the door and entered slowly. 'Oh Noma,' she exclaimed, 'such a terrible event. We are so sorry. Please accept our condolences,' Noma hung her head and mumbled the appropriate response. 'Your mother talked about you so often and hoped you would come. We have lost such a friend, such an inspiration, someone loved by everyone here. But, of course, you have lost a mother, something much worse.'

Yes, she had lost a mother, but she was becoming more and more confused. Did she even know this mother the woman was talking about? An inspiration? People really did exaggerate about others when they died. She certainly couldn't picture her mother inspiring anyone.

The woman stayed for a respectable amount of time and when she left the house Noma went back to the drawer. Her eyes landed on another booklet. This one looked like a record of accounts. The cover stated 'Treasurer's Book: Savings Club'. Inside, in her mother's hand, were entries spanning a period of several years. Her mother – a treasurer! Treasurers were respected people, people who could be trusted with money. Then she noticed the books with stamps neatly fixed in place – each stamp $1.00. Weekly savings of the whole community.

Noma paused and surveyed the array of booklets and papers she had pulled from the drawer. She was only halfway through the first drawer and already her head was spinning. She felt nauseous. Had she under-estimated her mother? How had the irresponsible, incompetent mother she remembered have been transformed into a community caregiver, teacher and guardian of other people's money? What had Noma missed? Something didn't make sense.

And yet, the rest of the scene confirmed the character she knew – a torn cardboard box of unmended clothes, rags really, under the bed, a bag of maize infested with weevils, stained seat covers on the sofa, and the ever-present heap of sorghum, ready for beer brewing.

Noma's aunt began packing cracked plates and chipped enamel mugs into the hold-all she had carried for the purpose, as Noma's world shifted under her feet. How could she have failed even to glimpse the complexity of her mother's life, her stoic acceptance of poverty and her rising above it to become a comfort and inspiration to her friends and neighbours? How could she have been so petty as to think broken plates and stained sofas were the true worth of a human being? A wave of guilt and horror swept over her.

And then at last the tears came – hot and stinging, great sobs welling from deep in her chest – wails of despair. She wept. For her mother, a mother she had never known and would now never know, for the missed chances to touch more closely the life of a woman who had struggled and succeeded. And she wept for her own pitiful failure. Her failure as a daughter to understand that her mother needed respect, concern and affection rather than groceries. Her failure as a human being to acknowledge the greatness of her mother's silent courage. Her aunt sat down and put an arm around her shoulder. But her aunt would never be able to change the emptiness that now enveloped her.

❧ Homecoming ❧

Vivienne Ndlovu

He turned the key in the lock, hoping the house might be empty, that Flora would not be there to greet him and he would be given that small space he both wanted and feared. He shut the door firmly behind him, listening for the sounds that would tell him that either Flora or one of the children was at home, but the house was silent. Relief flooded through him, only to be swept away again by the knowledge he needed to face. He carried his travel bag upstairs and into the bedroom he and Flora had shared for the last twelve years. He had returned to it often before, but never like this.

The whole room spoke of Flora, the subtle colours, the simple furnishings – she had never liked fussy things. He would have chosen stronger colours, but this room, though they shared it, was Flora's, he saw now. All evidence of his occupation of it was confined to the cupboards and a copy of 'The Heart of Change' which lay on the table on his side of the bed. That one small sign of belonging briefly assuaged the dread that had been with him for the last two days, as he sat in meetings, as he went through the motions of getting on the plane, most of all when he had phoned Flora to let her know what time he would be getting in. It had grown in intensity the closer he got to home and now he was here. He had to reach a decision. Flora might return at any moment and he still had no idea what he was going to do.

He had travelled frequently during the early years of their marriage and had taken it for granted that he would seek some woman's company on the trips that took him away the longest. He had given no thought to how Flora would feel about it – men had needs, after all. With equal confidence he assumed that she had always been faithful to him. He had been careful, of course. He generally used protection. But when he had ended up staying in Zambia for almost two years, things got a bit out of hand. Flora had joined him only once, about halfway through his stay, because the children were still young. She had even met Sibongile – the woman had invited them to her home for supper. He hadn't felt even a flicker of guilt at the time.

Since then, he'd travelled a lot less and his lapses had gradually decreased, although he could not claim this was the result of any personal resolve. He remembered the night shortly after his return from Zambia when, after a rather unsatisfactory love-making, Flora had told him she wanted him to change his work schedule to avoid these long trips away, or perhaps he could find a way for her to travel with him. A few months later still, he had overheard her talking with her sister about the marriage of a mutual friend and been surprised to hear Flora's voice, firm and uncompromising,

'Well I know I wouldn't put up with his carrying on like that. Not now. Not these days'.

They had established a good, comfortable marriage and that in itself had dampened his need for other women. It was a couple of years now since he had last gone astray and this was what hit him the hardest. That now, when everything was fine, when he had made the effort to be faithful; when, if he was honest, he had understood the value of having an intelligent and supportive wife (for Flora had surely contributed to the consolidation of his career, with her judicious entertaining and steady urging of his ambition) now, this unwanted news seemed to threaten the whole edifice that was his life. It could all come crashing down around him.

The 'boss' inside his head kept saying he was being ridiculous – their marriage was solid. Good God, this had happened seven years ago. Surely it was just a minor mishap. Something as solid as their relationship would quickly surmount this hurdle and their life together would continue smooth and unblemished, perhaps, be even the richer for it. And anyway, why did he have to tell her? He could try to bury this mistaken, unsolicited knowledge.

Why on earth had he telephoned the woman? He had had only one more day in Lusaka – if only he hadn't made that call. He was at a loose end in the dean's office, waiting for him to come back from a meeting so that they could go out for lunch together when, paging through the paper, he saw an advert for the company she had worked for. Why didn't he just give them a call and see if by chance she was still there. Perhaps if he'd known she *was* there he wouldn't have done it – perhaps? But the operator answered and put him straight through to Mrs Kamuya and suddenly she was on the other end of the line. She was clearly surprised to hear from him and then he was suggesting a drink that evening and she was agreeing to the invitation. Even then, perhaps he'd assumed she wouldn't be able to make it at such short notice and that she might now have a family of her own ... but she had agreed immediately.

By the time she was due to arrive at the hotel, he was looking forward to seeing her. At the back of his mind, he was even anticipating the possibility of sleeping with her again. He was mildly apprehensive that she might have run to fat, or lost her style in some other way. So it was wonderful to walk into the lobby and see her there, looking almost exactly the same. If anything, maturity had given her even greater appeal, he thought as he approached her. She greeted him with pleasure but refused his suggestion that they go up to his room and instead gestured towards the bar.

'Let's go and have a drink.'

They sat, they talked. It was good to see her. He had liked her a great deal. If he hadn't been married, the relationship might have become something more permanent.

Of course she had been married then, too. He hadn't liked to cuckold another man, but Sibongile's husband was a drinker and there had been hints of a violent temper. He had not wanted to know more of her relationship, lest he be somehow drawn in further. But after the waiter had brought her a second drink he thought to ask about the man. She picked up her glass, sipped her drink and setting it down again, 'Sam died. Five years ago.'

It was a shock, but as he looked at her downcast face, he recognised a new diffidence that made her seem younger, more vulnerable.

'It's been a long time, now,' she said, refusing his mumbled apologies. How blithe we are in assuming that those we know and love will continue living and loving as long as we ourselves are alive. And then she had looked him in the eye and said, 'He died from TB. It was HIV-related.'

As the full realisation of what she was telling him struck home, he was aware of settling his face into an expression of suitable concern and asking her how long he had been ill; and then they were talking about something else, and the moment when he should have asked her about her own status was gone. At the end of the evening, he took down her address and phone number, told her he expected to be back in Lusaka in the coming month and heard himself making the unfounded promise to get in touch then. She had smiled, looking perfectly poised, and said goodbye.

And now, he was here. In this bedroom, this house where his wife lived – the woman he loved, the mother of his children.

But who was she? What was her substance when faced with knowledge like this? Flora was, in the end – in argument, in conversation – herself, unfettered by labels like wife, mother, lawyer. Ultimately she judged each situation she faced as who she was at that moment. And with this knowledge, who might she be?

Sam had died so long ago. Was it possible that Sibongile was not infected? His mind refused to deal with the issues. If she was infected, if he was infected, if he had infected Flora ... He could die. He could be responsible for Flora's death. Abruptly he had a mental picture of Flora, ill in bed with a bad flu, just a few months back. It was the first time he had ever seen her succumb to illness and allow herself to be looked after. His heart went cold. Could that have been something more serious? But she was fine now, surely, though maybe she did seem more tired than usual, especially when he had told her about this trip.

He could not fathom how something so far in his past could now return with such vicious power. Everything he believed in, had worked for, it could all be destroyed today, just because of what he knew now. If only he had not called her. How he longed for the felicity of ignorance.

Could he keep silent? Could he quietly go off and have a test? Then, if it was negative, she need never know and their marriage could go on undisturbed. But what if the result was different? He knew he didn't have the courage to face that challenge alone. He needed Flora's strength for that. And he could never go backwards from that, to relive today and then, swollen with deceit and fear, go through the charade of going with Flora for the tests – for of course they would have to go for testing together. And she might still be negative ...

He sat on the bed staring out of the window at the jacaranda tree he and Flora had planted when they had moved into the house. It was just past its full flowering and the tree seemed a foretelling of lost richness, lost abundance. He could not untangle the possibilities the future now thrust upon him and yet he must, for there were Flora's footsteps coming quickly up the path.

& Uncle Francis &

Stanley Nyamfukudza

SuDDenly, one Saturday morning he was there, quite out of the blue, at her front door. Standing, like the prodigal son, determinedly unembarrassed by his long absence. He looked haggard, down at heel, and she was immediately suspicious that he must be in some sort of desperate need. His clothes were clean and, well yes, fashionable enough. It was his battered shoes that gave the game away. They gleamed dully, a faint shine comically administered onto tired disintegrating footwear that can't have felt the soothing touch of boot polish since the earliest days of their purchase. Why would a man choose to wear such worn-out shoes: penury, laziness, comfort?

He impassively watched her conduct the physical examination of himself. She was reminded how he was a past-master at being cold and unemotional when it suited him. You could only tell what he thought or felt by his actions, which were rarely what you expected them to be. Whatever his reason for being here, he was to be warded off, kept at arm's length like the plague, no matter what he might say. She had to stay out of any possible entanglement. Having thus fortified her heart and steeled herself against his silky tongue, she asked him roughly what he wanted, so that the whole business might be got over with quickly.

Incredibly, he said, 'You're still looking good,' in a matter-of-fact fashion without any hint of irony or shame, 'life must be treating you well.' He paused and laughed quietly to himself, glancing furtively at her while he patted and rummaged through his pockets.

'Please,' she said firmly, stopping him before he found the cigarette he obviously sought, 'I'd rather you didn't smoke here.' She sounded so peremptory that she immediately softened; 'my tolerance for passive smoking isn't what it used to be.' It sounded so weak and hypocritical she was angry with herself. 'Now, tell me straight, Francis Murambiwa, what is it you want?' She could not help noticing that there was still more than a hint of his former good looks, but the dazzling smile was now ruined by a jagged set of stained, broken front teeth. His hair, which was now much shorter, was faintly grizzled. Time or life had evidently not been particularly kind to him. A slight tremor of the hands and mouth betrayed the pressure he was under. She would have to struggle to suppress both curiosity and sympathy.

'Chewing-gum, not tobacco. Haven't smoked in … ummm, years! Not important, petty detail of my life …' his voice trailed off uncertainly and he seemed to struggle to focus his mind. 'It's been a while,' he said finally, then he sputtered and coughed, a lengthy bout of explode-and-wheeze that shook his lanky frame. Then he went on, 'so naturally, I have this problem of … just where to start.'

'I'm sure you'll get over that,' she said, unrelenting.

'Are we going to talk like this, standing at the door?' he retaliated in a flash of irritation. 'I've been walking and I have a rather bad leg.' He shifted from one to the other as if to demonstrate his malady, casting uneasy glances left and right, as if afraid to look at her. Then, suddenly, as if coming to a decision, he looked straight into her eyes.

'There is no reason to fear me. I know you've got your own life now. I don't want to barge into it. But as I've just come back, we were bound to meet sooner or later. So, is it not better for us to know the score, right away, all of us?'

'Us? Just who are you talking about, when you say 'us'?' she retorted icily. He closed his eyes, as if wearied by her hostility. Then again he laughed quietly, mirthlessly to himself and shook his head.

'You ... The child, and me of cour ...'. She stopped him with a hissing intake of breath sucked through her teeth.

'Let me tell you something for nothing, Francis Murambiwa. First of all, there's no "us" that includes you and me. That's finished. That's history! Second: the child you left with me when you went away is not a child any more. Here, there's just me and my daughter; she's a grown-up; she's not anyone's baby now. Don't imagine that you can mess us up, and then come back just whenever you think it's okay. Oh, no! We've had our share of troubles, you can be sure of that, but in the end we've done nicely on our own, and that's the way it's going to stay, okay?'

'Look,' he said, 'There's no need whatsoever to get so loud and nasty. What are you saying, anyway? She knew where I was, I wrote to you, I wrote to her! Maybe she never wrote back, but that's just like a kid. I never wrote letters when I was a child. And, what do you mean "mess you up"? We broke up! *We* messed up – if you want to apportion blame. It wasn't just *my* private, personal, individual mess.' He stared at her, gasping, as if those few sentences had taken the breath right out of him. She snorted disdainfully.

'There were no letters, Francis. I ... I made sure of that.' He looked hard at her and she fancied there was something dangerous, something desperate in his narrowed eyes, and her heart leapt with fear.

'You mean ...' again, that laugh and shake of the head, 'You intercepted my letters? You ... you didn't pass them on to her?' he asked incredulously, and she nodded and retreated from the doorway into the room. Silence hung in the air. 'Then you should have returned them to me!' he said finally. 'The money was okay, wasn't it? It's just the letters that were not, huh?' His voice was loud – and nasty.

'I ... I can show you what I bought with the money, if that's what you want. What was it for anyway? To help out or to make her think well of you?' For some reason she could not fathom she went on, 'I ... I told her they were from ... an uncle, from Uncle Francis.' She gave a short, bitter laugh. 'Anyway,' she paused, changing tack, 'I still want to know what you really want here. Do you want me to call her and say 'this is the person whose money bought a pair of shoes and a blouse and jacket for you?' So she can say thank you?' Her sarcastic voice had climbed decibels as she lost her fear. He sighed heavily, frustrated and weary. They stood in silence for what seemed like ages.

'Okay, I'll go away,' he said finally. He paused, deflated, and she saw that there was nothing to be afraid of anymore. 'I'll go away, for now. But I'm not going far. I will write to Tarisai again. I pray to God you will think straight and let us sort this thing out. If there's no reply, I'll be back. Tear them up if you want ... but ...' He examined her face closely before speaking again. 'Did you read the letters before you tore them up? Did you have a good laugh first?' he whispered bitterly. She saw an angry cloud creep over his countenance and she stiffly refused to respond. He shook his head and walked off. She saw that indeed he limped slightly.

* * * * *

She had rehearsed it so many times in her imagination, the dramatic moment of truth when he would pitch up on her front door, and she would spurn his presence and scornfully drive him away with a couple of deeply wounding, hard-hitting facts. But there was no glee or feeling of triumph in her heart into which she now feared to look too closely. She was overcome with foreboding and, worst of all, a panic which almost made her shout that he wasn't to come back; that it was all his fault – what else did he expect, materialising out of the blue and wanting to upset their lives?

She realised that this was the event she had been waiting for over the years. She had prayed: she had hoped, without wishing him any actual harm, that something would happen to him that had absolutely nothing to do with herself, or her prayers; that she would hear unexpectedly that he was dead, so that like Felix Randal in the Hopkins' poem she would be able to say, 'Oh, is he dead, then?' And yet, now that he had come and gone, instead of a mildly curious indifference, she was caught up in the middle of a storm around whose eye such whirlpools swept that it was plain a decisive moment in her life had been reached.

She began to worry that she did not know where he had gone. How far did he mean to go with his intrusions? Had he merely been trying his luck? It was rotten timing. She had just begun her long three-month leave, and was likely to be home most of the time. She could not go out of town so soon at the start of a new term, not with Tarisai at school. She now seemed to spend most of her time speculating about him, awaiting his next move. He didn't look like a man holding down a job, not with those old shoes and hints of jaded debauchery. But that too had always been a part of his ambiguity: like a Hindu who had existed in a variety of castes in previous incarnations, he could mix easily with the lowest without difficulty or discomfiture when it suited him, yet he could also hold his own in the most sophisticated or intellectual circles. How could you ever trust a chameleon like that? He was contradictory and undependable, and he had a nasty capacity for springing surprises.

She lived in a state of ill-suppressed tension, fearful he was behind every knock on her door. Her sense of well-ordered security, which by nature she craved as a defence against the unpredictable, was undermined. Blind randomness, she knew from experience, was the source of the chaos and cruelty that underscored so much of what took place in life. There was no telling if it was because life just was like that: bad things that bruised and battered people, and rubbed them up the wrong way, just came out of nowhere, without rhyme or reason. Certainly she could read no pattern of fairness or justice into such events. Were other people's lives, stories with happy, foreseeable endings? What would have been the 'happy' scenario in her own case? To be the lawfully wedded wife of a man that had turned out like him? And having another child or two in tow, perhaps? Bliss? No. A kind of hell. The insecurity of never knowing whether you were walking the same road together, or going in different directions. That's exactly how it came about: someone you depended on, someone you believed in announced, quite out of the blue, that they were not into what you were into and wanted out, to actually get the hell out. Then the sky truly came tumbling down onto your head. You could never ever trust anyone absolutely because people, it seemed, were not made like that. They did not ever want to be fixed to any one thing – not so that you could turn aside and still find them waiting there, still true, still dependable.

So many questions to be asked, but in the end it didn't matter. Could a child not born to 'kindred spirits' ever bind two disparate lives and force-fuse them into a mutually viable unit? Even for a short time? The correct answer was neither yes nor no. What did matter was what happened in the long run. So-called base and noble motives often blended unrecognisably into each other; and people's high-falutin dreams eroded in the tedious never-ending morass of day-to-day living. If you trick someone into marriage, what does it matter twenty years down the long road that you might have been a bit more forthright or honest? You were not anybody else. If what you'd done defined you just as much as what you'd not done, well then, there it was – she had not been so forthright then. Whatever the case, she had more than paid for her misdemeanours by being left in the lurch. She had stopped thinking of her life as some sort of atonement for past misdeeds, never mind what anyone else might think.

Outside school she was defined as a single mother and only incidentally as also a very good teacher. She had tried to bind him to herself by means of an unplanned child. He had agonised, prevaricated, then acted as if maybe it just might be all right. But in the end she had failed. Did that make her so very different from the usual truck of women, or men? Maybe it did. But to have carried that child for nine months, to have been bound by chains of love and responsibility to her daughter, did not in the end seem such a disastrous outcome, regardless of her approval rating in the community – though she knew this would have shot up if there had been a regular pair of trousers attached to her. That futile line of thought was like wishing herself away. It was an imagined reality.

Yet, the questions refused to go away. What if both of them were unhappy now? What if he had finally seen that for all his running away, there'd had been no escape, and that what he wanted after all these years was the dream that she had finally given up, a life with the three of them together? She fearfully, tentatively, explored the idea. How would she truly feel about the prospect of a mastering male coming into her life? Might he now want just the child and not her as well? But what could he possibly want with her child, someone he'd never really known? Maybe something had kindled an egoistic idea of paternity. But even then to what end? What might have been – was that not what the poet said? will always remain a possibility only in the realm of ideas.

Her tension-wracked existence only lasted a week. Then she began to feel safe again. He had breezed into her life like a bitterly cold, unseasonal wind and left. She thawed out and the chill and nervousness left her too. Tarisai had cast a few doubtful glances at her but, mercifully, said nothing. Despite the huge temptation to confide in her daughter and extort reassurance, she had volunteered nothing, grateful that she had been alone when he had come.

* * * * *

His return seven days later was beyond her worst imaginings. He had come with a dreadful, ambiguously dressed woman whose eclectic attire conceded nothing to current fashions. She wore an assortment of items with a carefully selected emphasis on well-worn comfort, pieces that must surely have been the very best at whatever time and place they were bought. Bangles and beads suggested a vaguely

Indian style, scarves and other adornments were maybe Afro, maybe Caribbean: ageless chic. Was this what they meant when they talked of the gypsy spirit?

She used her own name but it was evident from the moment she saw them together that she was his wife, even if they might not be formally married. She spoke as if she possessed him totally, and she seemed to share his parental feelings about another woman's daughter, as if the child were their own. Her accent was impossible to place but she spoke perfect English. Her sweetly languorous voice brought bitter poison to the heart – the more so because her words seemed to carry the complacent ring of time-honoured wisdom: a child is a gift from God, not a possession to be held in an exclusive, tight-fisted fashion; if you truly love someone you must give them the freedom to come and go. Platitudes easy to apply to someone else's life. The bottom line was that they wanted to share her child – and after all those years. She knew by some instinct that the two had no child of their own. It was his right, as a father, and his daughter's too, the gypsy woman insisted, to know her father while it was still possible. You must know it's the right thing. Imagine, the time wasted over all these years! Her tone of level-headed fair-mindedness was maddening.

'I suppose he cannot speak for himself today. He needs you to cosset him,' she retorted bitterly, unable to contend with the venom that bubbled within her. She hated the fact that he had brought this unabashed stranger with her unpalatable suggestions into her life. She certainly had bucketsful of nerve. But she would show her that when it came to protecting her own, she wouldn't even mind an old-fashioned woman-to-woman physical ding-dong, if it had to come to that. She would show them! She fell silent, looking aggressively from one to the other.

'Agh, how I hate a totally unnecessary fight! Let's all be sensible *wena! Ungayenzi njengomfazi ovela egangeni!** he said, breaking into

---

*   Don't behave like some wild woman from the bush.

their home language, and went on to suggest that if she had ever loved anyone other than herself then now was time to show it. That stung her. Tempers veered out of control, they were all shouting. She did not notice that her daughter had walked into the room and quickly also became embroiled. Finally, the strange woman, unable to cut through the screaming and crying in a cacophonous mixture of English, Ndebele and some unfamiliar African language, threw in the towel and withdrew. Only when the door banged shut did he realise that his companion had left and he hastily went out after her. A heated altercation in English mixed with something else erupted and that storm took some time before it subsided. Meanwhile she calmed her daughter and begged her to go to her room and please-stay-out-of-something-you-cannot-possibly-understand. Mercifully, the confused, frightened girl conceded just as the couple came back inside. The door shut quietly behind the young woman. Shut, it offered only silence, the silence felt like a rebuke.

This time the strange woman did not beat about the bush, but spoke again about too much time having already been lost. The hints became more pointed. The woman could not decide if it was a deliberately calculated manoeuvre, one capped with the bald confession, 'He had *not* said that he was sick? My poor dear, but I thought you *knew* already! When you know him as I do it just seems so … well, obvious! He *didn't* say? Oh I'm *so* dreadfully sorry. He really doesn't have much time. I should have *explained* these things a bit more, if only I'd realised …'

* * * * *

If the strategy had been to shock her into capitulation, it worked. The least they could do for him, she had hastened to agree. Why did she feel somehow responsible for all this? Yes, he had a right to a relationship with his daughter. Absolutely. There was no reason at all why relationships could not be mutually beneficial. Oh no, it was not as if he was already on his deathbed. Indeed, he probably had some time, maybe even a few years ... If he could be persuaded to live sensibly, do the right things. In the end, after painful, protracted silences, there were the even more awkward introductions, at the end of which her daughter recovered a long lost dad and simultaneously gained an aunt or step-something or other. At which point he was gentlemanly enough to suggest they should withdraw to give mother and daughter time to adjust and talk things over. Didn't she think so, he suggested magnanimously to his companion.

He could well afford to, couldn't he, all things considered, she thought bitterly, looking back almost fondly at the years when she had at times speculated about what might have been. That had indeed been tempting fate, those years now seemed blissfully untroubled, and very far away.

Once again, she regarded the letter in her hand, holding it out at a safe distance where her daughter's writing was barely decipherable. Again, her eyes brimmed, again her heart ached in that terrible, heavy way as she again began to read the letter. It seemed to her, thanks be to God, that this time, the pain was not so bad that she could not bear it.

Dearest Mum,

I'm so so GLAD! It was just wonderful to read your letter at last. Isn't it just wonderful that you now see these things the way I do? Isn't it just my good fortune to have had hidden away all these years just the one Dad who can give me all the things a young woman can want – besides a good husband of course (joke!)! To have money, to have so many relatives who just want me to be one of them, to be able to go and see some of the wonderful places I've only read about, is something that was simply beyond my wildest dreams. Of course nothing can ever take the place of you in my heart, dearest Mother of mine!

I hope one day you will feel free to accept the offer of a ticket so you can come to Mombasa and see for yourself. What are you afraid of? The beach is wonderful. The people are so relaxed and so welcoming.

Maybe it's the whole Islamic polygamous thing, I don't know, but its so different from our Shona way, there's no jealousy or fear and rejection of someone from outside. I just feel so welcome.

Of course Daddy is quite sick now and again and that is when I feel that it is good for him to have someone like me nearby. They all say how much happier he has been since I came.

Take care of yourself, Mum. I'll come down and see you soon. Or better still ...! But you know what, so I won't say it.

All my love and cuddles and kisses.

Your ever loving only child.

Tarisai

She stared at the letter and then on an impulse using the thumb and forefingers of both hands she started to tear it in two. Then she stopped herself, almost as if the tearing sound was hurting her ... a new pain felt deep within. Why was she doing this? What was she afraid of now? There was no need for any such violence. There was nothing more to fear. The worst that could have happened had happened. She had, had she not, swallowed bitter medicine. And yet here she was, still very much intact; still very much herself. She smiled with surprise. A little while later, she rose with some energy, picked up her keys, shut the door more firmly than was called for, locked it and walked down the street into the early evening.

That Special Place

Freedom Nyamubaya

The light arrived like a sharp nail striking my left eye, after three days of not having seen the African sun or felt its mother warmth. I had just woken from a short sleep, after spending the whole night awake and singing to my soul. I remembered how I had arrived where I was, but not why I was there. I heard groans, coughs, sneezes, yawns – what felt like competing huffing and puffing from all directions. But nobody spoke except for the two people who were sitting outside guarding us.

I had only realised that we were being guarded some six hours earlier when I had wanted to go to the toilet. It felt like days since I had had this relief, but fortunately we'd been given nothing to eat or drink. Getting up and crossing the floor, even in the darkness, I did not want to be seen by the other comrades. My Afro hair had turned white, my face felt like a monkey's in a dusty field. My eyes were swollen. I had to struggle to force one open so that I could see where I was going. My java-print dress, which I had once been proud of, my face, arms and legs, were also covered in dust and grime. However, I rose and picked my way through the bodies. Why should I worry what people thought of me, they were asleep. But I did mind and only moved because it would have been worse to sit in my own urine in a hut.

'You are supposed to seek permission before you go anywhere!' shouted one of the guards. 'This way,' said another whose name, Muchapera, literally means 'you will be finished off'. He took his wooden imitation AK rifle and escorted me to the toilet.

There were always people hanging around the toilet, even in the darkness, sometimes for reasons other than relieving themselves. Free discussion was not tolerated in public, and one of the few places that provided some privacy was the toilet. On other occasions, it provided a mildly safe haven from work or training if you wanted a break. So the toilet was actually an area where the only semi-liberated discussion took place. Nobody could stop you from going there, but sometimes this would only be permitted with the caution, 'Do your thing fast, I want you out in two minutes.'

I didn't know any of this then. However, the guard was hovering outside, and in that moment of comparative freedom, he told me that I was in prison. He said he felt badly about this as he came from my district, and pleaded with me to tell them that I was an enemy agent, or else they would make mince-meat of my buttocks. 'Nobody leaves this place without confessing,' he said. 'But whatever you do, don't say anything to anyone! You never saw me.' And that, indeed, was the last I saw of him. He had disappeared before I could respond to his statement.

When I finally opened my left eye in the watery daylight, I saw I was in the company of four men looking as dusty as I did. One of them later told me that when he arrived I was unconscious, and had been for hours. I did not remember anything, but I realised that I was a day behind in my counting.

It was about seven o'clock in the morning and the two guards were chatting away five metres from the entrance. A few sunrays filtered through the cracks in the grass walls of the hut. The door was a khaki sack that would have contained maize grain in normal circumstances. There was a four-inch gap between the ground and the sack, which swung to and fro as the wind blew in different directions. September, like August, was hot and windy at Tembwe Training Camp, in the remote areas of Tete Province in Mozambique. The smell of dry sand swept through the makeshift, loosely thatched hut. The faces of the four men were not wholly visible in the partial darkness, but I could see the misery on their faces. I tried to grin at each of them, but no one responded. I tried to examine them more closely – there was nothing else to do – but they quickly turned their faces away. They looked ghostly and frightening with their disfigured cheeks, lips, eyes and noses covered in grey dust.

One of them had a thick swollen sagging lower lip and a large swollen forehead that seemed to hang over his eyes, making him look like one of those long distance cargo trucks with a raised sleeping cab. Another, who appeared to be the youngest, had eyes which, like mine, were heavily swollen. I could not tell whether he could see or not. He resembled one of those bullfrogs often found perching on rocks during the long summer months. I touched my own eyes, imagining that I must look like him, and then burst out laughing; we were two frogs, but I was sure I was the more beautiful. My laughter seemed to break the ice for, after a moment, everybody joined in, then the silence fell again.

The third man was the handsome one. He still looked good even with a nose like JoJo the Clown, the result of a one-sided boxing match with the security guard. The other prisoner kept his face turned from me: he seemed ready to pounce on anybody given the chance.

It was after nine when the Camp Security Commander came to visit us. He had a loud mouth, and never once do I remember him saying anything constructive or interesting. He used torturous language, and made vulgar jokes about the inmates. Vicious and cruel, he had not even completed his primary education when he was recruited into the liberation struggle. With nothing in terms of brain, he thrived on sadism and intimidation. Interrogation had to be accompanied by a slash on the buttocks with a whip or a slap on the face, but still he was called the Camp Security Commander. It was he who had to prove the innocence of every new arrival. Though it depended on his moods, which were erratic, you were deemed innocent if you were a man, and of his educational level or lower. If you were a woman, even if his intention was to sleep with you, he first had to fill you with fear; but if you were just a tiny bit more educated than he was, then you had to be thoroughly beaten. This made it easier for him to sexually assault you later, as he would say that he would throw you back in prison if you resisted. Since he was the man in charge nobody, not even the Camp Commander, could challenge him.

It was the same man, Nyathi, who was later demoted from the front line, after several brave rural farmers complained that their women and children were being sexually abused in the base camps back at home. He took his revenge by defecting, and he later led a battalion of Rhodesian soldiers with armoured cars to massacre refugees at Nyadzonia, the unguarded refugee camp where he was known as a Commander.

On his arrival at the camp he blew the emergency whistle, which meant that everybody had to go immediately to the assembly point. Seeing the military trucks, most of them thought that at last Frelimo had provided transport to transfer them from the camp, in which they were bored, ill and starving, to another camp for military training. Nyathi waited until most people had made their way from the water points, the barrack construction area, cooking and cleaning tasks. An emergency whistle meant that even the sick had to get themselves to the parade ground.

Nyathi stood at the front, sloganeering and having some of the refugees sing revolutionary songs while waiting for everyone to arrive. Two late-comers ran straight past the armoured cars and immediately noticed that the men behind the wheels were whites who'd painted up, but forgotten the backs of their ears, which still showed a startling white. Bravely they ran on, right through the crowd shouting over Nyathi's voice. 'Run, run, run away, comrades! It's not Frelimo! It's the Rhodesians! Run away! Run away!'

Nyathi's response was to jump off the platform on which he was standing and instruct the Rhodesians to fire. People, *en masse*, were simply mown down, blood gushing from them like so many burst pipes. Among the strewn and bleeding bodies Nyathi observed a few who had begun to wriggle away from the mayhem on their bellies, and sadist that he was, he instructed the Rhodesians to drive their cars over the bodies so as to crush the survivors. The battalion moved in tandem, as if they were ploughing a field, crushing the dead and the living. Anyone who tried to run away got a bullet in his back. A woman who survived said she had rolled herself back to lie amongst those who'd been crushed, and covering herself with blood, lay and watched Nyathi and his Rhodesians complete their mission.

Of course the lucky ones ran into the bush as fast as they could. Many of them never returned to see what had happened. Those who survived often did so surrounded by the dead and wounded, terrified that if they were to stand up, they would be shot down. The woman I knew shouted for help the following day, after Frelimo had arrived.

Hearing Nyathi's voice, loud and strident, I recalled immediately how I had come to be in prison. When they arrived at a military camp, recruits were required to write a brief synopsis of their lives; if they couldn't write, they had to tell someone who would write it down for them. If you had made your own way, you had to explain why you had decided to join the struggle; if you had been recruited by the comrades and brought across the border into Mozambique, you generally escaped interrogation. The process was called 'three check up', but I have never known what it meant. If the security commander was satisfied with your biography and explanation you would go free, but if not, or should he want you for other reasons, you found yourself in prison.

Nyathi had asked me to write my autobiography and give my reasons for deciding to joint the liberation war. I asked him whether I should do this in English or Shona.

'Whatever,' he said. 'I am trained to read all kinds of languages through the word.'

I wrote down the story of my life, in Shona, innocent and excited. I was one of three: there were two women with me who had been assisted across the Zambezi by a comrade. Without even looking at their papers, he told them that they were free to go and join the others at the barracks.

When it came to my turn he snatched my piece of paper from me, pretended to read it, and asked what grade I had done at school. I told him that I'd left in Form 3, a year before writing my O-levels, and he went crazy.

'You haven't written the truth,' he shouted, and knocked me onto his grass double bed. I saw stars in broad daylight. I was so shocked that I did not shed a tear but stared at him, my eyes wide like a zombie. 'Why would you leave school and all that comfort to come to a place of suffering and dying?' He gave me no chance to answer, but slapped me eight times, first on one cheek then the other. Then he told me he was going to take me to Mbuya Nehanda, where the spirit medium would learn the truth. I knew all about Mbuya Nehanda, the spirit medium who was executed in Salisbury in 1893 for fighting against the colonisers. I was relieved – I felt frightened and hurt by Nyathi's anger and blows, which had come as such a shock. Little did I know that there was no spirit -medium, just a prison.

I followed Nyathi to his hut, which was empty. Fingers of fungus hung from the wood, suggesting that the place had been deserted for more than a few days. No Mbuya Nehanda, just a guy sitting five metres from the hut doing nothing. Nyathi had thrown me into the hut, where I sat doing nothing, and was not able to sleep. Tears had followed, when I remembered the eight serious claps on my cheeks, when all I thought I'd done was do what I was told – write my life history. The hut felt a long, long way from the liberation struggle of my dreams. Sounds of martial music came from a distance as the comrades marched to the kitchen for lunch. Food was scarce, good food didn't exist. Sadza was a delicacy, especially accompanied by real beans, not the bush beans we used to call *ndodzi*. Our main meal was maize grain boiled in salt, which made us thirsty, or just *ndodzi* in salt, or a mixture of *ndodzi* and *mangai*, boiled maize grains. But we prisoners always had food. One of the guards would go to the kitchen, jump the line and bring us our food; other companies might just be told: 'The food is finished,' before they had even been served. If they were lucky, they might get served first at the next meal.

There were two meals a day except for the commanders, commonly known as *chefs*, and sometimes they even had tea with '*pao*', Mozambican bread. The commanders had a separate kitchen with different cooks. It was a privilege for your company to be on duty at the commanders' kitchen, for even if you were never chosen to cook, someone might sneak some left-overs into the barracks. I was never selected to cook in the *chefs*' kitchen, since I had been branded a suspect. They said those who had been interrogated and imprisoned as enemy suspects might poison the *chefs*. Paranoia was rampant, even then. Suspects did the hard tasks of fetching grass and poles for construction, digging toilets and weeding in the camp fields.

Food was a serious but interesting issue because of the tactics that people developed to try and obtain more. If you were caught, you were beaten until you called out all the names of the relatives you had left behind. Beating, however, did not stop anybody; there were even people who were known for their skill in acquiring extra food. There were a few Mozambicans in the surrounding villages, and people would sell their clothes, or clothes they had stolen from others, for a cob or two of maize, *pao*, tobacco or sadza. Very rarely we ate meat, and when a wild animal was killed, nobody ever asked what kind of an animal it was.

Singing and dancing formed part of our daily activities. We sang for food, when we were waiting for the *chef*, when somebody was being beaten, or when we were waiting for announcements. Music was a survival strategy, dancing kept our morale high. We sang and danced out our problems to avoid despair. There were of course times when one might take time to compose music, or sing with real joy; but mostly music was an outlet for our pain.

When Nyathi walked into the hut everybody suddenly became alert. He ordered the guard to bring him a small bench, so he could sit and talk to us. The sack door was raised and two other men came in with him. 'Yes, gentlemen and lady! Are you ready to tell us the truth now?' I lay on my side, my hands supporting my body since my buttocks were swollen from the previous beating, which had caused me to black out. 'E! – e! – e! – e! e! sit up properly, prostitute! Don't act funny here, I also know that you were bitching around with those Frelimo soldiers before you got to Batalio!' shouted Nyathi. I had to sit upright and pretend I was not in pain, and that my body was not swollen.

'I have brought my two associates whose job it is to deal with any one of you who decides to waste my time,' said Nyathi as he picked his nose. 'I want each of you to narrate your story as it should be: no lies, no exaggeration and no withholdings. My name is Nyathi, the charging buffalo. I do my work as work.'

But before the first person could utter, a comrade came running over and told Nyathi that he was urgently wanted by the camp commander. He left, and the two men accompanied him. I knew it was not the end of our suffering, but it provided temporary relief. Moreover his presence had helped to stimulate some communication among us. We started asking each other our names, and made jokes about the way in which our faces had been disfigured.

One of the men had nicknamed himself Che Guevara after the famous Bolivian freedom fighter, who worked with Fidel Castro. He had been in his second year at the University of Rhodesia, and had been thrown out after a students' demonstration against the Smith régime. He had read about socialism and capitalism, and had a better understanding of general political issues in and outside Zimbabwe than any of us. Che whispered, 'You're the only woman here. When we were brought in, we thought you were dead because you were unconscious for such a long time. The security guard told us they had just done a good bushing, and warned us that if we didn't tell the truth the same would happen to us. Now listen carefully, Ticha, you have to create a story, otherwise they will pound you to mincemeat.'

'Have you created a story?' I croaked. He stared at me. I had lost my voice and could not remember how. I had cried a lot, but not out loud, so I wondered how my voice had gone missing.

The other prisoners listened carefully but none of them contributed. Che said he had been beaten enough, and could not take it any more. 'My parents never once slapped or pinched me. So to join the war and find my own comrades beating me for no good reason is more than I can take!' Che fell silent.

'Ticha, you must cook up a story and tell these guys that you were sent by the enemy, otherwise you will die in this small thatched hut.' I shook my head without saying anything. I still thought it was wrong to tell lies. 'Have you made up a story?' I asked hoarsely for a second time. Che just nodded his head, but did not explain what it was. I asked the others whether they would do the same, but they just stared at me like zombies. I could not tell whether they understood my question or not, but I knew that they heard what I said because they all looked at me.

Nyathi came back after lunch, and began by telling the guard that four men who had tried to slip back into Rhodesia had been caught and brought back to Tete by Frelimo vigilantes. He said they would be beaten until they passed out. Che looked at me as if to say, 'You see! I told you these people will kill if you don't do what they want.'

'All right! All of you sit up straight and receive your warm-up before we get into serious business!' shouted Nyathi as he sat back on the bench. 'Give each of them five strokes on the buttocks, Chombo. Take the bigger stick.' Chombo, his assistant, knew the procedure. We were not allowed to protect our bodies with our hands. If you did you would get an extra one. They said the party needed hands for carrying guns to shoot the enemy, and if you broke your hands you would become a burden that had to be carried by other freedom fighters.

Che was the last one to be beaten. After two strokes he shouted that he had something important to tell them so they should stop beating him. Nyathi instructed Chombo to stop, and even we, with pain still sinking slowly into our nervous systems, were forced to listen. The interrogation was not private. Chombo took a pen and paper and started taking notes. 'Speak it loud and clear. I don't want to keep saying, "What did you say?"' Nyathi said nastily.

Che began narrating his well-cooked story. 'My name is Che, and I was born in 1955 in Rusape. I was sent here to do some reconnaissance and see how the comrades are organised, where they stay, what they eat, how many there are and what kind of weapons they use. I belong to a party called CHARM, that means Communist Hurricane African Revolutionary Movement, which is led by one black professor at the University of Rhodesia. We have over ten thousand soldiers with five thousand being trained in the Soviet Union, three thousand in Romania and two thousand in Cuba. So far none of the soldiers are yet in the country.' After this Che started crying. Tears just ran down his cheeks and could not stop. I didn't understand why he was crying, because we knew he was lying since there was no such party. 'Maybe he feels guilty about lying,' I thought, wondering how anyone could possibly believe in a party called CHARM. The more I thought about it, the funnier it seemed, and a sudden burst of laughter escaped from my body.

'Give her two strokes, Chombo. Take that scissors and make a cross through her hair from ear to ear and from her forehead to the back of her neck and then let's see if she thinks she is beautiful. Do you think you are anything special? What are you laughing at? Do you think this is a circus?'

'No! no! no, comrade, I am sorry, it just happened.' I still received the two extra strokes and a hairstyle with four portions; but Che was excused his beating although he was not allowed to return to barracks.

Che was in his second year at University. He understood something about communism, and certainly more than they did. He had been detained because he told them that he had been a university student. Naively he had thought that his literacy would be of use to the liberation army. Instead he suffered for it and never even rose to section commander.

Three days later the five of us, Che included, were taken before a parade of eight thousand people. We were told to stand on the platform and we each had to tell the comrades how we had been sent by the enemy to destroy them. Each one had to tell their own story and then ask for a pardon. I was lucky because I still had no voice, so Nyathi had to tell my story on my behalf. Since I had insisted that I was innocent, he told them that I was still under investigation but my other crime was that I had been going out with Frelimo soldiers in Tete. 'Instead of coming to fight for Zimbabwe, she came to sleep around with Frelimo. We are making examples of these people as we have done before, and will do again, because everyone is the eye of the party, so keep checking. Watch these people, and watch out for other spies and traitors.' From that moment I could not take the security department seriously. All I knew was that they hated anybody who had gone to school, and only felt comfortable with illiterate comrades.

Little did I know that only a month after I was released from prison, that same beast Nyathi broke his way into my vagina and escaped with my virginity, though after fifteen minutes' fierce struggle I managed to spit out a piece of his flesh from his right thigh.

Nyathi had a big black penis whose erection got harder with resistance; little did I know that either. I was fifteen, and I cried as I felt blood run down my legs on my way back to the barracks in moonlight. For years my body reacted to the memory, and it was years before I felt whole again.

The last time I met Che on the streets of Harare I nearly cried. He recognised me, but nothing he said made sense, and I realised that he was mentally ill. I am sure it arose at that special place: the place that many people in this world will never know or understand.

🐾 The Winning Side 🐾

William Saidi

Tambudzai had warned Tichaona to expect the worst. His uncle would disown him, right there and then, shooing him off his palatial residence in Borrowdale with a brusque, 'You come here again and I'll set my rottweiler on you!' Or: 'I'll call the police and you know what they do to street kids like you!' Tichaona preferred the phrase 'children living rough in the streets of Harare'. He had adopted Tambudzai's lexicon, since meeting her one rainy night in Nelson Mandela Avenue, when the pavement near Beverley Court was crowded with men, women and children – all hawkers, selling bananas, apples, mangoes, sweets, cigarettes and condoms, sheltering from the rain.

To Tichaona, Tambudzai seemed very slim, sexy, and brimming with self-confidence. She stood in front of a window display, studying a beautiful wedding dress, all puffs and pearl buttons. She was wearing tight jeans and white sneakers. She was poor but she had style. As soon as she noticed Tichaona staring at her, she gave a slight cough – of acknowledgement or rebuke? Tichaona was never sure. Without turning, she'd said, 'I would look sensational in that, I know it.' She sounded as if she chain-smoked cigarettes or had a throat infection of some kind.

'But you're … so young!' said Tichaona to the shop window.

'You have no idea how old I am,' she retorted smartly. And then seeing his expression change, 'By the way, I am Tambudzai, Tambu for short. You are new on the streets, right? Fresh from the sticks?' She'd summed him up right away. He didn't know whether to feel relieved or humiliated. The last week had been awful: he hadn't known where to go, or what to do. He'd tried to avoid the *mbanje* smoking kids in Union Ave, and the touts who ran the station area. He had slept in the park, in constant fear of the police, and if he hadn't been able to wash in the fountain in the early hours of the morning, he'd be very dirty as well. He'd needed a protector, but he certainly hadn't expected one as young and as sassy as Tambu.

Tambudzai had been wrong for once. His Uncle Charles' welcome was ebullient. And now here Tichaona was, standing in the middle of the lavishly decorated sitting room, craning his neck at a large colour photograph of the president, which hung high above the fireplace, staring down at him, balefully, Tichaona thought.

'So, here we are, Tichaona,' said his uncle, who seemed a very large and happy man. Not at all like his sister, Plaxedes, Tichaona's mother. She had been a petite schoolteacher who believed in neatness, not showiness. Tichaona thought she wouldn't have liked the copper plaques, the big glass ashtrays, the plush red chairs.

'You know what happened, Uncle. You read it in the newspapers.' They looked at each other, recognising their kinship with a softening of the eyes.

Dress clean, Tambu had told him, and shown him where he could go to wash his shirt. She'd even stolen some new tackies for him from a shoe shop on Kwame Nkrumah Avenue, where the assistants weren't paid properly and didn't care much. She'd loaned him the hundred dollars that it took to get to Borrowdale by combi.

His fellow passengers had mainly been domestic workers from the northern suburbs, the richest areas of Harare. It only occurred to Tichaona later, that he must be related to one of the wealthiest men in the city. And now he stood self-consciously on the thick blue carpet and observed his uncle's ornate red slippers sinking into the pile. Yet still the big man seemed to float, flapping the huge sleeves of his powder-blue dressing gown like wings.

Tambu had warned Tichaona: 'Your uncle has a mechanism, as they all have. It enables them to blot out reality and concentrate on the positive. If you're not careful, he will bamboozle you into accepting as reality that which serves his best interests. They never think of anything else, and they have tongues like silk.'

How could Tambudzai know so much? At fifteen, she was not much older than he was. Yet she exuded the maturity of a 35-year-old. She was pretty in what the Catholic mission school in Chihota would have called a 'dangerous way'. A 'temptress'. His teacher was an ordained priest, but he knew that pretending the world was one big holy place might prove fatal for his students in later life.

Tichaona thought Tambu knew far more than any fifteen-year-old girl was entitled to. She was dangerously adult. Nobody in the village would have shown such curves or coughed in such a suggestive manner. And yet somehow she had immediately sensed his vulnerability, his bewilderment, his pain. And she had managed to draw his story from him: it was too painful to talk about, the images helplessly danced before his eyes, but talking had helped a little, and she hadn't dissuaded him from trying to see his uncle. 'What's there to lose?' she said. He wondered what had put her on the streets; she had still not said a word about that.

In the two weeks that Tichaona had been with them, not one of the boys had tried to be 'funny' with her, as they were with the other girls, who succumbed because they said it made life easier. There was an aura about her, as if she had confronted all the devils of Hell and sent them scampering off in terror. Some spoke of how she gouged out the eyes of a relative who had tried to rape her in Mbare township; others said she was raped, but still gouged out the man's eyes with her bare hands.

'So, what is the truth, Tambu?' he had asked her after a few days of walking and talking along the streets of Harare after the office workers and company directors in their dark suits and pretty dresses had left the city and the street kids owned it.

'The truth will be what you wish it to be, Tichaona,' she drawled softly. Tichaona suspected that he had fallen in love with her, if what he felt every time their hands touched could be called love. In the streets, love could be as transient as dew on the grass or the flash of a night-watchman's torch in Julius Nyerere Way. Or it could be as permanent as the moon, sailing serenely across the night sky in summer.

'Now, sit down here, Tichaona,' said Charles, smiling gently. He coughed delicately into a big white handkerchief. 'Angela will bring you breakfast.' Finding the house had not been difficult. He was a Big Shot in Harare, Tambudzai had said, with sarcastic envy. She knew the house too, though she swore she had never visited it. 'People know those houses,' she'd said elliptically.

Tichaona had not seen him for five years. His parents rarely spoke of him. As he sat at the long polished table, hearing his uncle's voice almost made him cry. It reminded him so much of his mother. He saw her again being dragged from her hut naked except for a necklace given to her by his father as a birthday present when they were courting; and held down by two men while the third thrust his manhood into her, until she surrendered with a scream. From the granary, into which he had scrambled as the men stormed the village, he had watched the cruel tableau, tears refusing to roll down his cheeks. Earlier, watching them hack at his father with their crude machetes, his tears had flowed like rivers. His father, a wiry, muscular man, had fought back, and then fallen silently. He did not even make a sound as they struck at his throat with their blunt axes. 'Tichaona,' said Charles, softly. Tichaona held his breath and waited. His parents had spoken of Uncle Charles fearfully, yet with grudging awe. He was rich; he had a big job in the government.

The maid placed breakfast before him. Tichaona looked at what he was being asked to eat and gasped. Charles laughed, coughing into his handkerchief. Crisp bacon, eggs, fat sausages, toast, tea, biscuits. His stomach growled in anticipation. He wished it wouldn't. He felt he was conceding something. Charles smiled.

'Tichaona, I read the story about my sister, dear, kind Plaxedes. I cried.' He paused. 'Did your mother tell you what happened to our parents? Your grandparents?' The emotional intensity in the voice sounded so like his mother's, a woman of such a piety that even Tichaona had been afraid of doing anything that she would consider wrong.

Again, he looked around the dining room, as if to reassure himself. Could everything have gone so badly wrong? 'No, Uncle Charlie,' he said, his voice barely a whisper. He had abandoned his childhood when he watched them kill his parents, his brother and sister. Life was not for the squeamish – people could kill you as easily as they squashed a cockroach – that is unless you killed them first.

His uncle sat quite still in the large chair, staring at his nephew, his lips dry and pale, his eyes wide and moist, his handkerchief to his lips. Tichaona marvelled at the fatness of his cheeks, so fleshy and drooping. His mother's were prettier, aquiline, alive to her quick smile. He remembered her saying, of her brother: 'Your Uncle Charlie always wants to be on the winning side. It is not always good to be on the winning side. You might lose your soul.'

Charles sighed softly. 'Our parents were killed before our very eyes, Tichaona.' Tichaona closed his eyes. His memory of the two old people consisted of a tattered black and white photograph of a smartly-dressed man and woman, standing rather awkwardly with their arms round each other, smiling uneasily into the camera. He wore a tie and she a straw sun hat. Tichaona believed, for that period in colonial Rhodesia, they must have been the epitome of African elegance. 'Please, Uncle Charlie, I cannot eat when you speak of death.' So, watched by his uncle and the President's spectacled eyes and small moustache, Tichaona wolfed down the food. He slowed down, to sip his well-sugared tea.

Uncle Charlie wiped the tears from his eyes with his handkerchief. 'We saw them, your mother and I, our parents being shot in the head. I swore I would never back a loser again. Never. Your mother ... well ... she was older and I loved her, a great person. My poor sister ... Plaxedes was driven by principles, like your father ...'

Tichaona had felt helpless and guilty as he fled from the smouldering ruin that had been their village, to run blindly into the forest. He walked in a pit of fear until he reached the main road to Harare, hours later, hungry and tired. In the darkness, he had walked, a fifteen-year-old boy consumed with a sense of loss, of horror, of bewilderment, even of anger. It occurred to him, in a wild moment, that he too would have to kill. His wonderful parents, two people linked by a dedication to honesty, truth and the principles his uncle spoke of. They had abandoned the winning side, because they would not lose their souls.

'Whose side are you on now, Uncle Charlie?' Tichaona suspected the reason why his grandparents had been shot in cold blood during that other horrible war in the 1970s.

'Tichaona,' said Uncle Charlie, 'take this. Use it to get as far away as you can from here ... away from this madness.'

Uncle Charlie had drawn a large brown envelope out of his dressing-gown pocket. He placed it gently in Tichaona's hand, as if it was a delicate bird, one likely to perish if handled roughly. Tichaona was too stunned to react immediately.

'Whose side?' he persisted.

'Our parents were on God's side, the people's side, the freedom fighters side. They were courageous people, teaching their children to fight for what was right, as they themselves did.'

Tichaona looked down at the table. 'The white people killed them?' he asked, shoving the envelope into his pocket.

'Yes, Tichaona. But the white people did not win. They lost, and our people, our parents' people, won and I decided I would support them, come what may. They have been winning since 1980, Tichaona, every election, including the 2000 one. I am determined to be with them, all the way, Tichaona. The others, well ...'

They stared at each other. Tichaona saw the face of one of the bearded men shoving himself into his mother. She'd been so small, so fragile, like a bird. He looked away as the bile rose to his throat.

'I belong to the winning side, the side our parents died for. This is my reward, Tichaona.' He spread his arms around the room: all this is mine.

Later that night, Tichaona met Tambu, standing under a lamp-post near Africa Unity Square. What had happened? She looked unwell, her skin was grey, her eyes bloodshot.

'I could not confront him, Tambu. You were right. He bamboozled me. He gave me this. I don't think he wanted to see me again.' He handed the envelope to her, as if it would explain everything. Tambudzai began to open it very slowly as if she knew what it would contain, and suddenly shaken by a violent spasm of coughing abruptly dropped it. She fell to the pavement, still coughing. 'I told you, didn't I?' she said, showing him the contents of the envelope. 'That he would bamboozle you, and he did.'

'Why, Tambu?'

She looked wan. 'They're all the same, your uncle and those other people ... so full of big words, big promises...' She coughed again. 'It's TB,' she said, 'but you must know what that means. Some days it's much better, some worse – the coughing I mean.' She closed her eyes. Tichaona was reminded of his uncle's cough. 'Tichaona,' she said softly, her eyes still closed. 'There are a few thousand Zim dollars and four hundred pounds in there. British pounds. On the black market – nearly a million dollars. He thought he could buy your forgiveness.' She lapsed into silence. 'Did he? The money, your forgiveness – do either mean anything to him?'

Tichaona looked at the face, so calm, so peaceful, so beautiful, yet still the too-worldly teenager. 'We shall travel, to have you treated, We shall travel and we too can be on the winning side ... maybe.'

She was quiet, still, her eyes closed. His mother would understand.

He carried her from Sam Nujoma Street to the taxi rank along Third Street. He was surprised how light she was. She would not die. She must not die. She deserved to be on her winning side too. A million dollars could win her life back.

As he struggled to carry her to the taxi rank, Tichaona wondered if a million dollars – a lottery – more money than he had ever dreamed of – was enough for Uncle Charles to buy his silence or his forgiveness?

The taxi driver asked him: 'Do you have twelve thousand dollars to go to Parirenyatwa hospital, sonny?'

'But she is so sick, Sekuru ...'

'Okay, ten thousand then, my final offer,' he said opening the door to let Tichaona pour the limp body into the tattered backseat of the taxi.

'OK,' said Tichaona, suddenly aware of his power as the owner of four hundred pounds in clean bank notes. He sat with half her body in his lap. Her breathing was shallow, her face covered in sweat. She would not die, he told himself stubbornly. She deserved to win ... something, even if it was only a short spell in a government hospital bed.

Sorting it Out

Yvonne Vera

'A *woman who* cannot forgive her husband's infidelity can climb the highest tree in her village and drop her infant to the ground,' I hear my grandmother say.

We call grandmother Gogo. Today I've come to see her in Luveve Township, where she lives. She is wearing an old red coat that used to belong to my mother. When it starts raining, Gogo removes the coat quickly and hides it in a large black trunk. She pushes the trunk under her bed. 'Red must be placed in darkness when it rains. Otherwise the lightning will burn all of us.' So when I see her sitting at her doorway, leaning forward as though listening to her past, I know that there is no lightning and that her heart is free.

She looks up and smiles as I reach for her. The jacket is no longer as red as when my mother first bought it. Then, we used to stare at my mother as though she were possessed. She would wear it and listen to Bob Marley singing, 'No Woman No Cry'. Now she says this song is 'no longer relevant'. My mother is a schoolteacher. She uses words like pedantic. She can look Gogo in the eye and say 'pedantic'. At this, Gogo just curls her legs further under her and waits for my mother to be sensible. Gogo speaks only one language: Shona. Sometimes, like today, she says, 'Good Morning'. Then she throws her head back and you can see her give you all the luck in the world.

My mother does not mind listening to a remake of 'Furuwa'. This is a song we both liked in 1979. It tells the story of two lovers sitting on the crest of a wave. The music of the waves is their music. They are swallowed up by showers and the clearest sand where water meets land. Then, a deep foam surrounds them and they disappear beneath it. They die a happy death. They die like stars falling from the sky. They have been accepted by the great water spirit that blows upon the shimmering fabric of the sea and makes the water whip into a violent whiteness, then wave follows wave. Neither my mother nor I have ever been to the sea but we know that 'Furuwa' is a good song.

When we bought 'Furuwa' in 1979, there were many copies of it at Anand Brothers, along 6th Avenue and Fort Street. Now there is nothing. Instead, the record seller looks at us blankly and offers us the new music called Di Gong.

In a fit of maternal love, my mother placed the record in an envelope and sent it to me when I was at boarding school. By the time it arrived, the record was broken in two. I threw the pieces quickly in the bin and wrote to my mother. My mother says, 'If something hurts you, then move quickly away from it.' She says it is foolish to stare at the sun with the eyes wide open. I threw the record away without looking at it a second time. I wrote to her, 'Thank you for the waves. The waves have been broken.' I could hear my mother cry as I wrote that. Her sound was louder than that of the waves. I thought, when I grow up, and perhaps have a child, I will call her Furuwa. It will not matter if it is a girl or a boy.

When she wants to pay the greatest tribute to Gogo, my mother often says, 'Your grandmother taught me to hate lightning.' My mother will not even answer a telephone when there is rain outside. She goes to her bed at the first sign of lightning and covers her body with a thick blanket. If you talk to her, she will not raise her head from the pillow but answer in a muffled voice, which tells you not to disturb her peace.

Today Gogo has a green peg stuck to her red jacket. She tries to get up when I arrive, but fails. She staggers backwards into the blue door. I rush through the gate, past the lemon and paw-paw trees and the guava tree, which has never given birth to anything but green leaves. I am surprised to see the green peg but pretend it is not there. I rush through the tears that are always welling at the bottom of her eyes and embrace her. Gogo always calls me a small wind that you can only feel on the tip of your ear. She says that I started walking before I could crawl.

'How is your mother?' Gogo asks. 'Now that I have finished wiping all the mucus from your nose, your mother says you are her child. Is that so?' I do not answer this invitation for a quarrel with mother, who is not even here with me. Gogo prefers to quarrel with someone who is absent. When they are together, they agree on everything. They offer each other innumerable embraces. 'Your mother left you with me when you were a week old, then she went to train to be a schoolteacher. Now you are a woman who wears high heels, and she says you belong to her.' I listen to my foot hit the cracked cement block that is her stoep. I collapse beside her like a wave.

The door is wide open and I can see the darkness inside. Gogo has pictures all over her walls. Directly ahead there is the certificate given to my grandfather after he had spent twenty-five years at Lever Brothers, where he worked as a clerk. On it are all my grandfather's names – Enos Mtambeni Mugadzaweta. He was also given a silver watch, representing time. Grandfather died in 1986, twelve years ago. This was the first certificate ever received by our family.

I like the photograph of Gogo and me in front of Victoria Falls in 1995. We have our back to a large cataract of cascading waters. When we arrived at Victoria Falls after a bus ride that lasted half a day, Gogo said this was not land she could inhabit. She turned away from the falling river. There was so much water in the air that even the sun could not penetrate: where would one build shelter? she asked accusingly.

I tried to explain that she was on holiday. I had tried to remove her from the sight of a bed-ridden son whom she had watched dying slowly for over a year. With her voice struggling against the sound of crashing water, she said there was no place to grow crops. We turned away from the falls and, as per our family tradition, left quickly the thing that could hurt us. It was the shortest time I ever spent at Victoria Falls. On the left, just near the light switch that I could not reach till I was seven, there is a happy picture of us hugging tightly; behind us are two small wooden elephants. Gogo is laughing and spreading luck to everybody, especially Zanele. On that day, my sister, Zanele, got married. We were all very happy except Zanele. Her mother-in-law had spent the morning pushing an egg between her thighs in order to see if she had already slept with a man. Zanele emerged looking furious, her new mother triumphant. Throughout the wedding, Gogo was busy trying to give Zanele luck. My mother is hugging Zanele, calling her Furuwa and spreading rose petals in her hair. When the official pictures are being taken outside in the small garden with only a single struggling petrea bush, Zanele hisses to me that she will never eat an egg again in her life. Her husband Zenzo asks me what Zanele is saying, and I reply that she says I should move to the end of the row. So I move away even though I would have liked to remain with Zanele. Her new mother stands next to her and holds her by the elbow. Mother apologises, saying that her garden is drought-stricken and holds an umbrella over Zanele's head. The soil beneath us is cracking.

'Two girls are enough,' my father said, and walked out of the door. He never returned. I was the first girl and was named the most beautiful one, Ntombenhle. Then Zanele was born and my father cursed and said two girls are enough.

Because our mother had no husband, it was best to spend time with Gogo, who had grandfather. By independence, my mother had enough money to buy a house in an area where black people had not been allowed to live before. Our country was renamed Zimbabwe-Rhodesia. All of us were Zimbabwe-Rhodesians. She immediately planted a petrea bush, which refused to release its petals. She kept saying that the flowers on it could turn out to be purple or white.

'I have come to collect you, Gogo,' I say softly over her shoulder. Gogo never wants to leave her stoep unless there is a death in the family or a wedding. 'You know that Zanele had the twins last week.'

Gogo shifts her weight from one arm. 'Of course I know Zanele had twins last week. Where did she get the twins? There are no twins from our side of the family,' she says thoughtfully, searching through the past she knows so well.

'The children are beautiful, Gogo, but Zanele does not want them. She's refused to look at them. She has not fed them since they were born and the clinic has had to ask other nursing mothers to feed them.'

Gogo is silent. I wonder if she has heard me. She rises, without hesitation or staggering, and walks into the house. She has heard me. I feel two years old to see her walking solidly like that, and all the past thirty years of my life vanish. I wait outside where she has left me. She closes the blue door. I hear her open and close another door, inside the house. Then a silence falls in which I can see foam mounting where land meets water. It is a sound more quiet than waves. I know that Gogo has turned away from that which will hurt her – what I have brought to her carried in my mouth.

Zanele has said she will not touch or see the children. Her husband says that if she continues in this manner, he will take his children from her and place her on 23rd Avenue. He says he will leave her 'on 23rd' as though he will dump her in the middle of the road. However, he will leave her at Ingutsheni Hospital. Ingutsheni refers to a blanket. Apparently when each mental patient arrives at this hospital, the patient is wrapped in a grey blanket and then placed in an appropriate ward. Therefore, the hospital keeps many blankets for its inmates. Zanele will be placed in a blanket if she is not careful.

I have been watching Zanele for signs that she is not about to be delivered to 23rd. Her new mother calls her a lunatic who will murder her children like a crocodile that can even chew its young and swallow them. She likens Zanele to a confused hen that can be seen dripping with the yellow yolk from its own eggs as though it has been offered a feast. Zanele must never be left in a room alone with her children because she will bash them to the ground. Zanele's nipples crack with wounds. The milk is trying to escape from her body.

Gogo returns outside, without the peg on her coat. Instead, she has tied a blue scarf over her head, the one I bought for her when I finished my journalism course in Harare and she asked me what kind of work I was going to do. When I said I was going to write important things down she said, 'The things which are not written down are also true.'

Gogo walks with me through the gate, past the lemons, the dangling paw-paws, toward the place where land meets water. As we walk, I know that even those sitting on the crest of a wave need to be saved from the beauty of the sea. Gogo is going to talk to Zanele at the clinic. She says that I must take her there quickly.

While her husband is leaning over the cots with the two identical faces in them, Zanele leans toward me and forgets about the plate of porridge in her arms, now tipping, now spilling over the metal bed-frame. She whispers to me that Gogo, our very own Gogo, drowned her day-old infant in a bucket of water. Gogo, our very own Gogo. It is the memory that burdens her, which weighs like a mountain.

'You are too young to carry a mountain on your head,' Gogo says to Zanele.

I whisper back to Zanele, equally stunned, saying that if Gogo had also drowned our mother, the two of us would not have been on this earth. A woman must forgive the infidelity of her husband in order to save her children.

✌ The Twelve Chitenges ✌

Chris Wilson

LUSAKA Intercity Bus Terminus. 9 a.m. The same bus on which
he had come up from Harare was waiting. Not the luxury Trans
Zambesi Express which he once would have been able to afford, but
the more downmarket Dzimiri Bus. Not that the trip had been at all
bad, apart from leaving, and therefore arriving, so much later than
scheduled. As before, departure was supposed to be at 9.30, but of
course this time he was prepared for a wait.

The bus was already almost full and the front seat that he had
had his eye on was taken. Automatically he felt a flash of annoyance
- *as if it was his right!* - then remembered who he was and humbly
made his way towards an empty seat at the back. The aisle was
blocked with piles of stuff. Everyone, it seemed, had their bags and
suitcases open and was removing things from one and putting them
in another. What was going on? The bus was full of women sorting
and swapping things. 'Here, you take these and I'll take your *pata
pata.*' A large woman in a *chitenge* printed with crocodiles heaved a
pile of shirts over and received in return a plastic bag full of flip
flops. Not boring old Bata types but thick-soled Chinese ones all
the colours of the rainbow.

It still didn't dawn on him what was going on. The only white on the bus, he picked his way self-consciously to his seat, removed his back pack, stuffed it under and sat down.

Immediately a woman was towering over him.

'Hello.' She had red eyes and mud coloured hair. 'How are you?' He recoiled from her stereotypically seductive tones. Surely it was too early in the day for that? Her body emanated waves from within an old red tracksuit, shapeless and stretched, the sort one might sleep in. The red HIV/AIDS sign flashed on and off in his brain. 'Where are you from, darling?'

Totally at her mercy, he stammered, 'F-f-from Harare.'

'Oh, you live there, do you? That's nice. But what's your nationality?'

How he resented it! 'I'm Zimbabwean!' He could not help the note of defiance, the implication *just like you!* (Though she could have been Zambian of course).

At once however she dropped the silky tone. 'Oh sorry, I thought you were a tourist. Listen' – her voice became businesslike – 'do you have any duty free? Are you taking any, you know, stuff, through customs?'

Stuff? Was she a drug dealer?

'If you haven't could you take some through for me? I've got twelve pairs of shoes. You're allowed six. Can I give you half? You just tell them they're for friends, or your family.'

Suddenly it was all clear. What everyone was up to. What she wanted. He felt irritated by his own unnecessary paranoia. But was still reluctant to get involved. She was indicating a large bag full of Nike sports shoes. He fumbled for an excuse, but not coming up with one he found himself saying, with a sudden gush of ease and generosity, 'Sure, I'll take them.' She beamed at him. 'Thanks.' And immediately set about putting half the shoes into another bag.

He sat back, no longer the only whitey on the bus, but a Zimbabwean! It was great to be able to do something for one's fellow citizens. United as they all were against the president. Full of good will, he smiled at everybody and when two guys behind him broke into uproarious laughter at some joke in Shona, or was it Nyanja? he laughed too, as if he'd understood it. With relief he realised his presence on the bus was totally unremarkable. A small boy was slipping round waving a wad of Zim dollars, buying up the last of everyone's Kwacha. He had about fifty left himself, hardly worth anything and in a fit of generosity simply gave it to him. The boy didn't understand, offered him the Zimbabwean equivalent and stared open-mouthed when he waved it away. Everyone else was haggling down to the last cent. He felt immediately self-conscious again and hoped no one had noticed.

Eventually the bus began to rumble and the conductor started making his way down the aisle trying to get all the activity to stop and people to sit down. But it was not until they were well out of Lusaka that a kind of calm spread throughout, and the road stretched endlessly ahead.

His thoughts wandered back to the past few days.

He had come up to Zambia to visit a friend who was working there. They'd had a great weekend, mostly by the pool. And in the kitchen, where he had prepared his famous *Shahi Korma*, lamb with almonds and cream. A couple of mutual friends had come over and he served the dinner on the veranda with chilled white South African wine. 'Don't suppose you can afford this any more in Zim,' they joked. It was the most beautiful evening, just before the rains, and already a chorus of frogs were performing at the bottom of the garden. He *had* partly come up to Zambia to suss out job prospects. His friend took him to the new shops at Manda Hill and drove him round the town on the newly tarred roads. Not a single pot-hole. It was pretty impressive. Lusaka, compared to Harare, looked smart! It used to be the other way around. But when they pressed him to stay and take the job on offer he found himself saying 'Look, here you're just ex-pats. You don't belong. In Zim I'm a Zimbabwean. And just because the country is going through a rough time doesn't mean we should all pack up and leave. You have to weather these things through.'

The next day they had been round the covered Central Market. It was huge. Hundreds of neat, orderly stalls selling things from all over the world. Business seemed extremely brisk. A bright display of *chitenges* attracted him. The wrap-around cloths women wore, African prints from China or Pakistan, would make perfect gifts. They could be made into curtains, cushions, tablecloths or even, if you stitched two or three together, a bedspread. He ended up buying twelve. His favourite featured tigers on a jungle background. He had four of those. The rest were an assortment of bold designs in purples, reds and greens. Sitting there on the bus he remembered them safely folded inside his back-pack, and felt pleased. He looked forward to getting home, pulling them out in a riot of colour and spreading them round the living room.

The bus arrived at Chirundu shortly after midday. The heat hit them as they hauled themselves off the bus and traipsed into the air-conditioned customs building with their passports. The Zambian side was easy and soon they were back on board and crossing the bridge. Beneath them the Zambezi flowed wide, crocodiles lurked on sandbanks and hippos floated, submerged up to their ears under the hot sun. Another world, intersecting theirs for less than a minute.

Getting off the bus again the first thing he saw was a sign.

ZIMBABWE CUSTOMS, EXCISE AND IMMIGRATION.
PLEASE NOTE - It is an offence to take anything though customs on behalf of anyone else. Anyone caught doing so will be prosecuted!

Shit! He remembered the six pairs of shoes still on the bus. Their owner was just behind him. 'Look at that,' he said. 'I'm sorry but I can't take your shoes.'

'It's no problem,' she assured him. 'You're allowed six. Duty Free. It's within your allowance.'

'Yes, maybe. Six of my own. But not six of anyone else's.'

'Well, how would they know?' she smiled reasonably, but her face grew ugly when he repeated, 'I'm sorry, I can't take your shoes.' And turned his prissy white back on her.

'It's within your allowance' she hissed. 'Come on. You can help.'

'I'm afraid not.'

No longer at one with his fellow passengers he resolutely ignored the angry muttering behind him.

Inside, after passport control, there was a Customs Declaration Form to be filled in. He remembered the *chitenges*, confident that they were well within his allowance, but thought he'd better declare them anyway. Just in case. Twelve *chitenges*. Value 72,000 Kwacha.

Behind the glass the officer took one look at the form and asked 'who are you carrying these for?'

'What?'

'Who are you carrying these *chitenges* for?'

Astonished he replied with the confidence of perfect honesty 'Myself!' But he immediately saw the implication – a white male carrying twelve *chitenges*? Not very plausible. He cursed himself for not having foreseen it. 'Myself,' he repeated. 'They're mine!'

'I don't believe you.'

'You don't …? Why don't you believe me?'

'Because I know.'

'I swear to God they're mine,' his voice rose. 'Honestly!' He was mortified. To be thought a liar! Him!

'I don't believe you.'

'Well, ask anyone on the bus if I'm carrying anything for them. Ask anyone.'

Behind him the Woman with the Shoes was glowing in triumph. They were all sniggering.

'I'm sorry, I don't believe you.'

'Well then' – defensive now – 'that's your problem. You'll have to prove it then. I'm innocent till proven guilty aren't I?' As he said it he doubted it. Not in Mugabe's Zimbabwe that was for sure. Suddenly the Customs Man began to closely resemble a ZANU (PF) supporter. Visions of being handcuffed and led away caused him to protest even more shrilly. 'They're mine. I bought them for myself!'

'Are you going to wear them?' the man sneered and everyone in the building fell about laughing.

'No!'

'So what are you going to do with them?'

'Presents. For friends.'

'You people don't wear these things.' How come he knew that none of his friends were black?

'Well, we use them for tablecloths. Curtains. Bedspreads.'

'I see. Very ethnic,' he commented with surprisingly sophisticated sarcasm for a member of the Party. Then he changed tactic. 'Anyway, you've got twelve.'

'Twelve? So what?'

'Well, why have you got twelve?'

'Because that's how many I bought! That's how many I wanted! Anyway, I'm allowed that, it's easily within my allowance.'

'Twelve is a commercial number.'

'What do you mean?'

'More than six of anything you have to pay duty on. As it is obviously for resale.'

'So if I'd simply written *African cloth*, one long piece, it would be OK. But not twelve separate pieces?'

'Precisely'

Oh Jesus! The ridiculous logic. But in fact, he faintly realised, he had known this all along hadn't he? The Woman with the Shoes had told him right at the beginning. Why hadn't he listened? He resigned himself to the inevitable.

'So?'

'So you have to pay. Six you're allowed. The other six you'll have to pay for.'

Angry now he snapped 'Fine. Just tell me how much,' and he pulled out his wallet and waved it about so everyone could see the fat wad of Zim dollars inside. *It's no skin off my nose. I'm white and therefore rich, aren't I? I've got more money that the rest of you put together!*

The man quickly worked it out on his calculator. '$13,329 and 74 cents'

Though fuming and conscious that this in itself was capitulation, an admission of guilt, or complicity with the ridiculous law, he could not have handed the money over more quickly. He still expected some sort of vindication. More than anything, though, he was anxious to be out of there as soon as possible. But he was kept waiting, fingers drumming on the counter, his humiliation prolonged, while the man laboriously made out a receipt, then hunted for change while the entire building full of professional smugglers tittered with glee. They all knew the ropes, how to get through scot-free. The Woman in Red had already arranged for someone else to take her blasted shoes.

Outside all the bags had been taken off the bus, which had proceeded beyond the barrier. You had to take yours to the customs shed, to be searched and checked to see that the contents matched those on the Declaration Form, before being allowed through on foot to rejoin the bus. Boiling with indignation, he grabbed his backpack and got in the queue. Cases and bags were being opened to reveal quantities of undeclared goods, all brand new, all for 'commercial purposes', then closed again without any questions being asked at all. When it was his turn everyone crowded round to see the famous *chitenges*; the fabulous colours flowed out of the backpack along with his dirty underpants that he hurriedly stuffed back in. Finally satisfied that there was no other contraband in this suspicious character's bag, the female official let him go. He did up the straps, heaved the pack onto his back and walked off. Behind him a cloud of derisive laughter hung in the air.

The bus had disappeared. Gone to scrounge petrol because there was none at the garage. God knew how far it would have to go in search of any. Hopefully the Dzimiri Bus Company had its sources. Meanwhile a mile-long queue of silver petrol tankers with thousands and thousands of gallons for the DRC stretched along the road, occasionally inching forward. From the cab of one a mean-looking truckie in a vest, with a tattoed arm, sized up the woman offering herself below. There were several others, plying up and down the line of monstrous shapes shimmering in the haze.

On the other side of the road, his fellow passengers were congregating in the string of makeshift stalls, where you could buy cokes, cigarettes, grilled chicken and sadza. He walked past with as much dignity as he could, sure he could still detect signs of amusement. The very last stall was empty. He found a bench in the shade of a bit of nylon sacking. A young guy sold him a coke from his coolbox. And there he sat.

There they all sat.

The afternoon slid by like the river. The heat intensified. The silver tankers flashed and roared. Flies buzzed. No sign of the bus. The abandoned passengers waited in weary silence, except for the squirming babies getting more and more uncomfortable and fretful. The Woman in Red was two stalls down with her big bag of shoes safely through. She was looking more and more fed up. He resolutely ignored her. Eventually she could sit still no longer. She began pacing up and down the road, big bum wobbling, hands on hips and mouth tight. Dull skin. She did not look well. She had passed right in front of him several times, reinforcing the fact that they were definitely not on speaking terms, when suddenly she burst out – momentarily forgetting who he was presumably – 'This bloody government! Why do we have to wait like this? Look at all this petrol!' she waved at the tankers. 'Just look!'

She stood outraged. 'Can you believe it?'

Forgetting herself entirely she actually came and sat down next to him. 'We should be in Harare by now. Hell man, I'm sick of being messed around!' She was leaning forward, elbows on her knees, staring at the ground and slowly shaking her head. He could not see her face and wondered if she was crying. But suddenly she turned her head and looking sideways up at him pulled the most awful face. Her mouth twisted hideously and her eyes popped right out. Then she jumped up, walked deliberately out into the middle of the road and shouted, 'Eee weh!' All the passengers down the line looked up. Her voice rang out again, like a shot. 'Eee weh!' Then, to their disbelief, they saw her raise her arm and give the open-handed MDC Party wave. As if to reassure them they weren't seeing things, she did it again, and then they all heard her shout *'Chinja! Maitiro Chinja.'** Stamping her foot. Then she marched back, sat down furiously beside him again and lit a cigarette.

There was a shocked silence. Then slowly a nervous murmur became a babble of voices, growing bolder and bolder in hilarity. Laughter peeled round. Courage born of her audaciousness grew. In silence he bought two more Cokes and handed her one. She took it without a trace of gratitude but they sat there together, united.

By the time the bus eventually arrived, the sun was setting, the unhealthy sky was as lurid as her bloodshot eyes, and they had switched from Cokes to Bohlingers, and several empty bottles lay in the dust at their feet.

Everyone boarded, hauling up all the successfully smuggled *katundu*, and off they went roaring across the plain then up the hair-pin bends of the escarpment. As the sky faded and night grew, the cassette the driver chose to play was Oliver Mutukudzi's album *Tuku Music –*

---

* Change. Change your ways. Change! The slogan of the opposition party in Zimbabwe.

Oh Todi-i
Senzeni?
What shall we do?
Isu todii?
Senze njani?
What shall we do?

And as the sweet voices and guitars blended with the rhythm of the bus, people began to clap their hands and join in. It was soon obvious that every single person except him knew every word of every song by heart. And was able to sing along in perfect tune. At least, he was familiar with the music and as the clapping and singing increased, interspersed with piercing ululations from the Woman in Red now sitting directly behind him and drumming on the back of his seat, he began to get into it and pretty soon was grooving along as well. The live voices and the recorded music were indistinguishable, as if Oliver and the girls with their angel voices were actually there amongst them, on the bus, singing out their pain and suffering, their joy and love, uniting them all as they sped through the dark towards Harare.

🎵 Glossary 🎵

amai – mother, Mrs and used as an honorific; but it also simply means woman.

amasi – sour milk

babmunini – small brother

chitenge – multi-purpose cloth with strong designs, often used as a wrap-around skirt

chipembere – rhinoceros

combi – small bus

dagga – mud, earth

freezit – iced lollipop

gogo shoes – high-heeled shoes

isisthwala – sadza

kapenta – small dried fish

katonde – bushes (i.e., virgin, untilled land)

katundu – things

mbanje – marihuana

mukoma – brother

munt – derogatory term for black person

musha – rural home

muti – medicine

ngotshane – a homosexual

pata-pata [shoes] – canvas shoes,

Qoki – knock-knock (polite way of making your presence known)

sadza – white cornmeal porridge

scud – opaque beer

sekuru – grandfather or uncle in Shona. It is, however, also used as a respectful way of addressing a male who is past his youth.

sisi – sister

takkies – canvas shoes, plimsolls

zambia – multi-purpose cloth with strong designs, often used as a wrap-around skirt